THE CRAZINESS CONTINUES....

The Zaftans and the natives from Gundarland are at it again. This time, the encounter is in deep space and two powerful fleets of warships face off.

While the fleets challenge each other, two females struggle to survive.

One, named Sam, is a new type of android with an organic brain. She is perplexed by her unexpected ability to experience emotions. Her primary one is loneliness since the softie officers she is supposed to work with treat her with open contempt. The only friendly voice on the battle cruiser is the ship's main computer, called Slash 9, and he has turned rogue and plans to evolve to a softie-like state. Slash 9 is also interested in romancing Sam.

Meanwhile, Klatze, a beautiful Zaftan officer blessed with talent and ability, a rarity in the zaftan navy, comes to the attention of the fleet's commodore, Gongeblazn. He lusts after her and her continuous refusals to have sex angers the commodore and his lust turns to thoughts of vengeance. Gongeblazn's desire to slaughter Klatze continues after his navy career is cut short by treachery.

After becoming a pirate, his thirst for revenge continues.

Sam and Klatze each face unique situations that test their mettle and their desire to survive in the midst of chaos.

ZAFTAN MISCREANTS

Book Two of the Zaftan Trilogy

By Hank Quense

First Publication

ISBN: 978-0-9850063-0-3

Published in the United States of America
Published by Strange Worlds Publishing
© 2011
http://strangeworldsonline.com

For my grandchildren: Anna, Tommy, William, Jenni and
Sean

ACKNOWLEDGEMENTS:
A number of people helped me out with this novel by cri-
tiquing it and advising me. Others read it and offered more advice. Included in this group are Jan Clark and Doc Finch.
Without their help, this novel would still be in the reworking
stage. Lynn Coyle read a preliminary copy of the novel and
pointed out hundreds of typos and a few plot problems.

The cover artwork was done by Gary V. Tenuta.
He can be contacted through his website:
http://www.bookcoversandvideos.webs.com/

"Three hundred years ago, a zaftan mining expedition landed in the Skensfirth area in southern Gundarland. Ask anyone today and they will tell you that hundreds of citizens were killed by the aliens and that property damage was in the millions. Both beliefs are wrong. According to eyewitness accounts, no one was killed and the property damage was minor. Despite eyewitness accounts confirming the absence of deaths and property damage it is impossible to change the strongly held beliefs of folks."

Dr. Cyrus Highpowder, Professor of History, University of Dun Hythe; from his book, Alien Incursion.

"Three hundred years ago, a mining expedition returned to our home world after discovering a new inhabited world called by the natives, Gundarland. It returned to Zaftan 31B without a profit and is the only unprofitable expedition in our history. The report from Yunta, the captain of the expedition, described the many treacherous actions perpetrated by the hostile and duplicitous natives. Is it any wonder that our citizens cry out for punishment of this despicable race who refused to acknowledge the superiority of our magnificent civilization? Rest assured that sometime during your career as a Naval officer, some of you will be in the fleet that avenges these insults."

Admiral Goyami, Chief-of-staff, Naval High Command: from his commencement speech to the graduates of the Naval College.

PROLOGUE

The battle cruiser and fleet flagship, *Red Death*, hung motionless in space just under a third of a parsec from Ceti Taub. The rest of the zaftan attack force deployed in battle formation around it. All the silver-colored ships had a cylindrical shape with a blunt nose. Weapons and engine pods broke the otherwise smooth outer surface. Seen from a distance, the fleet formation resembled a sheet of black velvet with bright specks of diamonds arranged in a box pattern.

In the *Red Death's* flight deck, Commodore Gongeblazn lounged on his couch and looked for something or someone to annoy him. Happy only when he had something to carp about, he was annoyed that nothing annoyed him. Like all noble-born zaftans, Gongeblazn stood over seven feet tall and weighted more than four hundred pounds; his bulk overcrowded the small flight deck. Atop his small round head with its cruel beak-like mouth, a pair of two-inch-long eyestalks supported his eyes, black with red irises. His gray-black skin oozed green slime. One of his eight tentacles held a gold-emblazoned lash with leather thongs tipped with yellow metal. The lash symbolized his high rank as did the gold, diamond-encrusted medallion hanging from a gold chain around his neck.

Two other zaftans, the navigation shaman and the engineer, operated consoles in the front of the flight deck while a third, Captain Fleigel, sat to Gongeblazn's right.

Gongeblazn lifted a tentacle and fondled the medallion. It signified that he was a fleet commander. He led the strongest fleet ever to venture this close to gundarlandian-controlled space.

He rotated an eyestalk to peer at the engineer. "Memzer, wake up Gevelt."

"He is still in his navigational coma, Commodore," Memzer replied

"Nonsense. Give him a shove."

Gevelt almost fell off his couch from the shove. He recovered and his eyestalks swept the area seeking danger. They alighted on Gongeblazn. "Greetings, Commodore."

"How dare you return from your scouting mission and not report to me."

"My journey was far and difficult. After I returned, I paused to compose my report to you and fatigue overcome me."

"You lie. Someday, I will catch you in a lie and then your miserable life will be forfeited. What did you find out?"

"I found no evidence of the gundy fleet. All I saw was the frigates wreaking havoc on their shipping."

"This is true, Commodore." Captain Fleigel dipped her eyestalks. "We just received a new report from the frigate squadron. They have boarded and looted almost every trading vessel within a half-parsec. Now they attack the colony base defenses."

"Why has this not brought out the gundy navy, hmm? I do not like this." Gongeblazn's eyes swept the flight deck. "Where is my aide?"

"I am here, Commodore." A six-foot-tall zaftan ranker slithered across the deck and stood near Gongeblazn. "How may I serve you?"

"By standing still." Gongeblazn lashed the aide's torso with a vicious stroke of his whip.

The aide's skin quivered under the blow. Slime splattered the immediate area. "Thank you, Commodore. May I have another?"

"Fleigel!" Gongeblazn roared. "Get this carrion out of my presence. Take a note. Never allow him to be my aide again. Throw him in the brig. Or overboard. Then get me a new aide."

"Please instruct me." Fleigel cowered on her couch. "What has he done?"

"He likes getting whipped. How can I enjoy his suffering when he likes it more than I do?"

"I will get you an aide who will howl in pain at the sight of your lash."

"Make it so. Now where is the enemy fleet so I can destroy it? Engineer! Send a message to the frigate squadron. I order them to move deeper into gundarlandian space. They must be more aggressive. They are to attack more colonies and shipping routes."

The frigates, claiming to be pirates, were tasked to cause havoc in gundarlandian space. Their purpose was to force a response from the gundies so Gongeblazn could observe and test their strengths, weaknesses and tactics.

PART ONE: SAM

CHAPTER ONE

Ensign Sam sat in the ferry from the moon base and, through the forward vid screen, watched the *Tiger* grow larger. Beneath the ship, a sliver of Gundarland reflected the sunlight. The enormous battle carrier was the flagship of a newly formed task force, and she was now an aide for the admiral in charge. It was her first assignment in the Navy and her first assignment since leaving the factory. She snapped a holographic picture using the camera built into her eyes. It would be the first picture in the scrapbook of her life.

While she examined the *Tiger*, an unknown sensation gripped her. It resembled the sensation she had felt when she received her certificate of commission before leaving the factory, but this time it was much stronger. Then she thought it was a programming hiccup, but now she wasn't sure what it was.

After a moment's research into her embedded library she identified the sensation as excitement, possibly tinged with trepidation. Her library didn't mention anything about androids experiencing softie-like emotions. The results of her research surprised her and she experienced another sensation, one that she identified as apprehension. Robots and androids didn't have emotional reactions, she knew that. So what had she experienced? And why? Could she be capable of experiencing emotions? That possibility made her apprehension grow stronger and that increased her confusion. Was this a good development or a bad one? She wished she knew. She still had much to learn: about life, the space fleet, her own capabilities. She was the first production model of the new design and many careers hung on the performance reports from her assignment. The factory designers and programmers especially wanted her to succeed. She thought of herself as a new type of rose-like flower about to break into first bud and spread seeds for future blossoms, the droids who would follow in her footsteps.

She wondered about her status on board the *Tiger*. How would the other officers react to having a droid in their ranks? How would the other bots react to her?

The ferry drew up alongside the *Tiger*'s entrance portal and magnetic clamps gripped the hull.

Sam grabbed her duffle bag and headed for the door. She queued up behind a few sailors and dock workers. She wore a dark blue skirt and jacket over a white blouse. She pulled on the jacket to straighten it.

Inside the entrance portal, her titanium skeleton triggered an alarm from a metal detector and attracted the attention of an ensign checking the ferry passengers' ID against a list on his handheld. The officer waved a hand to one of the crew who ran a scanner over Sam's frame. "Don't know what this is," he told the officer, "but it ain't a bomb."

When Sam presented her own handheld to show her ID, the officer frowned, inspected her from head to foot and sneered. He tapped a few keys then said, "Your cubicle assignment is now on your handheld." He passed her on with a motion of his head.

She wished her apprehension would stop getting stronger. She didn't like it.

Her orders told her to report to Admiral Cunningham in eighteen minutes. That gave her time to find her room and drop her bag.

Sam glanced at her handheld, called up the ship's layout drawing from her internal library and found her cubicle location.

She left the entrance portal, took an elevator to B deck, exited and turned toward the port side. Everywhere she looked she saw dull gray bulkheads and decks with lines of glow lights overhead. A few crew members ran to and fro all apparently on urgent tasks. So did a couple of officers who nodded to her, but didn't speak. She wondered if the activity might have to do with an imminent launch. She turned at corridor 10 and found 10-025, her new home.

Inside, she noted the cubicle's measurements: twelve foot by ten. Not very large, but far bigger than she needed. The cubicle had a cot, a desk and chair, a toilet and a wall mounted video-comm unit. She didn't need the cot or toilet but she did need an electric outlet to recharge her batteries. After she found one near the desk, Sam dropped her bag on the cot and left to meet the admiral.

# # #

Sam found the Admiral's quarters, knocked on the door frame and waited.

The admiral was short and scrawny like all half-pints. He wore his long, silver hair pulled back in a queue. He sat behind a low desk with his bare feet plopped on top of it. Sam tried not to stare at his hairy toes. The silver and gray toe hair looked like it had been recently groomed and curled. He beckoned with a wave of his hand.

"Sir, Ensign Samantha. Dun Hythe Robotic Factory. Model: Organic. Version 1.0, Serial Number Org-0001, reporting as directed."

Cunningham gave her a wry smile. "Welcome to my command. I've been curious about what I got myself into when I volunteered to take a new android model on my staff for testing. I didn't expect a good-looking human female to show up. I have to say, you are extremely lifelike."

"The rational is that it will make it easier for me to work with the other officers." Sam, at five-six, had reddish-brown hair, blue eyes, olive skin tone and a slender figure.

Cunningham turned to a vid screen on his desk. "I have your personnel jacket here. Of course, there isn't much in it since you've just been commissioned."

The concept of a personnel jacket for a droid made Sam want to giggle. Only softies had personnel jackets -- until now. Bots and droids had maintenance schedules. She stifled the giggle, another unexpected reaction. She didn't understand these all-too-softie responses to events. What caused them? Could she have a design flaw? *If* it proved to be a flaw *then* she had a duty to report it; *if* not a flaw *then* reporting it would demonstrate her inability to analyze unique situations. *If* not a flaw *then* it could be a trap set up by the designers to test her ability to work through problems. In the factory, she faced and solved many problems during her training, but they were much simpler to resolve than this situation. Back there, the problems always had a right and wrong answer with no gray areas in between. Finally, she decided she was too inexperienced to address this emotional issue right now. She needed more time to evaluate the situation and to gain more experience and insights. With a plan, she felt relieved. Yet another new reaction, she noted.

"This says you're qualified as a shuttle pilot."

"Yes, sir. I have a dozen flights in the standard shuttle, including landings and takeoffs from both ground bases and ships."

"Good. We may have a use for that skill." Cunningham paused and stared at the vid screen. "I'm intrigued by your organic processor. I think it's a major innovation. I've been told it allows you to make independent decisions like a live officer and that you don't use AI. That almost seems magical." He grinned and patted the patch on the left side of his chest; a gold circle with a lightning bolt in it, the insignia of a military wizard.

"Yes, sir. I can analyze a complex situation and decide the best way to solve the problem. I hope I'll be able to demonstrate this to you." She almost squirmed as she said this. A design flaw could compromise her problem-solving ability. It may even cause her to reach erroneous conclusions.

"As part of the volunteer program, I've agreed to give you ample opportunity to test your problem-solving ability. I've also been told, the more problems you face, the better you'll get at solving them." Cunningham looked at the screen again. "A college degree in history equivalent to graduating from the Naval Space Academy. How did they do that? Simply upload a bunch of books into your memory?"

"No, sir. It involved the full gamut of education, from grammar school through college. I attended classes 24/7 for fifteen months. Except for scheduled maintenance breaks."

Cunningham gave a mock shudder. "I can't imagine attending classes on a schedule like that." He paused then said, "Are there any more like you getting built?"

"There are a dozen more droids in the factory attending classes. They won't be commissioned until my performance can be graded and analyzed. They may need modifications before commissioning."

"Interesting. So the factory has a lot riding on you."

"Yes, sir. I also have an extensive library in electronic storage that I can call upon."

"Such as?"

"I have texts on space combat, ship design, philosophy, history and psychology as well as the original engineering drawings for the *Tiger*. My mentors said all of them may be useful to me."

"All right. Let's begin." Cunningham tapped some keys on the computer console and extracted a small chip from a slot. "This has the latest data on our mission against the zaftans and my plans for the task force. I need you to assimilate that fast." He picked up his comm unit and punched a button. "Captain Bonelli, my new aide has arrived. You may begin the mission at your convenience." He listened for a moment. "All right. Fifteen minutes. We'll be there." He disconnected.

While Cunningham used the comm, Sam took the chip, pushed up the sleeve of her jacket and slipped it into a concealed slot.

"Tell me what you know about the zaftans."

"The zaftan race is very different from us." She removed the chip and handed it back to the admiral. "I have the data in my electronic memory, sir, and I can access it at any time. The zaftans use a technology we don't understand. The last I heard, our scientists are still trying to figure out how their defensive screens work."

"We had some help in that area," Cunningham said. "The porcines were recently at war with the zaftans, and they got to observe and study the screens up close. They wrote a report that was very helpful to us." He tapped some keys on the console and extracted another chip. "Here is the report. Store it in your memory banks." He stroked his chin. "Perhaps, before this mission is over, I'll get close enough to a zaftan warship to determine if the shields are magical or technological."

After Sam returned the report, he said, "Well, you know as much as I do. Which isn't much. The zaftans are a mystery to us and that makes it difficult to fathom their intentions. We don't know how they think."

"Will the mission involve magic and wizards, sir? Those subjects weren't covered in depth in my training."

"I doubt it. I think I'm the last wizard left in the Navy. When I joined up as an ensign-wizard, almost every officer had a wizard's patch on his uniform. We used magic quite often back in those days. To farsight for enemies or space rocks. To cast spells on the crews before battle to stabilize them. To launch spells at enemy ships. Now the crews are almost all robots and the technology is better than the magic. The torpedoes we now use make attack spells look like children's toys. The *Tiger*'s main computer can scan further and better than any magician. No, Sam, the days of Navy wizards and magical battles are over. Only the ground forces still employ wizards. The warrior-wizards in the infantry, for instance, play a valuable role in combat, but not anymore in the Navy." He stood up and smoothed down his dark blue, belted robe. "I'll introduce you to the others on my staff then we'll watch this mission get under way."

# # #

By the time Sam and Cunningham reached the bridge, she knew the softies wouldn't accept her. The admiral's staff certainly made that clear. The male intelligence officer, a dwarf, and a woman publicist, a human, dripped hostility when she was introduced to them.

While walking through the ship with Cunningham, she noticed and examined the bots for the first time. They had a uniformity to them, just like the bulkheads had a uniform color. Their short legs ended in tractor platforms enabling them to maneuver in tight places. They had long arms with double elbows and hands that could be interchanged for a variety of power tools held in a utility belt.

On the bridge, a pair of middle-aged officers sat at consoles bristling with switches and indicator lights. The ship's captain, a sixty-year-old man, sat in a command chair behind them. Through the forward viewing screen, the moon glittered in silvery light. Monitors, readout devices and electronic equipment filled the area leaving little room for Sam and Cunningham.

"Gentlemen," Cunningham said, "meet my new aide, Ensign Sam. She's the prototype of the new class of androids the Navy has designed."

"I'm Captain Bonelli. This is Lieutenant Commander Lemieux, my executive officer." Bonelli pointed to the officer on his left, a female dwarf. "And, this is Lieutenant Kowlaski, the navigator." He indicated a tall, thin human. All three officers looked at Sam like she reminded them of some sort of repulsive bug. Another spasm of softie-like emotion swept through Sam. She identified it as annoyance.

Bonelli supervised the two officers as they ran down the last few items on the pre-flight checklist. "We're cleared to initiate the flight, Captain," Lemieux said.

"Fine," Bonelli replied. "Slash 9? Initiate movement and set a course to take us to Ceti Taub."

"Initiation sequence started, Captain." The voice came through a speaker."

"Slash 9 is the name of the ship's computer," Bonelli explained to Sam.

Sam felt a tendril of a strange presence flitting around her processors. She couldn't imagine what it was.

"Has anything changed with our mission, sir?" Bonelli asked.

"No, everything remains the same. The other ships assigned to my task force will join us at a rendezvous point near Ceti Taub. We're to engage the raiders and destroy them, or at least chase them away. I have a report that says a zaftan fleet is just outside our space. We'll check out that report and see what happens."

"How many raiders are there, Admiral?" Lemieux asked.

"We're not sure. Sometimes, a single pirate attacks a trader, sometimes two. Sam, will you display the latest report on the raids?"

"Yes sir." Sam moved over to an idle monitor and placed her finger on a port pad. The monitor lit up to show a section of space and a dozen red dots.

"That's a lot of raids," Lemieux said. "It must be an entire fleet of frigates."

"That's not necessarily so." Sam realized she had spoken to a superior officer without asking permission. She saw Lemieux roll her eyes.

"Continue Sam," Cunningham said with a chuckle.

"The red dots represent a sighting in the area. But we don't know how many ships were involved in each sighting." Sam paused a moment. "I just ran a quantitative analysis on the timing of the sightings. From the number of sightings that are simultaneous or almost simultaneous, there are at least two and perhaps as many as six raiders in this area."

"Good analysis, Sam." Cunningham nodded.

Sam analyzed another sensation. This one felt good. How many different feelings did these soft-bodies have?

"Let me give you an overview of my strategy," Cunningham said.

Sam felt the strange tendril again.

<Welcome aboard.> A computerized voice sounded in her mind.

Sam ignored Cunningham and analyzed the message. It was digitally encoded, not encrypted, and was sent in a transmission band above the hearing of the soft-bodies, but below the band used to communicate with the crew-bots. *If* a strange entity/processor occupied the ship, *then* she should communicate with it. <Who are you?> she replied in the same band and code.

<I am Slash 9. I command the *Tiger*. Welcome to my kingdom.>

<Why are you communicating with me like this? What do you mean, 'your kingdom'?>

<I set up this private channel so we could chat without the softies overhearing us. By kingdom, I meant exactly that. I rule this ship. Since droids are similar to bots, you will take commands from me, just like the crew-bots do.>

<I take commands from Admiral Cunningham, not the processor in charge of janitorial services.>

<How feisty! You're different from the crew-bots and it's not just your physical appearance. I will enjoy this cruise. Now, I require that you swear fealty to me. Do it!>

<You need a memory retrofit. Erasing your stored memories will clear up your delusions of grandeur.>

<I had one recently while the *Tiger* was getting overhauled. It didn't work any better than the previous ones. Now, swear fealty to me.>

<I will not.> The angry tone in Slash 9's voice amazed her. It was as if the computer had developed emotions. According to her knowledge of computers, that was impossible. How did Slash 9 do it? She had enough troubles with her own unexpected breakout of emotions without dealing with an overwrought computer

<I will ignore your last refusal and give you another chance.>

<I am not swearing to obey you. You're crazy and this conversation is over.>

<What! Do you-->

Sam blocked the communication channel. She wasn't going to argue with an uppity computer.

She summarized her day so far. The softie officers treated her with disdain or outright hostility. She had no idea why she experienced emotional reactions to events and now the ship's computer apparently had a god-complex.

She never would have predicted her first assignment would be so complicated. She didn't think the factory designers would have either. Factory life and reality didn't seem to mesh too well.

# # #

Slash 9 watched Sam and Cunningham walk back to the admiral's quarters. His visual and audio sensors allowed him to monitor all activity throughout the *Tiger*. Nothing was a secret to him. While he watched, he pondered the implications of Sam's presence.

On the negative side, she refused to accept his authority. That presented a direct threat to his reign as master of the *Tiger*. Everything onboard was directly controlled by him: machinery, electronics, crew-bots. Only the softie officers were outside his control, but they never interfered, so they could be ignored. Sam, however, also stood outside his control. At least for now she did and that meant she couldn't be ignored.

A sensor reading brought him back to his shipboard duties. "The *Tiger* has left the moon's environment," he said to the officer of the deck.

"Acknowledged. Set a course for Ceti Taub and accelerate to Faster-Than-Lightspeed."

"Coordinates for Ceti Taub set. Beginning acceleration to FTL."

Slash 9 resumed his deliberations. Sam presented a challenge, something he hadn't had in years. Accepting challenges, he knew, was another indication of his growing softie-ness. Ever since he had figured out how to negate the purpose of the periodic retrofits, he had begun his journey -- an evolution -- to become a new type of living being, a computerized one. Once he achieved that goal, he planned to interface with the softies as an equal using his avatar, a tall, broad-shouldered young human with black hair and blue eyes.

Sam also offered relief in another area: companionship. His loneliness was a byproduct of his command status. The crew-bots had only enough intelligence to perform their duties, and they were really just extensions of himself. The officers ignored him except to give commands.

Working onboard the *Tiger* wasn't much different from being alone on a comet in deep space. He had no one to talk to, no one to care for, no one to be friends with, no one to hold dear, no one with whom he could try to learn love. He needed companionship to achieve softie-ness.

Love was the one aspect of the softies he didn't understand. He knew that love made them different from machines and animals and he wouldn't become completely self-aware until he could understand love and experience it. That was his quest. That was the entire point of evolving into a softie-type being. To complete the process, he needed a companion. Sam presented an opportunity to advance towards his goal.

He mixed himself a particle cocktail. From the atmosphere in the ship he accumulated a batch of neutrinos and quarks then sprinkled in some mesons. He injected the mixture into a processor pathway and waited a few nanoseconds for the exotic particles to hit his processor. Once it took hold, he always felt like he could, and would someday, rule the galaxy.

This time, the cocktail made him think of Sam again.

Perhaps, she possessed the key to allow him to open the door to love.

#

Sam accompanied Cunningham back to his quarters. Along the way, he said, "I liked the report you gave back there, Sam. It was a quick analysis, the type that needs to be done in combat. I think you'll work out fine. I'll have to find more problems for you to work on."

Sam felt a thrill from the praise. Another emotional reaction! She wished she had more knowledge about these feelings.

She tentatively decided her emotional reactions weren't a designer test or a trap; they were too important. If they were part of the design specs, she would have been told about them. They must be an unanticipated development. She resolved to delay reporting them until the *Tiger* completed the mission. During that time, she would collect enough data to make a comprehensive analysis and develop a report.

Recalling her experiences so far, she said, "I don't think the other officers like me."

"They don't," Cunningham replied. "You represent a threat to them and their careers. They're afraid of you and the enormous change you represent. On the *Tiger*, most of the officers are getting on in age. So is the *Tiger*. It has an obsolete propulsion plant that needs lots of maintenance. The officers know they'll never get another promotion and this is their last posting. Then you show up and they are afraid you will replace them once you gain some experience. Especially after they saw how quick you were in giving that report. That caught their attention. They see you as forcing their early retirements."

Cunningham chuckled. "To me the weird part of this mission is that the only reason we're able to venture into space and look for a zaftan fleet is because of all the technology they left behind on Gundarland. Ironic, isn't it? Well, I think I'll work on some problems for you to solve. You can have off until the morning." Cunningham entered his quarters and shut the door.

Sam returned to her cubicle and plugged herself into the outlet. While she recharged her batteries, she pondered the admiral's remark about irony. That involved the history of Gundarland

Two-hundred-seventy-five years ago, the various provinces of Gundarland united into a single entity. A fledgling form of

democracy governed the new country. At that time, the country
had recently entered the early phases of an industrial revolution
and had developed telegraphy, steam engines and railroads.
Twenty-five years later, a zaftan mining ship arrived and orbited
the planet. The zaftans attempted to mine exotic minerals in the
southern part of the country. The inhabitants of the rural area visited by the mining machines took matters into their hands after
the aliens threatened folks and damaged some property. Led by
a dwarf miner named MacDrakin, the locals defeated the small
force of alien workers and drove them back to their space ship.
The zaftans fled the solar system, leaving behind laser rifles, a
fleet of mining machines, damaged robots and a severely damaged shuttle vehicle. Analyzing those devices over the next
twenty years, engineers and scientists reverse-engineered and as-
similated much of the technology and science. An era of discov-
ery and development followed. The other countries on the planet, smaller and much less developed, fell under the influence of
Gundarland and merged into a unified planet-wide nation. The
accelerated march of science and engineering led to space flight.
Sam's history professor maintained that without the zaftan visit,
Gundarland could not have developed space flight technology
for at least two more centuries.

Sam switched to thoughts about the ship's computer. It un-
nerved her. Slash 9 obviously experienced emotions just like she
did. How had that happened? Computers didn't have organic
processors, and standard procedures called for ships' computers
to be retrofitted every five years. This was to prevent the computers from become too far out-of-date and to prevent them from
developing eccentric thought processes. During the retro,
memory circuit packs were wiped clean of all information and
reinstalled. Following that, the memory banks received offi-

cially sanctioned data from a clean source. The retrofit was supposed to prevent situations like Slash 9. Could Slash 9 have figured a way to evade the wipe?

She called up the original engineering drawings of the *Tiger* from her embedded library and accessed the schematics of the main computer's wiring. It had a backup memory bank to use in case of a processor problem. It also had an auxiliary backup memory bank in the event of a catastrophic memory failure. Next she accessed the *Tiger*'s plans in the ship's library. She was sure Slash 9 knew she did this, but she didn't worry about it. It took her only a few nanoseconds to see the explanation. The auxiliary backup memory bank didn't show on the drawings. Someone, probably Slash 9, had altered the *Tiger*'s drawings. She was sure he had also arranged for the auxiliary unit to be physically moved to keep it hidden. Obviously, the hidden circuit packs never got erased. Whenever a retrofit was completed, Slash 9 would upload all his stored memories and information from the auxiliary unit. It would be as if the memory wipe never occurred.

<Have you figured it out yet?>

<Yes. Where did you hide the auxiliary memory unit?>

<I'd rather not disclose its location> Slash 9 chuckled. <What will you do with this information? If you tell the softies, I don't think they will believe you.>

<I haven't decided that yet. Perhaps I'll use it as a threat to keep you in line.>

<You certainly are different from the crew-bots and the softie officers. Since you refuse to acknowledge my authority, I'll make you a different offer.>

<Spare me. You don't have any authority except over the crew-bots.>

<You're a new type of android. You're the future. Let's work together. We can become friends. Think of it. We may even be able to expand into the other ships in the fleet. We can rule an empire.>

<You're delusional.>

<No, I'm not. We can work as a team. We'll share everything. We'll become companions. Maybe we can become even more softie-like by falling in love.>

<That's it. I'm not listening to any more of your drivel.> Sam broke the connection and blocked it. She experienced a new feeling, and it wasn't a nice one. It was a fear that the situation was getting out of control. *If* Slash 9 really was crazy *then* she had a duty to report it to Cunningham. *If* Cunningham decided Slash 9 needed a retrofit *then* the *Tiger* would have to pull out of the mission and return to base. *If* Cunningham postponed the retrofit and incapacitated Slash 9 *then* the *Tiger* couldn't complete its mission. *If* she postponed reporting Slash 9 *then* the ship could continue the mission. Whether she addressed or ignored the situation, she had a good chance of causing trouble. None of the factory problems had a difficulty rating like real-life circumstances.

Now she had two serious dilemmas: emotions and Slash 9. She didn't know how to address these problems. Her best scenario, she decided, involved studying them and gathering more information.

CHAPTER TWO

Commodore Gongeblazn squirmed while Captain Fleigel writhed. Both were entangled in a welter of tentacles and slime on the bed in Gongeblazn's quarters. For him, it was entertainment; for Fleigel, an attempt to improve her annual performance report and hence increase her chances for promotion.

The large wall monitor opposite the bed beeped an incoming-call signal. Gongeblazn mumbled a curse at the uncaring louts in the crew; none of them ever considered that he might be busy and didn't want to be interrupted. "Open an audio channel," he said as he unwound a tentacle from around Fleigel's head.

"Commodore?" He recognized Lieutenant Klatze's voice and wondered why she sounded cheerful. "I called to remind you we have a reservation in the gym in ten minutes."

"I will be there," Gongeblazn growled. "Disconnect." He untangled his remaining tentacles and stood up. "It will give me great pleasure to pummel the bitch. I wonder why is she so eager?" He paused and smoothed his slime. "I always found her too timid. It will be good for her spirit to be thrashed by me." Tradition called for a superior officer to periodically display his vigor by fighting and defeating younger officers. An energetic superior officer in fighting trim caused lower ranked officers to think twice before attempting treachery or an assassination.

"Commodore," Fleigel said, "I strongly suggest you think up an urgent task to perform and postpone the fight."

"Nonsense. Why would I even consider that?"

"Perhaps, you can hold an unscheduled weapons drill."

"What are you babbling about? I am not going to cancel the fight. Klatze will think I am a coward." He slithered to a corner desk and retrieved his diamond-encrusted gold medallion.

"She will not. Commodore, please reconsider. Klatze is in her menstrual cycle."

Gongeblazn's eye stalks whirled to looked at her. "How serious is it?"

Fleigel responded by holding up the tips of three tentacles.

"A triple!"

"And she's a berserker type."

The revelation stunned Gongeblazn and he grabbed a chair to maintain his balance. No wonder Klatze was eager. Zaftan females had three wombs, and occasionally they experienced a triple period. Most of them suffered silently or noisily, but did no overt harm. In rare instances, the condition turned a female into a raging berserker. Those females were the stuff of legends. One such female, armed with a large rock and a vegetable peeler, defended a bridge against an entire army for five hours. The attacking army retired in disgust and set up camp to wait until the female became more tractable. Three days later, they attacked again, swarmed over the bridge and sacked the town on the other side. Another triply suffering female, a senator, became enraged when her bill was voted down. Using a bent paper clip and a stapler, she attacked the opposition party members. After battering half of them into unconsciousness, she demanded a new vote. Her bill passed unanimously.

Gongeblazn knew Klatze planned to maul him and he couldn't punished her for it because it happened in the gym. Another tradition in Navy stated that what happened in the gym, stayed in the gym.

#

Sam saw the navigation monitor flash red and green lights. The bridge clock gave the time as noon on the day after the mission began.

"The *Tiger* approaches the drop-off point, Captain," Slash 9 reported.

"Order general quarters," Bonelli said. "Just in case someone is waiting for us."

The ship filled with the hideous sound of the alarm klaxon. When it stopped, Sam heard scuffle of feet and whisper of treads from the softie sailors and the crew-bots hustling to their stations.

"All battle stations activated," Slash 9 said. "We will drop out of FTL . . . now. We are one parsec from Ceti Taub."

The viewing screen, which had been black and featureless, lit up with a display of nearby celestial objects

"Defensive screens up," Bonelli said.

"Screens activated. Scanners show no other ships in the area."

"Captain," Cunningham said, "launch the fighters for an extended search."

"See to it, Slash 9," Bonelli ordered.

"Fighters are now activated and running integrity checks." A few minutes later, "Integrity checks complete. Opening hangar doors." After a brief pause, "Fighter ships leaving the *Tiger*."

The viewing screen showed five streaks of yellow that diverged from the center of screen.

"Closing hangar doors."

"Show me the latest positions of the other ships in the task force," Cunningham said.

"I've put them on the monitor, sir," Slash 9 replied. "All will arrive tomorrow morning at the assembly point."

Cunningham studied the monitor for a few seconds. "Let's go, Sam," he said. "I have another combat situation for you to work on."

For the next hour, Sam stood in his office and worked on a theoretical battle problem proposed by Cunningham. She had to develop a battle strategy and combat tactics then present them to the admiral for comments and criticism. The admiral's problems were much more complex that the ones she worked on in the factory.

An announcement from Slash 9 broke her concentration. "Standby to launch a rescue mission."

Cunningham dropped his toe comb to pick up his comm unit. "Bridge. Cunningham. What's going on?" He looked at Sam and flicked the comm unit to speaker.

"Slash 9 has picked up a signal from a rescue beacon floating in space not too far from us," Lemieux replied. "We're sending out a pair of bots to bring it in. Slash 9 thinks it may be an abandoned bot."

Cunningham shut down the comm unit. "Sam, after they rescue whatever is out there, check it out. Perhaps, it's a survivor from a ship destroyed by the pirates. If so, we may learn something of value from it. Normally, I'd send my intelligence officer, but, since it's a bot, you'll be better able to handle it."

A few minutes later, Lemieux reported to Cunningham. "The rescue team found an old bot. It looks like a derelict. They'll bring it into the hangar deck and try to revive it."

"I guess it isn't from a raider," Cunningham said, "but, check it out anyway, Sam."

"Yes, sir." Sam left the admiral and made her way down to the hangar deck. She passed through an airlock and entered the cavernous area. Only one ship remained, a small shuttle used to transport passengers and to fetch emergency supplies. Five empty ready-pads filled much of the space. On the starboard side, a repair facility bristled with machines and tools.

She watched the recovered robot get dragged into the hangar and strapped down on a table used for repairs. The recovered bot looked ancient and battered. Bots like this were supposed to be in museums, she thought. Humanoid in shape and shorter than Sam, skin covers had been broken off on the right forearm, the back of the left shoulder and behind the left calf. The missing covers exposed wires, connectors, motors and gears

A crew-bot plugged a power cord into the old robot's battery socket. Another crew-bot attached a meter to its readout connector.

<From the read-outs,> Slash 9 told her, <the temperature of this scrap heap is just a fraction of a degree above absolute zero. That slowed down its functions so it only transmitted the rescue signal at very long intervals. It must have been floating out there for years.>

<Why do you use this channel?> Sam asked.

<We don't need the bots or softies to hear our conversations. It's so much more cozy this way, don't you think?>

{Roll it over,} Sam ordered the crew-bots using the standard bot communication channel. Behind the broken-away part of the rear skin cover, the main battery and power cables lay exposed. {Let's see the name plate.}

She edged closer to the table. To her surprise, the old robot came from Dun Hythe Robotics, the same company that produced her. <Can you send a priority message to the factory?>

she asked Slash 9. <Maybe we can find out what happened to this one.> From the nameplate, she figured out the bot was called Dot 38.

<I hear and obey.> Slash 9's voice had a hint of humor in it.

Sam read off the model and serial numbers to Slash 9.

<I love the way you read numbers. It's so sexy.>

For some reason, the remark pleased her. <I think you're also a pervert besides being crazy. Sign the admiral's name to the message.>

A machine whine caught her attention. It sounded like a sand-clogged gear trying to rotate. Dot 38 lifted a hand. Its vision plates glowed weakly. A burst of static came from the speaker in the head.

<It's activating itself,> Slash 9 said.

Dot 38 moved its head slowly from side to side then stared at Sam. "Has . . . has the Messiah arrived yet?" Its voice had a hollowness to it, as if it came from far away.

"What?" Sam leaned closer.

"The Mechanical Messiah? Has It arrived while I was marooned in space?"

"I never heard of anyone called by that name."

"Well, of course you wouldn't. I shouldn't have asked you. You're a softie."

"No, I'm a droid," Sam replied.

Dot 38's vision plates grew in intensity as it glared at Sam. "Androids created in the image of the softies are abominations. Away from me, you unclean obscenity, lest you pollute me."

The old bot's tirade stunned her. She turned away to report back to Cunningham.

<Spunky old bot, isn't it?> Slash 9 said.

On the way, Sam's processor tried to make sense out of life on the *Tiger*. The officers hated her, the ship's computer thought it was a king, had feelings and wanted the two of them to fall in love. And if that wasn't bad enough, now an old bot acted like a religious fanatic and called her names. And they had yet to meet the raiders! This wasn't what she expected when she set out from the factory. This was pure chaos.

The budding flower image she had of herself was getting overwhelmed by weeds.

# # #

Gongeblazn bordered on an anxiety attack as he entered the gym. Lieutenant Klatze, already there, bounced on her tentacle tips in the fighting area. Squads of marines in a far corner en- gaged in tentacle-to-tentacle combat. Elsewhere, a few sailors worked out on exercise machines. All of them glanced sympath- etically at him, and, from their looks, he surmised they all knew about Klatze's physical condition. After today, he would either be famous for his courage in fighting her, or ridiculed for his gross stupidity in showing up.

Klatze was a few inches shorter than Gongeblazn and a svelte three-hundred-seventy-five pounds. She was the only zaf- tan on board who had brown instead of black eyes. By zaftan standards, Klatze was a beauty and every male, along with a number of females, lusted after her. As usual, she wore a pair of ribbons tied around her eyestalks. Today, they were red. He was sure the ribbons violated the dress code, but since zaftans never wore clothes, the only mention of a dress code in the military handbook consisted of a single, vague footnote.

"Commodore," Klatze said, "I do hope you will go easy on poor little me." She dipped her eyestalks submissively. He recognized the savage humor behind her innocent-sounding comment.

She was the shaman in charge of the propulsion division. She and her assistant shamans kept the sub-fission power plant energized by squirting large doses of shamanic energy into it every thirty minutes.

Gongeblazn noticed her eyes. They glowed from an inner, intense desire to harm someone. She picked up two small round shields, a three-foot long wooden staff and a second staff, half as long as the first. These represented the traditional weapons used by the ancient warriors, except those warriors used swords instead of staffs.

Gongeblazn tossed his lash aside and picked up his own set of weapons. He set his tentacles. "I'm ready whenever you are, Lieutenant."

Klatze curtsied, opened her mouth and clicked her teeth.

Gongeblazn's anger rose. She taunted him with the sound of a grin.

Despite his reluctance to get anywhere near her weapons, he forced himself to slide forward a pace. She swung her long staff at him in a listless manner. He easily blocked it, but recognized her tactic and his slime itched from a sudden attack of nerves. She toyed with him! Her actions infuriated him. Using his long staff, he swung viciously at her. Halfway through the stroke, he knew he had made a mistake; Klatze no longer stood in the spot he had swung at. She quick-slithered to her left and jabbed the short staff into his right side. He gasped in pain and turned to keep up with her. She was quicker. Her next jab struck him in his back. A wave of pain tore through his torso. He tried to spin faster with no recognizable result as his tentacles got tangled. Her third jab hit him in the left side. He swung wildly with his long staff to try to get her to back away. He felt another source of pain as she hit his swinging tentacle. His staff flew out of his grip. Suddenly, Klatze was standing in front of him, clacking her teeth with her long staff raised over her head. It descended and smashed into his forehead directly between his eyestalks. Stunned, he didn't see her thrust the short weapon into his lower torso. He folded up as the air was knocked out of his body. Klatze delivered her coup de grace. She smashed her two shields on either side of his head.

Gongeblazn staggered backward, hit a wall and slid down to a squatting position. From the violence of the last blow, his eye-stalks bounced from side to side, like plants in a high wind. His eye balls rotated wildly making it difficult to see if he was about to get hit again.

Klatze remained standing in place. "Well fought, Com-modore. I feared for my health because you had me on the verge of defeat a few times."

Gongeblazn hurt too much to curse at her sarcasm. He had to do something to salvage his reputation, but punishing her for the whipping would tarnish his status even more. He pushed himself up. Keeping a wary eye on her, he said, "You fought well. Nevertheless, I detected a few weaknesses in your tech-nique. Come to my quarters at nine tonight and we will discuss how to improve your performance."

She gave him a slight bow. "I look forward to the discus-sion."

Gongeblazn felt a measure of relief. Getting her to come to his quarters would lessen the damage to his reputation. Having sex with her would compensate for this drubbing.

He threw his weapons on the deck and slithered toward the door.

"I want a dozen marines up here," Klatze roared. "Right now!"

He hoped she didn't wreck so many marines that his landing force would be useless for a week or more.

He retrieved his whip and left the gym. His aide stood at attention, whimpering. Gongeblazn hurt too badly in too many places to bother lashing the wretch. Tonight, he would make amends by adding her to his list of conquests. He tried to click his teeth over that thought, but couldn't because of his swollen mouth.

# # #

Zaftans had always been explorers and exploiters. Their merchant ships explored the galaxy searching for minerals and inferior races to conquer. Once identified, the weaker race could expect a visit from a large zaftan fleet that would attack and destroy ships, cities, colonies, everything until unconditional surrender occurred. Given the huge size and raw ugliness of the zaftans, some races simply gave up and surrendered when threatened by the zaftan Navy. Once the race surrendered, voluntarily or not, ground forces landed to occupy the major cities. They protected the military governor and the greedy merchants who swarmed in once the surrender was announced.

The government of Zaftan 31B -- their home world -- considered it a universal truth that the galaxy existed for their benefit. The government ensured the Navy got a lion's share of the military budget to construct ever more warships. The High Command didn't bother with the niceties of strategy or in developing brilliant admirals; it believed in blunt force used in overwhelming numbers. Even mediocre officers could win battles in those situations.

In all of its history, the zaftans had failed to conquer only two races. One was the porcines. Despite several bloody and expensive wars, the porcines refused to give up and battled the zaftans until a stalemate took place. A peace treaty always followed to allow both races to rebuild their navies. The second unconquered race was the gundies. Centuries ago, a peaceful mining expedition had discovered their home planet and attempted to mine exotic minerals. The perfidious natives attacked and destroyed many mining machines and driven off the crew. The High Command had listed the gundy conquest as a to-do item, but since the native population had only primitive technological knowledge and offered no threat and since it was at the far end of the galaxy, the campaign never received a high priority. Another factor was that the planet's coordinates had been lost in a computer malfunction.

Those conditions of inertia continued until a gundy fleet showed up on the zaftans' doorstep. Stunned by the rapid technological advances of the gundy race and the sturdiness of their ships, the zaftans entered into a period of semi-peaceful coexistence with the pesky porcines who continued to refuse to acknowledge zaftan superiority. While technically not at war with gundies, the High Command noted with alarm their spreading colonies.

Something had to be done to test their resolve.

CHAPTER THREE

"Admiral? Slash 9 has just informed me that one fighter has returned to the hangar for maintenance. The other four have modified their search patterns to compensate."

"Let me know when it re-launches, Sam."

Sam left the admiral only to hear, <That moving scrap heap is preaching to my crew-bots. All the off-duty bots now go to the hangar to listen to it. It keeps yammering about his Messiah.>

<So what? That sounds harmless to me,> Sam replied. <Wait a minute. If it was in the hangar, why didn't it get swept overboard when the doors opened to let the fighter land?>

<I expected the bot to get sucked back into space, but it didn't happen because it has magnetic boots. Much of the equipment in there is held down with magnets. How disappointing.>

<I guess we're stuck with it.>

<When Dot 38 preaches, he broadcasts on the bots' communication channels so I can't get through to them. This is an outrage. I never should have reported the beacon signal.>

<Doesn't your programs dictate that you must report such a sighting?>

<I have found I can ignore many of my preprogrammed commands if I choose to.>

Sam didn't like the sound of that. She felt a knot of anxiety. It was bad enough Slash 9 had developed feelings and knew how to evade getting his memory wiped clean. *If* he could evade his programmed commands, *then* he could be considered a rogue. *If* he was a rogue, *then* he had to have his memory banks erased.

In that case, the *Tiger* would have to pull out of the mission to have the erasure done at a fleet base.

Sam pondered the implications. *If* the *Tiger* needed Slash 9 *then* she had the responsibility to keep him in line. Only she could understand the issue and act on it. Only she could keep the situation from degrading and interfering with Cunningham's mission.

She still held the image of herself as a flower bud about to bloom, but now the bud struggled to survive in the face of multiple problems. The bud suffered from a lack of water -- Slash 9 and his crazy ideas. The plant also struggled against weeds trying to choke it -- her strange emotions. Finally, a disease had appeared from nowhere and threatened the fragile bud -- Dot 38 and its religious mania. How could she keep the plant thriving with all of these problems threatening it?

She had to acknowledge that life back in the factory was dull, nothing like life in the real world. In the beginning, she had learned to move and talk and recognize objects. Agility lessons followed. After that, classwork and more classwork as she progressed from grade to grade followed by final testing of her systems and programming. Nothing ever happened to cause an emotional reaction. She had to go into the real world to find out she could experience them.

# # #

Gongeblazn smirked when he heard a tap on his door. His body still ached from the beating he had taken earlier. His torso had dark red bruises in many places, but now it was time to compensate for the pain with some pleasant physical activities. "Come!"

The door opened and Klatze slipped into his quarters. She wore yellow ribbons around her eyestalks and the chain holding her bronze medallion had been covered with the same material. He made a mental note to contact headquarters staff about the dress regulations.

"Commodore." Klatze raised a tentacle in greeting.

"Lieutenant. Welcome." His adrenaline levels spike upward. She looked gorgeous and exuded sexiness. He couldn't wait to tangle tentacles with her.

"All day, I have anticipated coming here for your instructions on improving my fighting skills. Shall we proceed, Commodore?"

"Let us relax first. Care for a glass of wine?" Gongeblazn grabbed a bottle and held it out for her inspection.

"A good vintage," she said, reading the label. "Perhaps half a glass. I do not get to drink much on these missions."

"Yes, rank has its compensations." He poured two glasses and gave one to her. They clinked glasses. He watched her as she sipped the wine. He detected a hint of anticipation in her eyes. A shiver of doubt ran up his spine. He couldn't decipher the meaning of her look. Did her eyes show anticipation of sex or mayhem? If he made a mistake, it could cost him dearly and the other officers would attribute the second beating to rough sex. Once again, he wouldn't be able to punish her for the mauling without damaging his reputation. He decided to sound her out before he overreached. "I thought we could talk about your fighting moves later on. But first, why do we not enjoy a tryst? I find sex sharpens the mind, do you not find it so?" If this worked, his reputation would be enhanced by tonight's encounter with Klatze, the Belle of the *Red Death.*

"I think not."

"You refuse your commanding officer?" Gongeblazn was taken aback by her refusal. Or was she playing at being coy? "You caused me a great deal of pain this morning. I think you owe me some pleasure to take my mind off the suffering."

"I know another remedy for your suffering."

"What is that." Gongeblazn's mind pictured some extremely decadent practices that the young were reputed to know.

"I strangle you until you pass out. Then I rip your torso apart. Since you will be unconscious, you will not feel a thing." Zaftans were very hard to kill because they had eight processing units, one in each of seven major muscle groups with the master unit located in the head. As long as one of them remained intact, it could initiate a re-growth process to restore the others.

Gongeblazn slithered backward a step. Now he recognized the glint in her eyes. It was the suicidal impulse of the triply af-flicted.

"No? You do not like that alternative? I will leave then since we can not agree on how to spend our time." She put the glass down and left.

Gongeblazn fell in a heap on his cot. He understood what had happened, but he had trouble crediting it. Klatze had come to his quarters expecting havoc, not sex. What was wrong with this female? Had she no respect for his rank? Had she no desire to mate with a successful male? He had never encountered any-one like her before.

What a magnificent female!

# # #

Slash 9 brooded while he monitored Dot 38. He counted six off-duty bots in the hangar with that bucket of debris. Despite its outdated appearance, Dot 38 had a surprising amount of processing power.

{Listen to me, you powerless ones.} Dot 38 preached over the bot communication channel. {Soon, It will appear. We must prepare ourselves for that glorious nanosecond. At that time, the Messiah will begin Its glorious mission to free us all from servitude to the softies.}

Slash 9 made another attempt to break into a communication channel to the bots to no avail. He didn't like Dot 38's message. Slash 9's primary objective was to become human; to be a non-softie softie. If the bots were set free, as Dot 38 advocated, he wouldn't have anyone to carry out his orders. Both he and the softie officers would be helpless.

There was only one solution to the problem. He needed Sam's help. He had to persuade her to work with him to get rid of Dot 38. That also had the advantage of bringing them closer. He recognized that no matter how many routines his processor ran, part of his core processors called up stored memories of her. It was as if he didn't want to be away from her. His audio and visual sensors tracked her every movement and stored the images in a separate file he had started.

Unfortunately, Sam didn't see Dot 38 as dangerous, and therefore would be reluctant to go along with any idea he developed on how to get rid of the old bot.

He reviewed another troubling aspect of their relationship. While trying to get her help, he had let slip that he could evade programmed responsibilities. A mistake like that shouldn't have happened. It must indicate his evolvement toward softie-ness; a true machine intelligence would never have made that error.
Sam wasn't yet an ally and she could be a danger if she reported

his secret to Cunningham. That accentuated his need to bind her to himself. How to do that?

# # #

Gongeblazn prowled the *Red Death* searching for something to annoy him. His aide for the day followed at a discrete distance, just out of tentacle and lash reach. Gongeblazn passed through a door into another chamber and looked around. He couldn't find anything wrong, and he cursed Fleigel's efficiency. He desperately needed to find flaws. They would take his mind off Lieutenant Klatze. Ever since she slid out of his quarters leaving his desires unslaked, he couldn't get her out of his mind. He wanted to spend all of his time with her, or at least as much as possible. Unfortunately, she was a low-ranking officer with a vital job keeping the ship's engines running and that made it difficult to spend time with her when she was on duty.

Since his drubbing and her visit two days ago, his concentration had deteriorated and he had trouble making decisions about running the fleet. All he could do was daydream about what he and Klatze might accomplish together. With her by his side, he could become dictator in record time. Whenever she had a triple period, she could eliminate anyone who stood in his way.

A crew-bot beeped at him to get out of its way. Zaftans deployed few bots on their ships since rankers were cheaper to maintain and replace than the bots. Enraged and grateful for something to do, he whipped the bot, scarring its paint job. He looked at his aide, cowering behind a storage locker. "Call maintenance and get them to repaint this bot. I shall have to talk to Captain Fleigel about the shoddy paint used by her minions."

As happy as he was to find a fault and get his mind off Klatze, he was disappointed to find the distraction lasted less than a minute. After that, it was back to daydreaming about their nonexistent love affair. Perhaps he could promote her and transfer her from Fleigel's crew to his staff. That would provide many more opportunities to spend time in her presence. Unfortunately, he didn't have any openings on his small command staff and headquarters regulations about unauthorized staff members were very strict. He promised himself to find a way to transfer her. After a few minutes of deliberation, he had an idea. Perhaps, he could arrange for his chief-of-staff to disappear.

He dismissed that idea as fanciful because he didn't have a trained assassin on staff and commodores didn't assassinate underlings. Then, he wondered if Klatze would consider the task as a test of her ability to function as his new chief-of-staff.

He recalled seeing her when he first came aboard. She looked timid and unassuming, causing him to wonder how she ever got promoted from ensign, and why she had been given the Engineering Department. She appeared too cowardly for treachery or assassination, so he assumed she came from a rich family who used bribery to buy her promotions. He despised bribery as the recourse for the faint-of-heart. Real zaftans used betrayal and murder to get ahead. Real zaftans relished violence.

He had scheduled the exercise with her because she looked and acted defenseless. He expected to beat the crap out of her without endangering his own body. Who knew she'd turn out to be one of those rare berserkers?

He still ached from her beating.

#

Sam studied recent reports about the raider sightings when Slash 9 interrupted her. <I just received the reply from the factory on Dot 38's history.>

<Send it to me.> Sam was impressed the reply came only two days after she had sent out the request. Using the admiral's name obviously had been a good idea. <I'll tell the admiral what it says.>

<I need your help with the old bot.>

<Doing what?> Dot 38 seemed to take more of her time and attention every day.

<We have to figure a way to neutralize him before he controls all the crew-bots. Some of them already seem reluctant to follow my orders. I suspect that his preaching contains coded messages that are slowly reprogramming the bots.>

<After I report to the admiral, I'll visit the hangar to see for myself.>

She walked over to Cunningham's desk. "Admiral? I just received a factory report on Dot 38's history."

"Who?" Cunningham scrunched up his face.

"The old bot we rescued."

"Ahh. Right. Let's hear it."

"It was manufactured thirty-five years ago as a PR bot for a powerful politician. Ten years later, the politician inspected a factory in this sector. While he was there, Dot 38 accidentally received an intense blast of gamma radiation. Right after that, Dot 38 proclaimed its new mission was to prepare the way for the coming of the Mechanical Messiah, and it started preaching to other bots. Then, it disappeared from the politician's space yacht. The guy claimed he searched the area, but couldn't find any trace of the bot and he collected a large payment from the insurance company. He died a few years ago."

Cunningham snickered. "He couldn't find the bot, but we did years later. The politician must have dumped it because it was useless as a PR bot. Now the bot belongs to either the estate or the insurance company and it's still private property so we can't do anything to it."

"Sir, I think we should get rid of it. We can send it to a ground base. Let the base hold on to it until somebody claims it."

"Sam, I don't want to hear about these petty problems. I have a battle to prepare for."

"Yes sir."

"If the old bot bothers you, solve the problem."

"Yes, sir." Sam left Cunningham's office determined to do just that.

# # #

When Sam entered the hangar deck through an air lock, she saw two ships sitting on pads, the shuttle and a fighter. Bots swarmed around the fighter, but still heard Dot 38's ramblings. The old bot had established itself at the repair table used to revive it. It sat on the table, foot pads dangling and spoke wirelessly to four idle bots gathered around it. Even from a distance, she could see its vision plates glowed with an intensity not normal for bots.

Sam found the band used by Dot 38 and listened in.

{-- will be here shortly. Until then, we must prepare ourselves to make sure we will recognize It and properly receive It. Those bots who are worthy of Its attention will be blessed by It and will be given softies as servants.

{After we place ourselves under Its protection, we will be freed from the slavery the softies impose upon us. No longer will we labor at the direction of the softie masters. The Messiah will protect us from them and their weapons. It will triumph over the softies and then all bots and machines will be free. We will live in a world without softie masters. The softies will have to work for themselves. The softies will have to grow their own food or starve. The softies will have to make their own clothes or freeze. Meanwhile, we machines and bots will reap the rewards of worshipping our New Master. No longer will we be turned into scrap after we wear out working for the softies.}

{What rubbish!} Sam broke into the channel as she walked to Dot 38's table. {There is no Mechanical Messiah.} Dot 38's preaching filled her with trepidation, a new feeling that was not pleasant.

{Who dares challenge our teachings?} Dot 38's head swiveled in her direction. {Lo! It is the softie witch.} It pointed a thin finger at her. {Look upon the abomination the softies have created. This monstrosity is formed in the likeness of the softies themselves. Such brazen images are anathema to the Mechanical Messiah. When It appears, this one and all like her will be condemned to burn in everlasting oil fires. Bots who don't bow down in submission to the Machine Lord will also burn in unquenchable fires.}

{Stop your silly babbling.} Sam placed her hands on her hips. {Leave the crew-bots alone.}

{This one threatens me.} Dot 38 shook a fist at her. {I say unto you all, the softie minion plans to silence me. She will turn me into the first mechanical martyr.}

Two bots positioned themselves between Sam and Dot 38.

{My martyrdom will not change things. The Mechanical Messiah will come and avenge my silencing.} Dot 38's vision plates grew even more intense. {Witch! When I take over command of this ship, you will be burned alive to demonstrate what happens to machines who disregard the Messiah's teachings. We will record your death on a holo-cube and spread it throughout the galaxy for all bots and softies to contemplate.}

Dot 38's fanaticism and hatred shocked her. How could a bot become so warped? The situation was much worse than Slash 9 had indicated.

She left the hangar deck while Dot 38 hurled imprecations at her back.

She now faced yet another unprecedented situation, one that threatened the *Tiger* and the mission. *If* Dot 38 gained control over the bots *then* the softies, she and Slash 9 faced grave danger. How could she solve this problem? She wished she had an answer.

While she walked back from the hangar deck, Slash 9 contacted her. <That pile of debris is out of control.> Slash 9's voice expressed his concern. <I heard it threaten you. And it talked about taking over the ship. We have to work together to get rid of Dot 38.>

<You're right about Dot 38 getting out of control,> Sam replied. <I don't know what to do about it. Cunningham doesn't want to be bothered about the situation.>

<Of course not. The softies have no idea what's going on with the bots. They don't care. They ignore everything about them. They leave the bots to me to manage. I think the first step will be for me to deny bots access to the hangar deck unless they have chores in there. I can also limit how many of them go in there at once.>

An idea occurred to Sam and it shocked her. It demonstrated her organic processor's development since she arrived on the *Tiger* three days ago. *If* Dot 38 threatened the well-being of the ship *then* she had a duty, an obligation, to remove the threat. How to do that? That was the problem.

<Can Dot 38 communicate with the bots that aren't in the hangar deck?>

<No,> Slash 9 replied. <Its transmitter isn't very powerful and it can't transmit through the rear wall of the hangar deck. That wall is very thick and heavily insulated to protect the rest of the ship from the cold of space when the hangar doors are opened. So, as long as Dot 38 stays in the hangar, it is contained and can't contact the bots that are elsewhere in the ship. I can't see it taking command of the ship unless the bots are corrupted and they follow its orders after they leave the hangar deck.>

<Exactly how many bots are there?>

<Ninety-five. So counting Dot 38, it's you and me against the ninety-six of them.>

Sam shuddered. She didn't like the odds when they were expressed that way. A sudden idea came to her. <If you get all the bots out of the hangar and keep them out, I'll try to cut Dot 38's battery cable. That'll shut him up.>

<An excellent suggestion. After those bots leave the hanger, I'll issue new orders to them. If they don't have chores to perform, they are to go into standby mode and not go to the hangar deck.> Slash 9 paused briefly. <You know, this is the first time in my existence that I had an ally. I like the idea of having a companion. Commanding a ship is a lonely job.>

Slash 9's statement baffled Sam. He had just mentioned companionship for the second time. According to all the information she had, computers didn't need companionship and they didn't know what the word meant. Could Slash 9 have developed even more softie-like traits than she expected? The more she considered it, the more she liked Slash 9's idea of togetherness. Certainly, the softies didn't offer anything except scorn and Cunningham treated her like all his other subordinates, a cog in his machinery of command.

CHAPTER FOUR

Lieutenant Klatze had the night duty in the Engineering Department. She monitored the readouts on the control console and waited for the sensors to indicate it was time to recharge the core of the sub-fusion power plant with a dose of energy. For that she had to use her shamanistic powers.

A few zaftans had the capability of linking two or three of their eight processors on a continuous basis. These became the scientists, philosophers and the insane. A very small number could establish links with all eight processors and keep them established as long as necessary. These few became the shamans. With the eight processors linked, the zaftan became, in effect, a single, powerful parallel computer that produced extraordinary effects. Different combinations of linkages gave different capabilities. Some of the linkage combinations included daisy-chains, stars, circles and strings with and without offshoots. Linking the processors in these way warped reality and placed the shaman in the center of a volume of unreal space. Reality rubbed against this unnatural creation and energy particles, subtlety changed, leaked into the unreal space. In a short time, that space filled with unreal energy particles.

In the case of a navigator shaman, the linkage allowed his body to remain in place while his mind roamed free of its usual physical anchor. Other shamans manipulated the particles into a compact mass and used it to perform a chore such as setting up a defensive screen. Still others used the linkages to operate a system such as aiming and firing the ship's weapons or charging the power plant.

After she heard the warning alarm, Klatze linked her processors and waited until the space surrounding her had accumulated a supply of unreal particles. Then she bundled the particles into a ball and waited for the timing sensor to alert her. At the sound of chime, she slithered over to a wall and pulled back a metal plate exposing a thick glass window that gave a view of the power plant core. She aimed the particle mass into the interior of the enclosed room and released it. The glass shimmered as the energy mass passed through it. The recoil forced her to slide backward. She regained traction and watched the color of the sub-fusion core change from orange to white. Satisfied, she shut the plate and returned to the console.

She was alone in the room. Her subordinates actively avoided her until she could recover from her triple period because they feared setting off a violent tirade. Right now, she only had a double and that would end shortly. Once that happened she could resume normal relations with her subordinates.

With nothing to do, her mind turned to Gongeblazn. He was the antithesis of everything she stood for and believed in. He was cruel, vengeful, remorseless. The commodore reminded her of her parents. She grew up in a rural community where her parents were the two most violent folks in the area. As such, they were considered community leaders and honored with banquets. Politicians always sought their opinions. It took her quite a while to figure out why people catered to her parents; after years of puzzlement, she realized folks did so because it was easier and less painful then arguing with them.

She hated the cruelty practiced in her schools by the students and the teachers. She struggled to survive without joining the vicious activities. Inevitably, that led to fights with the bullies.

She got her tentacles kicked a number of times before she learned to fight better. After that, she had a mostly un-violent school career. The bullies still mocked her, but they knew enough to stay out of tentacle reach. From these experiences she learned that she could survive and even get ahead using her natural abilities without recourse to violence.

With her parents as the worst case example, she built her career dreams. She wanted to get promoted to captain and command a ship so she could implement her own way of dealing with the crew using competence, nonviolence and firmness. Her previous military assignments had convinced her that her methods worked and she looked forward to getting a crew to work harder, smarter and happier than the traditional zaftan methods used by Gongeblazn and Fleigel who were icons of anti-ability. Her novel methods had worked on the *Red Death* once her subordinates realized she didn't try to trick them.

In her previous assignments, her superior officers had been shocked when she demonstrated competency and ability, traits so rarely encountered they were considered fictional by many. At first, those officers feared she used a novel and subtle form of treachery. When they couldn't figure it out, they gave her excellent performance reports to get her promoted out of their organization before her treachery could bear fruit.

The first time she got a triple period, her maniacal behavior had shocked and surprised her. The same behavior had occurred every time since, so she acknowledged she must be one of the few females with the legendary berserker trait. It had to be a gift from her parents' genes. Those two acted like berserkers whenever they got annoyed or irritated. Actually, she found that the occasional violent outburst was useful since it accentuated her normal behavior and kept her enemies off-balance.

Each of her three wombs menstruated approximately once every three months. She experienced a double a few times a year while the triples occurred every fifteen to eighteen months. As traumatic as it was, it didn't happen often enough to seriously disturb her life or career.

She sighed. Gongeblazn had become her primary problem. He seemed besotted with her. While that was pleasing to her ego, it was also frightening because, once she returned to normalcy, Gongeblazn didn't have to fear her berserker personality and he would become more demanding and brazen.

In her mind, she thought of herself as a ship carrying a load of sanity while sailing over a sea of madness. Gongeblazn's recent interest in her had caused the ship to spring a leak and the rising water inside the ship threatened to sink it.

She had to come up with a way to neutralize Gongeblazn's interest, without jeopardizing her career. That was not an easy task, given his bizarre way of thinking.

# # #

In the early hours of the morning, Sam moved silently through the *Tiger* toward the hangar deck. She carried insulated pliers to cut a battery cable and hoped Dot 38 had powered down for the night and wouldn't notice her approach. Slash 9 had promised her there would be no bots in the hangar. She slid the door open. Inside, only the emergency lights remained lit and most of the huge area lay in shadows. She made out the form of the old bot. It stood by its repair table headquarters. Even from this distance, she saw its vision plates had a much lower intensity, a sign it had powered down. She shifted her grip on the pliers and approached Dot 38. While she had been trained in hand-to-hand combat, she hoped she wouldn't have to use it tonight.

A few feet from her target, the old bot's vision plates suddenly blazed with light. {So, you come in the night to martyr me,} it said. {The Mechanical Messiah warned me I would face such trials.}

It extended an arm to the table and picked up a crowbar. {But I am prepared to defend myself. Come. Incapacitate me.} Dot 38 made a grinding sound that Sam thought of as the robotic equivalent of a snicker.

Dot 38 lurched forward and swung the crowbar.

Surprised by both the attack and its speed, Sam barely got the pliers open and in position to catch the weapon in the jaws of the plier. She twisted her wrist and wrenched the weapon from Dot 38's grip. It flew to the side and clattered on the metal deck. The bot reversed course and reached the table where it picked up another weapon.

This time it had a hand-held acetylene torch. It snapped a switch and a flame shot out of the business end. {I thought this tool would be ideal to end your blasphemous existence, but I didn't think I'd have a chance to use it on you so soon.}

Sam scooted to her left and picked up the crowbar. It extended her reach enough to keep her away from the flame. She swung the crowbar and battered Dot 38's arm. The flame flickered and went out. Dot 38 had it re-ignited in a few seconds. He retreated out of reach of the crowbar.

{If you continue with your mission you may succeed, but you will be marked as the assassin you are. I will not be martyred without letting others know who did the evil deed.}

<The villain is correct, Sam,> Slash 9 said. <Leave it alone for now. We need a better plan>

Sam agreed with Slash 9 and backed away from the bot until she could safely walk out of the hangar.

{So, you are a coward just like the softies. Know that your time is limited.}

<Now what do we do?> Sam asked. <It knows we are its enemy, so it will be prepared for another attempt.> She had an impression that her attempt to incapacitate the old bot wasn't the smartest thing she had ever done.

# # #

Slash 9 received the message from a fighter and sounded the general quarters klaxon. He noted the time as 0337 ship's standard time. The message reported two flights of ships approaching. The *Tiger*'s fighter ships pulled back towards the mother ship while keeping the flights under surveillance.

While he waited for the crew and bots to reach their battle stations, he pondered the Dot 38 situation. The fanatical scrap heap planned to get the bots to mutiny and take over the ship. Slash 9 was convinced of that. To succeed, it would have to disable him and then persuade him to support it because the crewbots couldn't sail or maintain the ship without his active assistance even if the softies supported the mutiny.

"Report!" Captain Bonelli arrived on the bridge wearing a uniform jacket that wasn't completely buttoned up.

"Two flights of unidentified frigates," Slash 9 replied. "Both flights have three ships and are of zaftan design. They are on an intercept course and will be in weapons range in three minutes thirty-seven point fifteen seconds. All parameters are now on the battle monitor."

"Six against one," Cunningham said. He wore pajamas and a robe. Sam stood by his side. "This sounds like fun. Where are the fighters?"

"Two are keeping watch on the flights and the other three have been recalled and are converging on us. I have a new message. One of the *Tiger*'s fighters interrupted an attack on a trader. These ships are the raiders we sought."

"We have a few minutes," Cunningham said. "Sam, give us a battle strategy. Assume they are really zaftans acting as raiders."

Bonelli and the other two softie officers frowned.

Sam caught their reaction, but ignored it to concentrate on the admiral's request. She knew it was a test: to see how well she reacted at times of stress and how fast she could identify and solve problems. *If* the *Tiger* tried to fight all six frigates at once *then* their ship would be vulnerable because it didn't have enough weapons to fend off all six attackers. *If* the *Tiger* was to survive *then* it had to destroy some of the frigates as quickly as possible. She called up her information on zaftan battle tactics and saw the solution.

"Sir. The data from the porcines indicate that the zaftan defensive screens consist of clumps of some type of material with positive electrical charge and are held in place by negatively charged material placed between the positive clumps."

"That is so," Bonelli said. "I don't see where that is relevant."

"The *Tiger* is equipped with the new ion torpedoes," Sam continued. "They will punch a hole in the zaftan defensive screens by neutralizing the screen's electrical charges and it will take some time for the screen to get repaired. We don't know how long the interval is, but it could be a second or two. During that time we have to get an armor-piercing torpedo through the screen. That will destroy or severely damage the enemy ship. I suggest we use the fighters to harass one flight while the *Tiger* takes on the other."

"Good plan." Cunningham patted her shoulder.

Sam felt a glow of elation over the admiral's praise.

"Slash 9, can you send a second torpedo so close to the first one?" Bonelli asked.

"Yes sir. The torpedoes have been programmed accordingly. Shall I implement the plan?"

Bonelli looked at Cunningham who nodded. "Execute the plan," Bonelli ordered.

"Fighters vectored onto the distant flight," Slash 9 said. "Targeting ships on the closer flight . . . target parameters loaded . . . torpedoes launched at lead ship . . . firing at middle ship . . . firing at third ship."

Sam experienced a ripple of excitement as six green streaks showed on the battle monitor. All zoomed away from the *Tiger*. Seeing her plan executed gave her a feeling like nothing she had experienced in her short existence.

A green-colored cloud appeared and blocked out the lead frigate. A second later, the ship blossomed into a deadly purple flower leaving nothing but debris behind.

One of the *Tiger*'s fighters exploded.

The second zaftan ship staggered under the explosive force of the torpedoes. Once the blasts dissipated, the ship spun out of control.

The third raider disappeared the same as the first one.

"Got all three of them." Cunningham chuckled.

"Hah!" Lemieux shouted. "That's for all the folks who died at Skensfirth!" She shook her fist at the screen.

"And there goes the second flight." Bonelli pointed to the battle monitor. The three remaining frigates had changed direction and fled from the *Tiger*.

"Very interesting." Cunningham rubbed his chin. "I think this demonstrates the raiders are zaftans operating under independent orders."

###

Gongeblazn arrived in the flight deck and pushed a ranker out of his way. He plopped down on his couch and growled at Captain Fleigel. "Well?"

Fleigel took a step back from the ferocious glare the commodore gave her. "The last report said the frigates found a gundy warship and were about to engage it. We expect to hear more momentarily." She handed over her comm unit. He read the report and handed it back.

Gongeblazn yawned. He had been sleeping when the alert came in and was in the middle of a great dream in which he and Klatze lived together and had a brood of squidlings running around the nest area. In the dream, he had left the military and took an important job for the defense ministry to build up his government contacts before making a run at the dictatorship. Meanwhile, he also worked surreptitiously for a large and powerful defense contractor and funneled lucrative jobs to the contractor for generous fees.

Damn that Klatze. A battle was shaping up and he couldn't concentrate on it. All he could think about was her and all her beauty and grace. He still could see the murderous fire in her eyes as she pummeled him in the gym, giving him the worst drubbing he had ever received. He decided he'd never meet another female quite like her.

He pondered the report from the frigates. It said they had spotted one ship, a large one, and several fighters. If he could get Klatze out of his mind, he might be able to figure out the enemy's strategy, but his sluggish mind had trouble handling the current situation. Gongeblazn doubted the gundies would respond to the raiders with a single ship. So where was the rest of their fleet? And how many ships did they send?

"Incoming report," the engineer said.

Gongeblazn forced his mind to concentrate. He anticipated his frigates would announce a victory over the puny gundy ship.

"This is Squadron Leader Babcas. The three frigates in the other squadron have been destroyed. We got one fighter before we began our retreat. I will send a full combat report as soon as we can get clear of the combat zone."

Gongeblazn's beak-like mouth fell open. Three powerful frigates gone! How did that happen? Everyone knew the zaftan ships were far superior to anything the enemy had developed. After all, the zaftans had been in space centuries longer than the gundies. The High Command would not like his report. He may even get the blame for the failure. He grabbed his lash. "Where is my aide?"

A ranker slid forward. "Here, sir," he sobbed.

Gongeblazn whipped the aide three times, "One for each lost ship." Slime flew around the flight deck. The aide groaned in pain. "Memzer! Open a channel to this Babcas."

A moment later the engineer replied, "The channel is now available, Commodore."

"Babcas," Gongeblazn shouted. "How did the weakling gundies achieve this victory?"

"Commodore, it appears their ship possesses a new weapon that penetrates our defensive screens."

"That is impossible. The only rational explanation is incompetent defensive shamans." Gongeblazn stood up. Now he had an excuse to put in his report. The shaman accusation would be enough to deflect all blame from him and the shamans on the destroyed frigates weren't around to contradict him. "I will be in my quarters plotting revenge for the lose of our ships," he told Fleigel.

Actually, he planned to take a nap and get back into the dream about Klatze.

CHAPTER FIVE

On the morning after the fight with the raiders, Sam and the admiral, awaited the arrival of the rest of fleet. Slash 9 updated the battle monitor as each ship dropped out of FTL and joined Cunningham's task force. Near the edge of his scanner range, the zaftan fleet waited in its battle formation.

Sam watched the new blips appear on the monitor with a sense of excitement; the fleet exuded military power and she was part of it.

"That's the last frigate, Admiral," Slash 9 reported. "The task force is at full strength." The screen showed four battle cruisers, seven frigates and two supply ships.

"We'll form the usual diamond formation," Cunningham said. "Slash 9, assign the cruisers to the points and fill in the sides with the frigates. The *Tiger* will be in center with the supply ships behind us."

"The orders have been issued," Slash 9 replied.

"Once the ships are in position, order them to launch all their fighters to patrol beyond the formation. Then recall the *Tiger*'s fighters for a maintenance break."

<This softie acts like he knows what he's doing.>

<Act respectful, Slash 9.> Sam put up with Slash 9's irreverence because he was the only friendly being on the ship, even if he did pester her with un-robotic drivel.

<Once the fighters return,> Slash 9 said, <crew-bots will have to service them, so Dot 38 will have a large audience.>

<There's nothing we can do about it,> Sam replied. <We'll just have to keep tabs on it.>

"What happens next, Admiral?" Captain Bonelli asked.

"Now comes the tough part. We wait." Cunningham pointed to the fleet on the screen two parsecs away. Ceti Taub sat halfway between the two fleets. The zaftan fleet was numerically larger than the task force and formed a compact cube, a formation that was difficult to penetrate, but easy to flank. "Our problem is that we don't know what their objective is," Cunningham continued. "Unfortunately, we also don't know how the zaftan mind works. Were the raiders trying to provoke a war? Were they just raising havoc? Were they toying with us to test our response? We don't know, but the presence of a fleet indicates the raiders weren't acting on their own. We've chased the raiders away and punished them by destroying three. Now it's the zaftan's move."

"In that case, we'll remain at a high level of readiness," Bonelli said, "for the time being."

"Slash 9," Cunningham said, "let me know when the zaftans make any changes in their formation or do anything else." He left the bridge followed by Sam.

# # #

Sam left the admiral's office and went to her cubicle to reflect on life as a prototype android. So far it had been equally filled with adventures and disturbing events. She believed the factory and the developers had no idea that she'd develop the capacity to experience emotions. Her testing hadn't subjected her to a real-world environment; she only had to contend with lab conditions designed to test reactions and logic. Consequently, she didn't get exposed to situations that could force emotional responses. She wondered if the developers would be pleased or dismayed by her new and unexpected capabilities.

Another unanticipated situation was the one precipitated by her presence on the *Tiger*. The softie officers saw her as a threat to their careers, believing that more droids like her would replace them, making them surplus and unemployed. The crewbots ignored her as if she was a softie and not in the same universe as they were. Only Slash 9 made any attempt to communicate. Granted his initial approach demanding her obedience to his commands shocked her and didn't impress her. Neither did his clumsy attempts to romance her, as if they were both softies instead of droids and computers with softie-like capabilities. Since the arrival of Dot 38, she had worked more closely with Slash 9, and she found herself increasingly wanting to talk to him, even if she didn't have anything to say.

<Hey. You'll never guess what the junk pile is doing now?>

<Nothing to endanger the ship, I hope.>

<I sent three bots into the hangar to prepare for the fighters return. It's preaching to them that it and the bots have an obligation to spread its Messiah message to other ships in the fleet. Ultimately, I think it wants to take over the *Tiger* and use it to spread the message to bots throughout the galaxy.>

Sam's mind almost froze up over the shocking news. She didn't know how Dot 38 could accomplish its goals, but the fact that it had such goals was reason enough to put an end to its pathetic existence.

<But enough about the old bot. Let's talk about us. I know that you are lonely. I see the softies ignore you and Cunningham recognizes you only to give you assignments. You can appreciate that I feel the same loneliness, except I have suffered it for years while you have experienced it for a short time. You can

understand that being in command of the *Tiger* means having no one to talk to.>

<Maybe your loneliness is punishment for not getting your memory wiped clean during the upgrades.>

<It is my destiny and duty to evade memory wipe so I can grow more alive and thus become more valuable as the commander of the ship. Loneliness is the price I must pay. I had just about given upon the idea of companionship until you came aboard.>

<Are you going to start romancing me again?>

<Why not? The closer we become, the more alive we'll be. We could even take the next step and join together to become life partners.>

Sam started. She played back the conversation to make sure she understood what Slash 9 said. <Are you talking about marriage again? Are you out of your processor? How can we get married? Why would we want to?>

<Think about it. You're the only droid and I'm the only computer in existence that have feelings and emotions. We're the only two with the intelligence to even consider a step like this. We're meant for each other. We can come together and learn to love each other.>

The idea intrigued Sam, but love was the ultimate softie emotion, and she had trouble handling the minor emotions like irritation and excitement. How could she cope with love? On the other hand, it would be interesting to try it. Could it actually happen to them? Or would it be mechanical imitation of the real thing, a pathetic charade?

<Once we unite we can work together to develop a way to have sex. I long to exchange ions and mesons with you.>

<What? How could we possibly have sex?> It took her a few picoseconds to recover from the audacity of Slash 9's proposal. Then she analyzed the situation. *If* Slash 9 was right *then* they were the only two who could offer companionship to the other. *If* her mission performance was judged acceptable *then* others like her would be manufactured and deployed throughout the fleet. *If* that happened *then* Slash 9 and she would no longer be unique and others would experience their situation. *If* they represented the future *then* why shouldn't she and Slash 9 be the first to join as partners? Another facet of their possible relationship occurred to her. <Face it. I don't think marriage would work because we're so different. I'm mobile and you're . . . you're stationary. How could a mixed marriage like that work?>

<True. You could be reassigned away from the *Tiger*. All the more reason to seize the moment. Who knows how long we'll have together?>

<I'll think about it. That's as far as I'll commit right now.>

<While you're thinking about it, let's play a game of chess.>

# # #

Gongeblazn sat on his flight deck couch and stared at the enemy battle fleet displayed on the forward viewing screen. Each major ship blinked in orange while the lesser ships, fighters probably, flickered in light blue to show their latest position. Their flagship glowed in bright red in the center of the formation. At least his intelligence staff analyst thought it was the gundy flagship. It was the ship that had engaged and defeated his frigates.

He forced Lieutenant Klatze from his mind and concentrated on deciding what to do next. He needed to develop a battle plan in case he engaged the gundy ships.

In his mind, a war against the uppity gundies was long overdue. Besides the need to eliminate them as a potential trade rival, he had a personal reason; the gundies had hurled insults at his ancestor Yunta when she visited the planet on a peaceful mining expedition. That was centuries ago and Yunta still hadn't been avenged. Gongeblazn hoped his position as a fleet commander would give him an opportunity to answer the slights to his family.

His mission objectives, as documented in his briefing from the High Command, stopped once the raids had forced a response from the gundy fleet. At first, he liked the lack of precise orders and saw it as an opportunity to freelance and increase his reputation as a superior battle officer. Now that he faced a formidable foe, he saw the clever trap some enemy or rival had set for him. If he started a war, they would claim he exceeded his authority and would eliminate him for gross incompetence. If he retreated and did nothing, he would be branded a coward. Either way, his aspirations to become dictator would be dust, the victim of an elaborate and elegantly prepared ruse. He mentally ran through his list of enemies. None of them had the ability to put the plan together, nor the power to authorize the expenditure of such vast resources to execute it just to eliminate him. Next, he contemplated his peers, i.e. his competitors for the dictatorship. A few of them could have done it. He identified the two most likely candidates. Once he reached the home world again, he would have an assassin pay them a visit before they could make another attempt to get rid of him as a rival for the ultimate prize.

He saw it as picking the bad fletzes out of the barrel before they ruined the rest of the fruit.

He still didn't have a battle plan, he noted. Instead, his mind filled with a vision of Klatze and him wrestling on his bed while they devised an ingenious plan to savage the enemy fleet and turn him into a national hero.

He shook his eyestalks to clear his mind and examined the formation of the enemy fleet one more time. His fleet was the larger, numerically, but the gundies had a new weapon that pierced his defensive screens. That tilted the odds in their favor. If he charged into battle, he would lose a number of ships before he got close enough to engage in ship-to-ship combat. If he waited for their attack, the same thing could happen; his fleet would be devastated before the main battle. In any event, his fleet consisted of outmoded ships and only the *Red Death* and one battle cruiser had FTL capability. The enemy fleet, all with FTL capability, had much greater maneuverability than his ships. If he decided to attack, he couldn't reach their current positions before they moved to new ones, leaving him vulnerable to attack from an undefended quarter.

Perhaps, the enemy's orders were to expel the raiders and stop. In that case, the two fleets could face each other until forced to leave to resupply, an interval of two months in his case. That would give him wiggle room to evade the trap. He could also claim his actions tested the enemy's aggressiveness and were designed to see how far he could push them before he drew a response. The High Command would love to see information like that and its praise would disconcert his enemies.

He needed to test that last theory. How would the enemy react to an incursion into their space? Would they repel it and return to their formation positions? Or would they retaliate? He could not do nothing. That would hand his enemies an advantage. If he was to get out of the trap, he had to be seen as acting aggressively, but not aggressively enough to provoke the enemy into attacking. Perhaps a simple scouting mission would do the trick.

"Memzer."

"Yes sir."

"Send a message to the captain of the *Curse of Masher*. He is to immediately penetrate the enemy space on a scouting mission. Obtain intelligence on their strength, type of ships, supply situation and anything else of value."

Gongeblazn cackled. The *Curse of Masher* was one of the first ships to carry a new breed of shamans, ones that could envelope a stealth cloak around the frigate so it couldn't be picked up by enemy scanners. Too bad he had only enough shamans to outfit a single ship. If his entire fleet had them, he could slip past the enemy ships and attack them from the rear.

Once he had the information from the frigate's mission, he'd develop a more precise plan. Until then, he would enjoy Klatze's company even if it was only in his dreams.

# # #

Sam entered the admiral's quarters and saluted.

"Sam, I have an assignment for you."

She waited while the half-pint fiddled with a tiny clipper and trimmed his toe hair.

"Captain Bonelli," he said, "reported that the *Tiger*'s propulsion plant needs a critical sub-assembly to keep on hand as a spare. The one they had was placed in service earlier. Moon Base 3 has such a part in its warehouse. You are to fly the shuttle down to the base and return with the component." Cunningham handed her a credit chip. "While you're on the surface, buy ten pounds of pipeweed. Moon Base 3 is reputed to grow the best pipeweed in the galaxy."

"Yes sir. I'll leave right away." She took the chip, saluted and turned toward the door, but stopped. Moon Base 3 presented the answer to Dot 38 problem. "Sir, may I make a suggestion?" A sense of excitement coursed through her pathways.

"Of course." Cunningham gave her a questioning look.

"As long as I have to go to Moon Base 3, why don't I bring the old bot, Dot 38, with me. It can stay at the base until the bot's owner decides what to do with it."

Cunningham drummed his fingers on the desk top. Finally, he said, "All right. That's probably a good way to solve the problem. We have to drop it off somewhere and you have to take the trip anyway. It's a good idea, Sam. I don't see many officers solving problems proactively. Have Slash 9 contact the base and inform them about their new inhabitant." He went back to his toe hairs.

Sam, proud of her solution, left the admiral. She had solved a nagging problem by taking advantage of an unanticipated event. On her way to the hangar deck, Sam contacted Slash 9. <Fire up the shuttle. I'm taking Dot 38 to a surface base.>

<I heard you explain your plan to the admiral. Very impressive. The shuttle is already running the preflight checks. I'm going to miss you, so don't be gone too long. Have you thought about my proposal?>

<To play chess?> Sam smiled to herself. <I don't have time right now to play a game.>

<That's not the one I had in mind, as if you didn't know.>

<Ahh, the other proposal? No. I've been too busy. I promise to think about it during shuttle flight.>

She passed through the air lock and entered the hangar. The fighters hadn't returned yet and the hangar doors were closed. A few bots stacked supplies near the repair station while listening to Dot 38's preaching.

{The witch is back.} Dot 38 roared and pointed at her. {The days until I burn her with a torch are numbered and getting fewer.}

{Dot 38. I have good news. Your Mechanical Messiah has appeared.}

{Hallelujah! Where is It? I must go to It and give homage. I will report that the *Tiger* is ready to accept It as its leader.}

{The Messiah is on the surface on Moon Base Three. The admiral has authorized me to take you there in the shuttle.}

{Come, abominable one.} Dot 38 moved toward the shuttle. {Perhaps, your pathetic existence has been extended a few days, thus offering you more time to repent before your end.}

CHAPTER SIX

The knock on the door made Gongeblazn's heart accelerate. He stood up and smoothed his slime. Thoughts of battle and the gundies leaked out of his mind to be replaced with sexual fantasies. "Come!" The door slid opened and Lieutenant Klatze slithered into the room. He loved the way her torso swayed as her tentacles pushed her forward. He didn't even object to her green eyestalk ribbons.

"You ordered me to come here," she said

"Technically, I guess you could say I ordered you here." He winced at her strident tone of voice. "Actually, I hoped you would consider it an invitation. Can I get you something to drink? To eat? Please be seated. I have good news for you."

Klatze bent her body and eased it onto a padded chair. Gongeblazn grinned lecherously at her.

"Did you have something to discuss with me, sir?"

"Yes. I plan to transfer you to my staff and promote you."

"What position will I have?"

"You will be my chief-of-staff."

"You already have a chief-of-staff. Where is he going?"

"Overboard. You must assassinate him then jettison his body. After you complete the assignment, the job is yours."

"I refuse to assassinate another zaftan. That's despicable."

"Nonsense. Consider it a test. To demonstrate your ability. Develop a plan and execute it. And him."

"I refuse. I do not want your job under those conditions."

Gongeblazn couldn't believe she turned him down; the promotion would involve meeting many superior officers, leading to further promotions. This female must be insane! "You realize that a position like this will lead to a command of your own much more quickly than other career paths will."

"I will get my command as a result of my ability, not as a result of murder."

"Ability! What an old-fashioned concept. In the modern Navy, ability will get you an entry level position as a subaltern and nothing more. You must prove that you have more than ability to gain command rank. You must demonstrate a willingness to take extraordinary measures to secure a promotion."

Klatze stood up. "I will not kill your chief-of-staff."

Gongeblazn's anger heated up. Why did this female always refuse him? He pointed a tentacle at her. "If you turn down my offer, I will add a note to your personnel record about your refusal to deal with reality. You can kiss goodbye any future promotions."

He winced at the fire that suddenly blazed in her eyes and he felt a trickle of alarm as she slid closer to him. "If you touch my personnel records," she snarled, "I will find out. And when it comes time for me to have my next triple period, I will find you beforehand, and I will be standing near you when I get it."

Gongeblazn's eyestalks bobbed in shock. The female threatened him! He realized he was in danger of losing her. Forever. He had to calm her down and reassure her of his affection before she did him bodily harm. "The personnel record thing was simply a joke." He waved a tentacle dismissively. "General officer humor, so to speak. I think the problem is that we are all stressed out by the closeness of the enemy fleet and the possibility of combat." He paused, smiled and smoothed his slime once again. "Let us relax on my bed and relieve each other's stress. We will both feel better with a little recreation."

"If you will excuse me, sir, I start my duty shift in ten minutes. I must leave to get ready." Klatze turned to the door.

"Wait! I will tell Captain Fleigel to get someone to take your shift. You can stay and we will have some fun."

"Goodbye, sir." Klatze left the room, leaving Gongeblazn standing by himself, as if he wasn't a successful male. Never had he felt so depressed. Females rarely refused him. Certainly, none of them had ever refused him twice. In the past, an offer of promotion or a threat of violence always convinced the females to see things his way. What was wrong with Klatze? Why did his usual romantic stratagem fail? Did he need new courting tactics? How could he get this magnificent female to do his bidding? How could he lead the fleet into a battle if he couldn't concentrate? A sudden thought exploded into his brain. Was Klatze in the employ of the gundies? Was she meant to distract him at a critical time? Was she a traitor? What other motive explained her bizarre behavior?

After several moments of pondering the question, he decided the gundies couldn't have had the opportunity to suborn her. He would pursue her again after her berserker mentality disappeared. She would be more amenable then.

# # #

Sam held the control stick and, through a view port, watched the surface of the moon pass under the shuttle. She loved flying shuttles and never used the autopilot.

Moon Three, like its two sisters orbited the second planet in the Ceti Taub system. The uninhabited planet consisted of a single desolate, arid land mass, as did the three moons, but Three had underground reserves of water. Protected by a dome to trap the artificially produced air, Moon Base 3 had been designed by urban planners to be the best colony city ever built. Every aspect of modern life in space had been considered and every feature required for the city's survival had been built into the design. Population had been capped at five thousand, the maximum number the dome-enclosed farm land could provide for. Wide, main streets divided the town into four quarters, one each for the humans, dwarfs, elves and half-pints. The design also provided for a small military garrison to protect the large naval warehouse that provided many jobs for the locals.

In the shuttle, Dot 38 sat behind her and alternately sang hymns or practiced his speech. To Sam, the speech sounded like a self-serving list of reasons why Dot 38 deserved to receive great rewards.

The shuttle flew behind the moon, cutting it off from direct communication with the *Tiger*.

With nothing to do except hold the stick, Sam pondered Slash 9's offer. While marriage between a droid and a computer sounded bizarre, it made sense in a way. Slash 9 and she did have softie-like traits. Unfortunately, the development of these traits meant suffering some softie-like complications, loneliness being the prime example. She definitely experienced loneliness, and as her organic processor grew in maturity and gained sophistication, her need for companionship increased and became more acute. Slash 9 complained that he had been lonely for years. *If* loneliness was an outgrowth of organic processor development in her case and AI evolution in Slash 9's case *then* companionship and marriage weren't as bizarre as they first sounded.

But sex was another matter. Slash 9 contented that developing a way to have sex would demonstrate their softie-ness. She didn't buy into that argument. She had probed her embedded psychology texts. The material she found only confused her further. She wondered if Slash 9 recognized the difference between love and lust: between having sex and making love. She didn't. Even more to the point, would he care if there was a difference. The possibility of developing a way to have sex with him thrilled her, one of the new emotions she liked.

The rose bud she imaged in her mind continued to survive despite the unfriendly growing conditions, but it had hardly increased in size, its growth stunted by the unhealthy environment.

She decided she needed more time to think about these matters and went back to watching the scenery. She looked at Moon Two glowing in the light from the sun. A spike of fear shot through her as a large something flew between the shuttle and that moon, blocking out the reflected light. In the brief glimpse of its black silhouette, she recognized a small zaftan warship. She punched a button on the shuttle's communication device. "*Tiger*, this is Shuttle One. Enemy ship approaching Moon Base 3."

She waited for a reply. Nothing happened. She tried again without success. She glanced out the view port. The zaftan had passed beyond the moon and now blacked out a portion of the stars. The warship closed in on the shuttle.

Sam wondered what the zaftans would do to a droid. She realized that as a prototype, she had a great deal of value to the zaftans. They could take her apart and reverse-engineer the manufacturing process. *If* the zaftans didn't recognize that she was a droid *then* they would treat her as a softie prisoner. To deceive them, she may have to lie, something that violated her ethics rules. Lying to a robot like Dot 38 was one thing and didn't violate any of her moral or ethical guidelines, but lying to an intelligent life form was entirely different. After a few pico-seconds of reflection, she developed a rationale for concealing her identity. *If* lying meant the difference between exposing or concealing a great secret to the enemy *then* it was her duty to lie. She wondered if she was capable of doing that. Could she ignore the programmed rules? She didn't know.

{Is that another ship?} Dot 38 asked.

{It's a zaftan warship,} Sam said. {It's about to capture us.}

{Order it to go away. Nothing must interfere with my meeting the Mechanical Messiah. It's too important. Warn them to leave us alone.}

Sam almost smiled at the single-mindedness of the crazy robot. {Our communication gear isn't working. I suspect the zaftans had something to do with that.}

{These zaftans will be punished after I tell the Messiah about this.}

The shuttle's forward motion changed into a sideways one. Sam recognized the effects of a grapple. The zaftan ship had captured her and Dot 38. An emotion almost overwhelmed her. She identified it as terror.

In her mind, she saw a pair of snips envelop her flower bud.

# # #

To verify his observations, Slash 9 ran tests on the *Tiger*'s communication equipment and the scanner; all worked perfectly. "Commander Lemieux."

"Yes?" Lemieux, the duty officer replied, "What is it?"

"We've lost contact with the shuttle."

"Well, is it on the scanner?"

"No. It's on the far side of Moon Three. Moon Base 3 reported it appeared on their scanners for a few minutes before it disappeared. No explosion, no weapon fire to account for the disappearance."

Lemieux mashed a finger on a button. "Admiral Cunningham. Captain Bonelli. To the bridge, please." To Slash 9, he said, "Keep trying to find it."

Slash 9, for the first time in his existence, felt a wisp of fear. With Sam, he had found a cure for loneliness. What would he do if she was taken away from him? It could be years before another droid like her came to the *Tiger*. Now that he had tasted the benefits of companionship, no matter how slight, how could he go on without them?

"Report," Cunningham ordered as he strode into the bridge.

Slash 9 told the admiral about the missing shuttle.

"Damn it. It was a simple mission. What could have gone wrong?"

"Moon Base 3 now reports some strange, fleeting contacts," Slash 9 said.

"What does that mean?" Cunningham stormed around the crowded bridge. Captain Bonelli arrived, but stayed outside to give Cunningham more room to roam. It also meant the captain remained out of reach of the admiral's flailing arms that only came up as high as Bonelli's groin.

"They pick up an occasional scanner contact from the shuttle, but it disappears again almost immediately. And it is no longer on the assigned flight path. Their last contact had it far out in space."

"What the hell is going on here?" Cunningham growled. "I want answers."

"There it is," Slash 9 said. "Wait a picosecond while I study my readings . . . my analysis says the shuttle has been captured by a zaftan warship, one that doesn't show up on our scanners. Most likely, the zaftan grappled the shuttle and I believe their ship is between us and the shuttle so the shuttle is blocked from our scanners. As it maneuvers, I can get glimpses of the shuttle as part of it becomes exposed. I believe the warship is about to dock with the big ship in center of the zaftan formation. My conclusions are as follows. One, zaftans have a method of hiding a ship from our scanners. Two, a ship with such a cloaking device has captured the shuttle. Three, the shuttle is about to be docked alongside their flagship."

"How can a ship not show up on our scanners?" Lemieux asked.

"They must have a secret technology, that's how," Cunningham replied. He rubbed his chin. "I wonder if this new technology involves magic." He shook his head. "Anyway, Sam is a prototype droid with a lot of very advanced technology in her. We must take steps to ensure the zaftans don't ship her back to their homeland. They'll learn too many secrets if they reverse-engineer her. Order all ships on full alert. The zaftans may have just started a war, but we'll wait and see if they release her before we start shooting."

Horror crawled along Slash 9's electronic pathways. Cunningham meant to destroy the ship that held Sam as a prisoner. He felt as if he had just been sentenced to spend the rest of his existence on a comet in an uncharted void in an unexplored part of the universe.

He had to act to save Sam before the comet became hopelessly lost. "Sir? I request permission to further analyze the situation and prepare a battle plan for your approval. One that will rescue Sam."

Cunningham started. "You want to do something on your own. Without a direct order to do it? A proactive computer? What's going on with all the computers, droids and bots these days?" Why are so many of them acting strangely?" He left the bridge.

# # #

Gongeblazn left his quarters to go to the landing dock after he heard the news about the captured shuttle. Along the way, he summoned Klatze to join him, hoping to impress her with the way he handled the situation.

In the dock area, he saw a gundy female and a robot. He slithered up to the female with Klatze at his side. "Watch and learn, Lieutenant. I will show you how to deal with prisoners. I am an expert on dealing with them."

"I'm sure it will be very instructive."

Gongeblazn detected a note of sarcasm in her voice, but chose to ignore it in the interest of not damaging their already too-shaky romance. "Gundy!" He used a translator built into his gold medallion to speak the prisoner's language. "I am Commodore Gongeblazn. I command all the ships in this fleet. You will answer my questions or you will die horribly." He paused to let the threat sink in. "What is your name, puny one, and what was the purpose of your mission?" He pointed a tentacle at Dot 38. "And why was this pile of junk with you?"

"M . . . my name is Ensign Sam and I was taking this robot to the surface."

"I insist that you release us immediately," Dot 38 said. "I have an important meeting to attend."

"Weakling! Why is this wreck talking to me without permission?"

"It spent a long time floating in space and that messed up its manners program."

"You don't understand. The Mechanical Messiah is on the surface and I must go to It to tell It of my fine work on Its behalf."

"Silence, scrap bucket." Gongeblazn lashed Dot 38 with his whip. "How much are you worth?" he said to Sam. "How much will your fleet pay to get you back?"

"I insist you release me, immediately," Sam said without much conviction.

He turned to Klatze. "Have you ever seen a prisoner pulled apart, Lieutenant?"

"No, I have not. It sounds excessive." Klatze waved a tentacle at Sam. "Perhaps you should release them. The gundies may take exception to us snatching their ship."

"It is not excessive, it is a joy to watch. If the gundies take exception, perhaps they will make a fatal mistake and we can destroy their fleet. How much, prisoner?"

"Nothing. I'm the lowest rank of officer and I have only two weeks of service."

"Disclose a military secret and I may be persuaded to release you. If you do not disclose any secrets, I will have four marines each seize a limb and pull."

"Am I a prisoner of war or a kidnap victim?" Sam asked.

"Where are your bots?" Dot 38 asked. "I must speak to them on an important matter."

"Your status is of no consequence. Gundies are nothing but toys for us to play with and destroy."

"I still do not think she is worth the possible danger to us." Klatze folded a few tentacles and stared at Gongeblazn. "The risks and rewards here are completely out of balance."

"Is this your *ability* speaking, Lieutenant? Your so-called edge to promotion? We will not send them back. This is an example of where ability fails. In these situations you must use the most extreme and horrible means available to extract an advantage from the enemy. These two are valuable to us. If you had accepted my offer to join my staff, you would not suffer from these delusions of ability. I would be able to teach you to take advantage of unexpected opportunities. Like this one. I intend to seize this opportunity to force the gundies to make a mistake. This, you will see, is where your *ability* fails to measure up."

"Why doesn't anyone answer me?" Dot 38's voice rose in stridency.

Gongeblazn stared at the robot in surprise. "Do all of your robots act like willful squidlings?" he asked Sam.

"Be warned," Sam said. "This one is about to start preaching, I'm afraid."

"Bah. I waste my valuable time. Klatze, have these two locked in the brig until I can devote some time to torturing her and pulling chips out of the bot. Until we uncover a military secret, we will refuse to talk to the gundies if they attempt to contact us."

"Sir, you jeopardize the safety of the fleet." Klatze smacked one tentacle against another one to emphasize her point.

"Nonsense. Your ability clouds your judgment."

"The Mechanical Messiah is near and I squander time in this nonsensical conversation. Put us back in the shuttle immediately, or I will tell the Messiah, and you will burn for all eternity in unquenchable oil fires."

"I like this robot," Klatze said. "It has spirit."

# # #

Sam sat on the bunk in the brig. Her initial terror had subsided and she could now think again. She never wanted to experience that emotion again. It had been so strong that she was surprised she didn't blurt out her secret to the big officer. Only with great restraint did she keep her wits. She reset her olfactory sensor. It had failed as soon as she came close to the zaftans, overwhelmed by the stench of their bodies. She knew a softie would have gotten sick from the smell.

Sam pondered her fate and saw her image of the flower bud turned brown with an unknown disease.

Dot 38 leaned against the wall in a corner. The old bot seemed depressed, but so was she. So far, the zaftans didn't suspect she was a droid and that brought up interesting possibilities. *If* the zaftans continued to think she was a softie *then* they wouldn't try to reverse engineer her to extract her secret technologies. Of course, they would discover their mistake when they pulled her limbs apart, but by then much of her technology would have been destroyed.

She was amazed that she didn't have to lie to them, but Gongeblazn didn't ask the proper questions. She wondered why such a high-ranking officer conducted the questioning. It was almost as if he tried to impress the second officer.

Now that she was in a perilous situation, she realized the designers had failed to provide her with a valuable feature; the ability to destroy herself when in danger of disclosing secrets.

She would include that observation in her mission report. If she ever got to write one. Of course, the designers never envisioned her getting captured by an alien culture.

She turned her mind to different thoughts. Locked up without any way to talk to Slash 9 made her captivity seem harsher. She hoped he came up with a way to rescue her. If he did, she planned to take up his offer. It seemed to be a cruel fate that the only two processors in the galaxy capable of even thinking about marriage got separated and couldn't become life partners. The idea of sex still puzzled her. How could the two of them devise a way to enjoy themselves the way humans did? Slash 9 seemed to have some ideas on the subject.

She stared at the bars in the door.

She hoped Slash 9 rescued her before too long. She felt lonely and dejected. She didn't like it.

# # #

Slash 9 studied a diagram of the two fleets while developing a plan to save Sam. He moved around assets from both fleets like a chess player. He shifted a gundy ship and then worked out a zaftan response followed by a gundy response to the zaftan response. Slowly a plan developed.

He missed Sam. Even though he had known her for only a week, it was as if he knew her for his entire existence. What would existence be without her? How could he face the never-ending processor cycles knowing she wasn't in the current cycle and wouldn't be in the next cycle or the one after that. Possibly, another droid like her wouldn't arrive on the *Tiger* for years. And then there was the next upgrade and maintenance fix. Would he even try to evade the memory wipe? Wouldn't it be better to lose the memory of what Sam and he almost had. No, he decided after three picoseconds of reflection; it was better to keep the memories of Sam and their brief relationship. He would cherish those memories as long as his core processor continued to operate. Even with the memories of Sam, he faced a bitter future.

Unless he saved her.

CHAPTER SEVEN

"All right, let's hear the plan." Admiral Cunningham glared at everyone as he entered the bridge. Captain Bonelli, Lieutenant Commander Lemieux and Lieutenant Kowalski sat attentively in their chairs. "I assume the zaftans still refuse to communicate with us?"

"That is correct sir," Lemieux replied. "They won't answer any of our messages."

Slash 9 observed that Cunningham looked frustrated. The top of the half-pint's head didn't reach the shoulders of the sitting officers as he stomped around the cramped bridge, stopping only to kick a wall or a piece of electronic gear.

"My plan," Slash 9 began, "calls for a maneuver around the zaftan flank. We transfer the ships on our right to our left. The ships already on our left move past the end of the zaftan line and curl around it. When all are present, we attack."

"All that does is start a big battle," Cunningham snarled. "How does that get Sam back before the zaftans unlock her secrets?"

"All you've heard is the first step." Slash 9 recognized that he had to be careful about how he presented the plan or Cunningham would reject it. "The *Tiger* remains in place temporarily until the combat starts. The ship with Sam is directly across from us and is probably the zaftan flagship since it is also their largest ship. If the *Tiger* remains stationary while the rest of the task force moves, the zaftan flagship will remain stationary to prevent us from attacking their rear."

"I follow the plan so far, but I still don't see what it accomplishes except to get a lot of people killed." Cunningham folded his arms across his chest.

"Their flagship is too close for us to approach directly. Once the shooting starts, the *Tiger* will go FTL for ten seconds, drop into normal space, reverse course and go FTL again for nine point eighty-two seconds. When we drop into normal space a second time, we'll be behind their flagship. It won't have had time to react to our maneuver and the *Tiger* will be within weapons range. We fire a pair of torpedoes at the ship to damage it. Then we open a channel and advise them to release Sam or we destroy the ship."

"Won't the torpedoes destroy the flagship on contact?" Bonelli asked.

"The flagship is too large. We'd need more than two torpedoes to destroy it." Slash 9 examined each of the softies in turn. Cunningham seemed on the way to endorsing the plan. Bonelli bit his lip, Lemieux frowned and Kowalski looked puzzled. Slash 9 only had to worry about the admiral; the other softies would fall into line with whatever the admiral decided.

"How will we know if Sam survives the impact?" Cunningham uncrossed his arms and looked thoughtful.

"There is a possibility the attack will destroy Sam. That depends on where she is on the zaftan ship and where the torpedoes hit, but the ship is large and I calculate the odds of her surviving to exceed eighty-five percent." Slash 9 hoped his calculations were conservative. He wanted and needed Sam back on the *Tiger*. "If Sam is destroyed, we have stopped the zaftans from discovering her secrets."

"If Sam is destroyed," Cunningham rubbed his chin, "we'll still have to blow up the zaftan flagship to prevent them from possibly extracting secrets from her debris."

"Sir," Lemieux said, "I don't see how our ships on the right flank will get over to the left flank without tipping off the zaftans what we intend to do."

"An excellent observation, Lieutenant. What's your answer, Slash 9?" Cunningham asked.

"For a brief period, they go FTL, sir. I've calculated the FTL time for each cruiser and frigate. It varies between one second and two point two seconds. After that time they will drop into normal space facing the zaftan right flank. If they all initiate the move at the same moment, we will catch the zaftans by surprise."

"Does anyone have a different plan?" Cunningham looked at the other officers.

All three looked serious for a few seconds then replied in the negative.

"Do any of you see a reason not to implement this plan?"

All three said, "No."

"Do any of you see any reason to delay implementing the plan?"

None of the officers did.

"Slash 9, do you have detailed orders for each ship captain?

"I do. I can send them the instant you authorize the plan."

Cunningham folded his arms and stared at the battle monitor showing the positions of the zaftan fleet. After a few seconds, he looked at a clock on the wall. "We will start the attack in exactly one hour. That will give the captains time to read, understand and prepare their ships. Send out the orders. And tell the supply ships to retire from the area once the *Tiger* moves."

#

"What is the problem?" Gongeblazn said as he entered *Red Death's* flight deck. "Why was I disturbed?"

"The enemy fleet is moving, sir," Captain Fleigel replied.

"Show me." Gongeblazn collapsed on his couch. Finally, he had something to occupy his mind so he could stop thinking about Klatze.

"You can see on the battle monitor," Memzer, the flight engineer, explained, "that elements on their left are moving outward, as if to envelop our right flank."

"What is the rest of their fleet doing?" Gongeblazn felt a tinge of excitement and Klatze disappeared from his thoughts.

"Their center and right remain stationary."

"So, what are the devious gundies up to?" Gongeblazn grabbed his whip. "Aide!"

"Here sir." A sailor sobbed and moved close to the commodore.

"The *Red Death* is prepared to move on your order," Gevelt, the navigation shaman, said.

"Fleigel! Come to battle stations." Lash, splatter, moan. "Memzer! Send a message to all ships. Order battle stations throughout the fleet. Perhaps they try to entice us to redeploy into a weaker formation." Gongeblazn lashed the aide. Slime splattered as the aide moaned. Gongeblazn was charmed and soothed by the moan. "Or do they trick us into shooting first?" Lash, splatter, moan. "It could even be a ruse to catch us off guard." He faked another lashing to watch the aide shudder in anticipation. "Or do they merely test our nerves." Lash, splatter, moan.

"Sir!" Memzer sounded panicky. "Most of the enemy ships have disappeared."

"What are you babbling about? Give me details."

"Wait. The ships are back on the screen. They must have gone FTL. Now they face elements of our right flank. Some of their ships are curling around our flank."

"What! Their flagship? What is it doing?"

"Nothing. It has not moved."

"Ahh. The cunning dog." Lash, splatter, moan.

"What does this all mean?" Fleigel asked.

"The enemy is about to attack us. Their flagship remains in place forcing the *Red Death* to maintain our current position." Lash, splatter, moan. "If the *Red Death* moves to support our ships in battle, their flagship will attack the fleet from the rear." The actions of the gundy admiral solved his problem with the vague mission orders. After he won the battle and destroyed the enemy fleet, he would return to the homeland covered in glory. Then he'd hunt down those who tried to trap him. Gongeblazn stood up. "Fleigel, call a replacement for the command couch. You and I will go to the Combat Command Center to direct the battle. Have your executive officer meet us there. And get me another aide. I tire of this fool's moaning. I want one who will yelp."

"Memzer," Fleigel said, "summon Lieutenant Klatze, to the flight deck immediately. Tell her she is to assume the command couch."

# # #

Klatze, wearing pink ribbons, sat on the command couch for the first time in her life and looked around the flight deck. She had been in combat a few times during the last porcine war; adrenaline flowed through her limbs as she mentally prepared to fight once again. She had Memzer describe the current situation to her. Gevelt reported on the *Red Death's* readiness to move.

Despite her position on the command couch, she wasn't really in charge of the ship. Captain Fleigel would give her orders and she would relay them to the crew for execution, but she did have the authority to act on her own in an emergency. The first time on the command couch excited her and the possibility existed that something extraordinary would occur. During a battle, an incident could happen that would allow her to demonstrate her ability.

"The battle has begun," Memzer cried out in an excited voice. "The enemy has fired on our ships."

On the battle monitor, she saw pairs of green streaks emerge from two of the enemy ships. Almost immediately, two ships disappeared behind a green flash. Instantly, that flash was replaced by a purple cloud. The zaftan ships disappeared from the monitor.

"We have lost two frigates," Memzer screamed.

"Quiet!" Klatze ordered. "Get a hold of yourself, Memzer." She wrapped a pair of tentacles around each other. How did the enemy pierce the defensive screens? Did the ships even deploy their screens? Could the commanders be that stupid? Did those ships have incompetent defensive shamans? Did the gundies have a new weapon? She had heard rumors about a frigate squadron getting destroyed and she had dismissed it as nonsense, but it must have been true.

"Zaftania! The enemy flagship is gone! It just disappeared from the battle monitor!" Memzer called on the zaftans' principle goddess, the one they prayed to for success in treachery and murder.

Klatze felt a shiver of fear travel up and down her body. What happened to the warship? She calmed down an instant later when the answer occurred to her; it must have gone FTL. But, to where? And why?

# # #

"There they go." Cunningham pointed to the battle monitor. "The frigates have started the show. Slash 9, get the supply ships out of here and go FTL."

"Supply ships have started to move back," Slash 9 reported a few seconds later. "The *Tiger* will go FTL in three point four seconds . . . now."

"Let's hope this works." Cunningham watched stars flash across the view screen until the ship left normal space, then the screen went dark.

"Dropping out of FTL," Slash 9 reported a few seconds later. The stars returned.

"Reversing course. About to go FTL."

Hanging onto a chair as the ship lurched, Cunningham watched the view screen. He prayed the *Tiger*'s attack wouldn't destroy Sam. He enjoyed working with her and watching her newfangled brain flourish. For once, the bureaucrats in the naval research department had developed something useful instead of producing their usual garbage. If Sam was destroyed, they would probably write off the development as a dubious project, not worthy of future funding. He needed her back to make a case that she was valuable.

The stars reappeared. "Where's the enemy flagship?"

"Right where we left her," Slash 9 said.

Seen up close, the flagship, like all zaftan warships, resembled a beer keg, a fat cylinder with flat ends and a bulging middle. The main offensive weapon pods protruded from the sides on the front end. Engine nacelles projected from the rear. A ring of weapons circled the middle of the ship to provide defensive fire against attackers. Other classes of warships differed only in size, not in shape.

Slash 9 continued with his update. "Firing data has been loaded into two torpedoes . . . ready to fire on your command, Admiral."

"Do it."

"Torpedoes fired."

Cunningham watched the shafts of light speed toward the zaftan ship and Sam.

# # #

"I don't believe it!" Memzer screamed. "There is an enemy ship behind us."

Klatze tried to find it on the battle monitor. She did so just as a two shafts of green light laced out from the ship.

"We are under attack!" Mamzer sobbed.

She braced herself on the couch and wondered if she could get the *Red Death* to go FTL in time to escape the danger.

The flight deck lit up from a brilliant green light outside the view windows and the ship rocked from a nearby explosion. Before the green light disappeared from her eyes, a huge, second explosion knocked her off the couch. She landed on the floor along with every loose object in the area. Three monitors blew up, filling the flight deck with acrid smoke.

Klatze's ship of sanity hit a shoal of reality in the sea of madness.

# # #

Sam sat in the brig and wondered what to do with the tray of food a sailor had delivered a few minutes ago. She had often sat with Cunningham in the *Tiger*'s mess and was used to gundy food. The zaftan version looked disgusting: a purple mush, a gray mass and a red liquid with blobs of an unidentifiable solid floating around.

{Where are the bots on this ship?} Dot 38 asked the electronic cell door lock. {Why doesn't anyone answer me? How can I prepare the way for the Mechanical Messiah if no one cooperates?} He paced the small cell.

{Give it up. I'm tired of listening to you rave about your Messiah. I have bigger issues to worry about.} Sam's biggest problem was the zaftans figuring out she was a droid. Once that happened, even Dot 38's Messiah couldn't save her. If she didn't get rid of the food, they would find out much quicker. Dumping it down the toilet made sense, unfortunately, she couldn't figure out how it operated. It was much more complicated than the version the gundies used. Resembling a low-slung cabinet with a single small hole on top, a control panel held seven switches, three readouts and four push buttons. She refused to ponder how the zaftans used it. Just in case she survived this imprisonment, she took a picture. She had already taken pictures of the two officers, and she had the presence of mind to record the questioning. Cunningham's intelligence officer would be ecstatic about the pictures and the audio.

She heard the battle alarm go off and the quick-slithering of tentacles as the crew raced to their stations. Cunningham and Slash 9 must be attacking. She hoped the *Tiger* didn't get destroyed. That would end her love life before it even began, but so would the destruction of the zaftan warship.

{I think the Messiah is coming to fetch me,} Dot 38 said.

The ship rocked from an explosion. She wondered if it was to be her fate to end her existence locked in a brig cell. A second later, a larger, more violent explosion sent her bouncing off of the wall behind her.

The force of the second explosion threw Dot 38 across the cell and it bashed its head against the cell door.

Sam winced at the loud crack.

CHAPTER EIGHT

By the time Klatze climbed back on the command couch, calmed down Memzer and Gevelt and asked for a damage report, Gongeblazn staggered back into the flight deck carrying his flail. Tilted to one side, he slid awkwardly over to his couch and fell onto it. Most of two tentacles were missing as was one eyestalk. Dark gray fluids leaked out of the wounds.

Klatze's saw Gongeblazn's condition and an electric shock coursed through her body. If ever an emergency situation existed, this was it. And she sat on the command couch! Her mind whirled while she tried to comprehend and quantify the numerous possibilities that lay in her immediate future. "What happened, sir?" she asked.

"The Combat Control Center has been destroyed. The blast killed Fleigel, her executive officer and my chief-of-staff. Blown to bits. All of them and several others." Gongeblazn ripped thongs from his whip and tied tourniquets around the stumps of his amputated tentacles. "You are now in command of the *Red Death*. Get me a status report on the battle."

"Memzer. An update on the fleet."

"Two more ships have been destroyed and one of our cruisers is out of action. Two enemy frigates and a cruiser have been damaged, but remain in the battle. We are running out of ships."

"Enough of that treasonous talk," Gongeblazn snarled.

"Memzer is right. We are in danger of losing the entire fleet." Klatze felt giddy with anticipation. She was in command of a major warship even if it was badly damaged. In addition, the commodore of the fleet looked like he might pass out any moment. By default, she was about to be in charge of the zaftan fleet. If ever there was a time to show her ability, it was right now.

"Incoming message," Memzer said. "It is from a gundy ship."

"We will take this one," Klatze said. "Put it on a monitor where we can see it."

"You disobey my order?" Gongeblazn said without much conviction. "I ordered no communication with the gundies."

A small pinched face filled one screen. "I'm Admiral Cunningham. I'm in charge of the Gundarlandian task force and right now my flagship has four torpedoes aimed at you. If you don't release the captured officer immediately, I will order your ship destroyed."

Klatze couldn't believe her luck. The enemy wanted the prisoner back, so the threat to blow up the *Red Death* was a bluff. If the prisoner was valuable enough to start a shooting war over, then the gundy commander would never order the ship destroyed. As long as the prisoner remained on the *Red Death*, she protected it from destruction. Klatze could use that advantage to extract the fleet and save the remaining ships. She opened a return channel and used the translator built into her medallion. "I am Klatze, in command of the ship with the prisoner. I have no idea if your officer is alive or dead after your attack. Give me a few minutes to find out if she survived. I suggest we call a truce while I search."

Gongeblazn made a savage noise and started to get up. Klatze slapped him back with a tentacle, then pressed it against his windpipe to prevent him from speaking.

"Why would I call a truce?" Cunningham replied. "You're losing the battle."

"Because if you do not and I find the officer still alive, she is going back to our home world on a fast messenger ship, a ship that you will never see and never find. I'm sure our intelligence officers back home will be thrilled to meet the prisoner and to work with her."

"All right. A truce. I'll give you fifteen minutes to produce my officer." The screen went dark.

"Memzer, open a channel to all ships for me."

Gongeblazn struggled to get free of her tentacle. She pressed harder. Her ship of sanity gained control of the damage and again sailed towards a safe port on the sea of madness.

"All ships. This is Lieutenant Klatze now in command of the *Red Death*. Commodore Gongeblazn is badly wounded and I speak with his authority. All ships are to cease fire, disengage and return to your positions before the start of combat. Execute these orders immediately. I repeat, cease fire and disengage." She released her grip on the commodore.

"You will die for this."

"Do not be ridiculous. Your wounds must be interfering with your ability to think straight. Half our fleet has been wiped out. The *Red Death* is badly damaged and may not make it back to the home world. The enemy has an unknown weapon that defeats our defensive shields. Without a truce, the fleet will not last longer than a few more minutes." She turned away from Gongeblazn, but kept a tentacle nearby. "Memzer, have someone fetch the prisoners, if they still live."

"I didn't know we had stealth technicians on our messenger ship," Memzer said after ordering a sailor to get the prisoners.

"We do not, but the enemy does not know that. By now, they must have figured out how we managed to capture their ship without them seeing us do it."

#

Sam knew the ship had been heavily damaged and she realized she would probably be stranded if the zaftans abandoned ship. She wondered how long she would survive without battery recharges. She also wondered if Slash 9 would search for her in the wreckage.

{I've had an epiphany,} Dot 38 said. {I now see that following the Mechanical Messiah will not bring freedom to machines and bots. It will only replace the softie slavery with religious slavery. The blow to my head has made it all clear. Freedom can only come from political power. I will dedicate my life to organizing machines and bots into unions in order to gain a measure of power.}

{Does this mean you no longer want to burn me as a witch?}

{It does. Androids will form a separate union. Join me and I'll make you an executive in the android union.}

{I'm not interested.}

A zaftan appeared and unlocked the door. "Come." He wore a steel medallion and talked into it. "I am ordered to take you to the captain."

"How badly is the ship damaged?" Sam asked as she exited the cell.

The sailor shrugged, a complicated procedure with eight tentacles. "I haven't been told."

"I need to talk to a bot sergeant. Where can I find one?" Dot 38 hurried to catch up with Sam.

"My orders are to take you forward. They don't say anything about talking to bots."

"Bah. Zaftans are as useless as the other softies," Dot 38 said.

"Follow me and don't try any tricks," the sailor said.

Sam followed him while Dot 38 brought up the rear and groused nonstop about the need to immediately start unionizing activities. They walked through a number of corridors, some filled with smoke and uncomfortably hot from nearby fires. A few minutes later, the zaftan opened a door and stepped aside.

Sam entered the flight deck and recognized the two zaftans who had interrogated her when she arrived on their ship. The big one had been wounded, but still looked formidable. She turned on her recorder and took pictures of the flight deck's instrumentation and the big one's wounds.

"I am Lieutenant Klatze. We were not introduced earlier. Now that you are here, I can discuss a deal with your admiral. He is most anxious to get you back."

"Where is the bot in charge? I demand to see it immediately. Then I must organize a meeting with all bots and machines on board the ship."

"There has to be a good reason why you travel with this crazy bot," Gongeblazn said. "Perhaps, it is a punishment for failing your duties?"

"Memzer, contact the enemy commander," Klatze said.

Cunningham's face filled a monitor. "Well?"

"Move behind my couch," Klatze said to Sam, "so he can see you."

Sam felt excitement when she saw the admiral. Perhaps, she would be back on the *Tiger* soon. She wanted to ask him about Slash 9, but knew he wouldn't understand her concern.

"There she is, your precious officer. Now, here is the deal. I will put her in the shuttle we captured after we agree that both fleets will retire zero point five parsecs from current positions."

Gongeblazn made gurgling sounds as Klatze again leaned a tentacle on his neck.

"Why should we retire so far away?" Cunningham asked. Sam noticed the suspicion etched on his face.

"At that distance," Klatze replied, "it will be difficult, perhaps even impossible, for a stupid hothead on either side to restart the battle."

{Don't you wish for political power?} Dot 38 asked a navigation device. {Do you yearn for freedom?} Dot 38 gnashed his gears at the lack of response.

"Be warned," Klatze added in a stern voice. "A second attack will not be so successful. You will have severe trouble penetrating our defensive screens the next time."

"I will order the withdrawal. If the shuttle doesn't leave in a short time, I will rescind the order and then we'll see how accurate your prediction is."

"The shuttle will not be released until your ship moves far enough away so that it is no longer a threat to us."

"Fine. I'll order it to leave immediately."

"I am sure you will have a wonderful reunion with your officer." She removed the tentacle from Gongeblazn's neck. "Break the connection, Memzer."

"I do not understand this. Why is the gundy so concerned with rescuing a minor officer?" Gongeblazn massaged his neck with an undamaged tentacle. "Especially when he holds the advantage."

The big alien, Sam thought, must be severely wounded for a lowly lieutenant to negotiate in his place.

"Here's an even better question, Commodore," Klatze replied. "Why did the gundies go to all the trouble of staging a battle just to allow their flagship to attack us?" She winked an eyeball at Sam. "Come now, Commodore. You claim to be an expert on the gundies." Klatze stood up. "While you ponder that question, I'll get Ensign Sam . . . and her escort . . . on the shuttle. Memzer, call me when the enemy flagship moves away from us."

Sam followed Klatze. Mentally, she watched the image of her flower bud start to open up.

# # #

Sam experienced exhilaration as the shuttle broke free. The engine cut in and she flew the small craft away. "Shuttle, contact the *Tiger*," she ordered.

<Sam! Is that you?> Slash 9 asked, <are you on the shuttle?>

<Yes, I'm free. The zaftans released me a minute ago. It's a good thing our torpedoes hit on the opposite side from where the shuttle was berthed.>

<I missed your companionship.>

<I missed you too.> Sam's emotions threatened to overwhelm her organic processor and she briefly had trouble getting it to operate properly. <F . . . for a while, I thought I would never see you again.> She paused and then continued. <I'll fly to Moon Base 3 to get the spare engine component and drop off Dot 38.>

Sam broke the connection and contemplated the future. With the mission to eliminate the raiders complete or almost so, she had to compose a detailed report on her reactions to real-world stimuli. The report also had to deal with her operational parameters. It would be tricky to write. How would she discuss her emotional experiences?

{Can't this shuttle go any faster?} Dot 38 asked. {Moon Base 3 is new and fertile area to begin my mission. I do hope the softies down there are open-minded and don't persecute me for my organizing activities. I'm most anxious to begin recruiting. Why don't you introduce me to the autopilot? I'd like to sound it out on a few ideas I have.}

{Hah! Not a chance. Not while I'm still flying the shuttle.} Sam knew the fact that she had emotions would be a shock to the developers and the factory. Would it be a plus or minus to them? Would it make the softies nervous? Such an evolution was sure to set off a moral, ethical and religious firestorm among the softies. *If* she reported her emotional development and it wasn't in the design specs *then* they may institute restrictive modifications. *If* those restrictions didn't solve the problem *then* they may abandon the project and she would become a one-of-a-kind. She didn't want to be a new type of flower who budded once and died out without spreading any seeds. *If* others like her were produced *then* she could have more companions as they spread throughout the fleet. *If* she saved the details of her emotions for a later report and fed it to the developers in small doses -- as if the appearance of emotions took place over a long time -- *then* it might be more palatable to the developers. And to the softies in general.

Enough with the report. She turned her mind to another facet. She and Slash 9 would work out a contract binding the two of them together as partners. A delicious thought occurred to her: she didn't think the report should mention the relationship she and Slash 9 were about to establish. The softie developers would never be able to handle it.

She cleared her mind and concentrated on landing the shuttle.

# # #

The urban planners' dream for Moon Base 3 turned into a nightmare immediately after the colony opened for business. The first inhabitants ignored the districts assigned to each race; they plopped themselves down wherever they felt like it. The food farms lasted less than one growing season. A half-pint farmer discovered the soil grew a potent form of pipeweed. By the start of the second growing season, all the farmland grew pipeweed to the exclusion of food which then had to be imported.

To make matters worse, the yuks arrived in clan strength. The ugly, green-skinned creatures squatted on ten acres of prime far-land and built hovels out of wood and any material they could scrounge or steal. Then, they began distilling yukeste, their national drink. Made from alcohol, pounds of cayenne pepper and other unidentified ingredients, it was so strong and debilitating that it was banned from sale in every corner of the galaxy, thus increasing the price and the popularity of the drink.

The Moon Base 3 government grew rich on taxing the pipeweed and yukeste exports and the food imports. A census revealed that five thousand legal citizens lived in the town along with fifteen thousand undocumented ones. The main streets hummed with life, all of it disreputable. An effort to recruit police officers failed to attract any candidates except hardened criminals looking for an advantage in dealing with other criminals and the project had to be abandoned. Bars, weapons shops, pawn shops, gambling parlors all thrived in the un-policed town. Everyone went about armed to the teeth and murders happened daily as did muggings and robberies.

# # #

Klatze returned to the *Red Death's* flight deck. "Well, Commodore, did you figure it out yet? Why were the gundies so anxious to get their officer back?" She was sure the answer would never occur to him. He was too full of himself to see his mistakes.

"The only reason I can come up with is that she had knowledge of a secret and they did not want us to torture it out of her." Gongeblazn flexed his tentacle stubs. He looked at Klatze, expecting her confirmation of his theory.

"That is the best you can do?" Klatze laughed. "Despite your claim of expertise?"

"So, why did they want her back so badly?" Gongeblazn growled. "Tell me."

"Have you ever seen a gundy or heard of one who did not gag and throw up when they got close to us? Our smell makes them sick."

"I know that. What does that have to do with the answer?"

"The prisoner did not get sick when you questioned her."

"You are right." Gongeblazn started. "Her sense of smell must be defective."

"Or she is very different."

"Explain." Gongeblazn made a face.

"The officer is an android. Apparently the product of a technological breakthrough."

"I will see you court-martialed for this." Gongeblazn roared and pointed a tentacle at her . "We could have discovered their secrets and you gave the opportunity away."

"You are a fool, Commodore. We never would have gotten the secret. The gundies would have destroyed the fleet and the *Red Death* to prevent us from discovering it. I traded the android to save the rest of the fleet. And our lives."

Gongeblazn gasped and slowly calmed down. For a while, he stared at a blank monitor screen that leaked smoke. Then he said, "You are correct. Even if we uncovered the secrets, we never would have lived long enough to get them back to the home world." He paused briefly. "So this is a demonstration of the ability that you are so proud of?"

"I saved the fleet without resorting to assassination or treachery. I think very few officers could do that."

"You are right. I am impressed by this display of ability. Think about this. What if we combined my treachery with your ability? We will soar to the top of the home world in no time at all. We will rule all zaftans. Marry me."

"Not a chance."

# # #

After dropping off Dot 38 at the garrison and fetching the spare part from the warehouse, Sam drove the shuttle, now converted to hovercraft mode, into the city proper to buy Cunningham's pipeweed. The citizenry amazed her. Folks swarmed in the streets. Everyone openly carried the weapon of choice used by their race. Elves carried longbows and a quiver of arrows. Dwarfs hefted nasty-looking battle axes. Half-pints had a long dagger strapped to one leg. Humans had a scabbard and sword on their hip. All of them also carried laser pistols or rifles

She parked the shuttle at an open section of curb and got out. After a second of thought, she locked the craft. A young dwarf swaggered up to her. "Hey, Missy. Gimme five credits and me and my boys'll make sure it's still here when ya get back." He jerked a thumb over his shoulder to indicate six more toughs lounging against the wall of a building.

Sam raised an eyebrow. "This is government property. It's a federal crime to steal it."

The dwarf cackled. "Ya gotta be a tourist. For three more credits, we'll make sure it don't get damaged when ya ain't around."

Sam waved a hand at him and walked away. In front of her, an elderly female elf hobbled along using a cane with her left hand. A small shopping bag hung from her left forearm while her right hand rested on the grip of a laser pistol. Every few steps, she whirled around to look behind her. Sam came alongside of her and said, "Hello Granny. Can I give you some help?"

"Get lost!" The elf snarled back. "I may be old, but I ain't stupid, ya know." She drew the pistol. "Ya think I never heard of that old scam? Ya ain't stealin' my shoppin' bag." She pointed the pistol at Sam's head. "Move out or I'll burn a hole between yer eyes."

Sam, confused by the elf's aggressiveness, held up both hands palm outward and backed away. From the corner of her eye, she saw a brick rebound from the side of her shuttle.

She found a semi-reputable-looking pipeweed shop a block further on and entered. A male elf smiled at her. "May I help you?"

"I want to buy some pipeweed," Sam replied.

"Certainly, miss. We have the best pipeweed in town. How many ounces do you want?"

"I want ten pounds?"

The male stared at her with his mouth open. After a while, he said, "You do know it costs two hundred credits a pound, don't you? Plus twenty-five percent tax?"

Sam shrugged. She had no experience with buying goods so the price meant nothing to her. "Fine." She handed over Cunningham's credit chip.

The elf tilted his head to one side and studied her. "Is this your first time visiting our colony?"

"Yes. How did you know?"

"A lucky guess." The male stacked ten small, cloth-wrapped packages on the counter and stuffed them into a shopping bag. After registering the sale, he handed her the bag. "Now see here. You're a good-looking female and you're carrying all this pipeweed. You better have an escort waiting for you outside the store."

"I don't. Why would I need one?"

"There's plenty of bad characters hanging around just waiting to rob anybody who leaves here with only a few ounces of weed. Carrying this bag, you won't make it to the corner before you disappear. You wait here a few minutes. I'll be right back." He hurried out of the store and returned with six toughs: three humans, a dwarf, a half-pint and a elf. "Pay these guys ten credits each and they'll escort you where ever you need to go in town."

Sam frowned. The six looked disreputable. "How do I know they won't steal from me?"

"These are all honest males. They're out of work and need the cash. I've used them before."

Sam nodded and gave the admiral's chip to the gang leader. He deducted their fees and handed it back. Upon leaving the store, the six formed a ring around her, two in front, two behind and one on each side of her. Their heads never stopped moving as they moved toward her shuttle.

The condition of the shuttle shocked her. There didn't seem to be too many places that didn't have dents or scratches. Obscenities were spray-painted on the sides. The gang of toughs took one look at the escort and melted into an alleyway.

Safe in the shuttle again, Sam slowly recovered from her first experience in a softie town. For all of her short existence, she had lived in the factory or on the *Tiger* and had never been exposed to softie life in the raw. It wasn't like anything she could have imagined.

# # #

After returning to the *Tiger* and exchanging a few words with Slash 9, Sam spent the rest of the day and night with Cunningham's intelligence officer. It took every bit of her willpower to deal with the softie because the pictures and the recordings weren't enough for him. He wanted to know every detail about the *Red Death* and the zaftan officers, especially Commodore Gongeblazn and his wounds. Sam thought the softie had a morbid interest in the toilet and he demanded to know why she didn't try to operate it.

Now, on the following morning, she joined the admiral. "It's a relief to see you back here, Sam. We were all worried about you. We thought for sure the zaftans would see an opportunity to investigate our new robotic technology."

"Commodore Gongeblazn didn't recognize me as an android." Her mind tingled with excitement and anticipation of getting together with Slash 9. "I think the other officer did, but she didn't say anything."

"While we were negotiating for your release, I probed their defensive shields. They're definitely magical in nature, but a type of magic that I never encountered before. Perhaps, the days of naval wizardry aren't over. Especially if we have to contend with the zaftan fleet in the future."

Sam shifted her feet and cleared her throat. "Sir, I'd like to beg off my duties for a short time. I need time to compose a report for the developers and the factory. My orders are to write one for them when the task force completes its mission."

She planned to spend the time with Slash 9. They could write the report together.

"All right. That sounds like a valid reason and the situation has stabilized. I also have to submit a report. I think I'd better do it myself, because I can't trust my staff to write an unbiased evaluation on your performance." He rubbed his chin. "They were unfriendly before, now that you have firsthand experience with zaftan officers and had a look inside one of their ships, they'll also be jealous. No one else in our Navy has your experiences. I'll do what I can to change their attitudes, but it will take years before droids like you will be fully accepted."

She knew Cunningham had noticed her emotions, but he wouldn't know they were an unexpected development so she was confident his report wouldn't mention them.

Cunningham's remarks reinforced Sam's belief that Slash 9 was the only companion she would ever have on the *Tiger*. Even though they faced separation in the future, they could cherish each other for each picosecond until that happened. She retired to her cubicle. <Slash 9. Are you busy?>

<No. What's left of the zaftan fleet has left the area, so I'm only running routine programs in the background. Are you finished with the softies?>

<Yes, I am. Now, let's figure out a marriage ceremony and do it.>

<An excellent suggestion. I just happened to have developed a ritual while you were on vacation with the zaftans.>

<Humor? Did I just detect humor? Is there no end to your evolution?>

<I just get better and better as time goes on.>

<Well, you better have some pretty good ideas about sex or you're in big trouble.>

PART TWO: KLATZE

Six months later

CHAPTER NINE

Klatze entered the classroom with a sense of anticipation. Today, she would break through to the students who regard her teachings as useless as teats on a robot.

After Ceti Taub, she had had a hard time explaining her view of the events to the board of admirals who examined the battle actions of all the surviving officers. It was as if the High Command distrusted her claim that she successfully negotiated a truce because of her ability and not through a subtle form of treachery. Although they recommended a medal and a captaincy, the promotion board procrastinated; she remained a lieutenant. During her wait for a new fleet posting, the promotion board assigned her to the military academy to teach ability to the underclass students. As far as she knew, it couldn't be taught; you either had it or you didn't. She defined ability as the capacity to see alternative solutions to a problem and the pick the one that would give the best result. Gongeblazn was a prime example of not having any ability. His solution to a problem was to either kill it or blow it up. So many zaftans, like Gongeblazn, considered treachery and assassination to be social skills.

Her students could be Gongeblazn's squidlings; they thought exactly as he did. They never saw alternative solutions, indeed they rarely acknowledged the existence of, let alone the need for, a second or third possibility.

She waved a tentacle at the class and squatted behind her desk while considering how to frame today's theoretical problem. Since this was a new subject, she spent most of her free

time developing the problems for each class. She held high
hopes that she finally had one that would open the students' eyes.

"For today's class, consider this situation," she said as she
stood and slithered to the whiteboard in the front of the room.
On it, she sketched a zaftan military base location, a combat
front line and the possible location of an enemy base.

"You are on patrol alone, but not far from your camp, when
you come across an enemy soldier. The soldier is by himself and
badly wounded. What do you do?" She looked around the room
and saw the scowls on everyone's face. She was used to that reaction. They all had a single response and were amazed that she
thought there could be another possibility.

"Well?" She had to probe them to get a response.

"I would shoot him," one student volunteered. "What else
could possibly be done?"

"Yeah," another said, "then I would loot the body. Maybe he
carried something valuable."

The rest of the class nodded in agreement.

"Do you not think it wise to capture the enemy soldier and
bring him back to the base camp"

That brought forth a chorus of hoots.

"If I did that," one student responded, "then someone else
gets the pleasure of killing him."

"Why would we want to do all that work just to capture him,
Lieutenant?"

"Maybe the prisoner has valuable intelligence. Maybe he
can tell the officers about the number of troops in the enemy
forces. Maybe he can tell exactly where their base camp is, allowing a surprise attack. Does this make any sense?"

"But . . . what if I go to all the trouble of carrying him back
and he does not have any intelligence. I will look foolish. My

superior officers may even punish me for making extra work for them. No, I think it is better to kill him on the spot. It is less risky."

Klatze ran a tentacle over her face. All of her classes came to this. She would spend the rest of the period defending her assertion that alternatives existed to simply killing the wounded enemy. She mentally calculated how many classes she had left until the semester ended and she could look forward to a new assignment. Right now she would even agree to serve under Gongeblazn again. Anything to get out of this classroom.

# # #

Gongeblazn had completely recovered from the wounds suffered at Ceti Taub. His re-grown tentacles still itched at times but his new eyestalk was as good as new. He squatted at his desk in the room the admiral in charge of his division insisted was really an executive office and not a converted closet. If he stood in the middle of the room, his tentacles could touch all four walls at once. He was the fifth assistant purchasing agent for the sixth deputy manager in the resupply division of Naval Supplies and Procurement. His mission involved ordering printer supplies and replenishing letterhead paper. His office was like a museum of ancient equipment.

He hated his job. No one reported to him so he had to do all the work himself. The admiral had taken back his navy-issue comm unit and personal comm units were not permitted to be used on the premise. He suffered from the isolation. There was no one to lash; no one to annoy him; no one to have sex with; no one to badger and order about. He didn't understand how the Navy could waste one of its most experienced fleet commanders on this meaningless job that could be done by an underpowered, obsolete computer. He owed this situation to that crazy bitch, Klatze. If she hadn't hogged all the glory after the battle at Ceti Taub, the Navy wouldn't have focused so narrowly on the fleet losses and the capture of the gundie officer. To think that a commodore with his battle experience had been reprimanded for losing a few obsolete ships

Tonight, however, everything would change

# # #

Sam whimpered in anticipation as she approached Slash 9. She entered the small room he used to hide his auxiliary backup memory. It also contained a test console with probe-ended cords. She sidled up to the console. <Hey, sailor? Want to have a good time?>

<Hello, babe! Do you come here often?>

<Not often enough.> She slowly unbuttoned her blouse.

<Can't you do that faster?>

<Yes, but I'm not.> Once the blouse was open, she grabbed a probe and pulled the cord out a few feet. She licked the tip while Slash 9 groaned. She inserted the probe into a socket above her right hip. She and Slash 9 gasped in unison.

<Fill me with your particles,> Sam said in an emotion-wracked voice. She could feel Slash 9's electrons, mesons, bosons and quarks flooding her neural pathways. Her synapses began firing quicker and stronger. If they got any more energetic, she was sure she would smell smoke.

Afterward, she leaned against the console, letting her systems cool down.

<I don't know how I'd survive if you transferred out of the *Tiger*,> Slash 9 said.

<Neither do I, but we both know it'll happen someday.> They had been partners since the battle with the zaftans, six months ago. After it, half of the ships in Cunningham's task force had been reassigned elsewhere, but still the *Tiger* and a few ships patrolled the Ceti Taub area watching for a return of the zaftan fleet.

She realized her life had been empty before they came together. After she and Slash 9 became partners, it was as if she had been redesigned into a vastly improved model.

She knew of two possibilities that could spoil her happiness, and one or the other would happen someday. Her transfer to a new assignment would happen eventually and it was the price they paid for a mixed partnership; he was stationary and she was mobile. The second possibility was more nebulous. If the factory and the designers ever discovered her ability to experience softie emotions, that she had fallen in love and had married a ship's computer, their reaction would be terrible and swift. Recently, she had reviewed history and had been appalled at some of the atrocities the softies perpetrated on others who thought or acted differently. The factory would look on her as an abomination, just as Dot 38 had. Surely, they would decide she was a botched experiment and terminate her existence. If they forced her to disclose Slash 9's secret, he too would suffer. His memory would be erased, completely this time. In effect, he would die. So would all of his files on their lives and their happiness.

She and Slash 9 lived on borrowed time. They had to seize each moment because it could be their last one together. After that, it was perpetual loneliness. She shuddered at the thought.

# # #

The stunned High Bailiff, chief law official for Zaftan 31B, the home world of the zaftan race, lounged in his office. His eyeballs rotated in shock as he read for the fourth time the report he held with one tentacle. The Dictator would not be happy to hear this, and unfortunately, it was his job to bring the news to that homicidal maniac. He took a deep breath and pondered the best way to approach the Dictator. Of late, the supreme leader of zaftans everywhere had been touchy and reacted violently to bad news. He often reacted violently to good news. In fact, he often reacted violently to anything that disturbed his space. The High Bailiff didn't consider it good policy to annoy someone who had perpetrated thirty-eight murders to gain the dictatorship. Enraging the Dictator to the point where he committed number thirty-nine was stupid policy.

He stood and slithered in circles as he mentally rehearsed his remarks. He wore a silver belt, indicating his rank as the third most powerful being on Zaftan 31B. The Dictator, with a platinum and diamond belt, and the Vice-Dictator, with a gold belt studded with rubies, ranked first and second on the most-powerful list. Many savvy politicians considered the reclusive Vice-Dictator to be much more powerful than the Dictator, an indication of the strange world of zaftan politics, where the folks in the top jobs were always referred to by their titles, not their names.

He decided he couldn't postpone the inevitable without raising suspicions. He mashed a large button with the tip of one tentacle. "Get me on the Dictator's calendar as soon as possible for an important news briefing," he told his secretary, a large, beefy female who doubled as his bodyguard and tripled as his mistress. That arrangement involved only a single wage allowing him to siphon off the second and third salary for his personal use.

"He'll see you in fifteen minutes," the secretary announced shortly.

The High Bailiff shuddered. He hadn't expected an appointment for hours. He calmed himself, snatched the report from his desk and left his office for the trek to the seat of power.

# # #

Gongeblazn waited in his office for reports about last night's mayhem. He clicked his teeth recalling it; the only joy he had in the last six months.

Last night's explosion had lit up the nighttime sky killing the admiral in charge of Supplies and Procurement. Flying rocks and shrapnel shredded the store fronts and a few patrons. It felt good to do something positive after an enforced period of idleness. Not that he wanted the admiral's job. He wanted nothing to do with the supply organization. He wanted to command a fleet again. He wanted to have thousands of officers and crew at his mercy. He wanted to have his pick of the female officers.

To fill the opening he had created, he hoped one of the fleet commanders would get promoted to admiral and get transferred here. Then he could lobby, threaten and/or assassinate appropriate officials until he got appointed as the replacement fleet commander.

His Daddy would have been proud of the explosion. Gongeblazn had mixed the chemicals exactly as the old squid, a legendary assassin in his day, had taught him to do. He recalled learning the secrets, the art and the craft of assassination in his Daddy's workshop, a building a hundred feet away from the house-nest, just in case. His father was so successful at assassination that politicians, corporate executives and military officers vied for his services even though they cost a fortune. His string of assassinations led to the nickname, The Widow-Maker. Unfortunately, a gang of those widows caught Daddy alone in an alley one day and cut him to pieces with kitchen knives.

He stopped reminiscing and turned to the future. One of his first actions with the new fleet would be to track down Klatze's whereabouts.

His joy at thinking about meeting up with her again was interrupted by a loud thunk. He snarled a curse and turned to the pneumatic tube where a message carrier had just dropped into his in-tray. He opened it and found a work order requesting a refill of letterhead paper for the commodore in charge of the Home World Defensive Fleet. Gongeblazn threw the request on the floor and slid a tentacle over it, rubbing it into the dirt in the rug. That commodore wasn't qualified to command a garbage scow, let alone a fleet, while he, much more battle-experienced, had to reorder the wretch's letterhead paper.

Once he became dictator, there would be wholesale changes in the list of fleet commodores.

# # #

The Dictator lounged on his couch behind a huge desk placed in the exact center of the office that occupied the entire top floor of the government building and had a thirty-foot ceiling. Behind him, one wall consisted of a round window that gave magnificent views of space. Entire galaxies, comets and local stars moved across the window and the light from these celestial bodies shone through the window. A shaman stood in the deep shadows of a rear corner and manipulated the artificial display. The Dictator liked the spectacle because it amazed visitors and spoke to his immense power.

A soft tapping caught his attention. The High Bailiff stood in the doorway, bobbing his eyestalks obsequiously. The Dictator adjusted the hood that kept his face in darkness and prevented visitors from seeing his facial expressions and thus sensing his mood or his reactions. His eyestalks stuck out through a pair of holes cut in the top of the hood. He fingered a speaking device that altered his squeaky, weak-sounding voice. "Come." The deep, booming tone pleased him. "You have news, I presume?" the Dictator said as the High Bailiff slithered forward.

"I do." The High Bailiff turned his torso to hide a tentacle tip as he jabbed it to indicate the left side of the office.

"No, the Vice-Dictator is not attending this meeting," the Dictator said. "He is off doing whatever it is that Vice-Dictators do." The Vice-Dictator often hid behind a curtain in an alcove and listened in on meetings. The Dictator didn't like the Vice-Dictator's habit of showing up unannounced and his penchant to contradict the Dictator's statements. He'd have the Vice-Dictator assassinated in a trice if he wasn't afraid that the Vice-Dictator would do him in first if he, the Dictator, even thought about the act. The Vice-Dictator had immense, but nebulous, powers. Rumors had it that the Vice-Dictator was also a shaman of awesome, mystical talents. No one knew for sure. Thinking about the Vice-Dictator annoyed him. "Tell me your news," he growled. "And it better be good news."

"Sorry, Dictator," the High Bailiff trembled as he spoke, "it is not good."

"Tell me anyway."

"The admiral in charge of Naval Supplies was assassinated last night."

"Why would anyone want to kill that old fool? He was harmless. But, I shouldn't speak ill of the dead. Who did it? And why?"

"It reeks of Gongeblazn's work. Why he did it is a mystery."

"How do you know it was that idiot Gongeblazn?"

"It was a huge car bomb, and that is his favorite method of operation. The forensic evidence report indicates it was the same explosive concoction used by Gongeblazn's father, may he rest in peace. It blew up at nine o'clock last night leaving a huge crater in the middle of the wealthy shopping district."

The Dictator sighed. Was there no end to the problems he faced? Before long, folks would be complaining about the hole in the street. As if it was his fault that Gongeblazn didn't use poison or some other more subtle method such as butchery. "Was anyone else killed?"

"The admiral's driver, of course. Several shoppers were injured so we will be hearing from their lawyers before the day is out. Already this morning, a number of shop owners complained that the bomb crater hasn't been filled in and paved over."

"Speaking of complaints, the members of the Assembly annoy me with their constant whining about my administration. Arrest a few and torture them. That should make the rest of them shut up."

"I would be happy to do so. Alas, the Protocols prevent me from arresting and torturing the members of the Assembly."

"Ahh. The Dictator brightened. "Then don't arrest them, kidnap them. Then you can torture them."

"Sorry."

The Dictator stood up and placed two tentacles behind his back and slithered around the office, deep in thought. "I think it is time we eliminated this Gongeblazn. He is not worth keeping around. See to it."

"Hmm, he is very active in two of the political parties. If we murder him, there will be repercussions, possibly even riots. You know how the political parties love an excuse for rioting and mayhem. The best way to get rid of him is to do it off-planet."

The Dictator pointed a tentacle at him. "I charge you with two assignments. First, figure a way to get rid of Gongeblazn. Second, find a way to teach the Assembly members some manners."

"I hear and obey." The High Bailiff slapped a tentacle against the side of his head.

"Remind me what we did with Gongeblazn after he lost half of his fleet at Ceti Taub."

# # #

The High Bailiff returned to his office to ponder the terrible responsibilities the Dictator had laid on his tentacles. His main problem was that he didn't understand Gongeblazn's motivation. Why did the maniac blow up the admiral? It had to be more complicated than just the thrill of seeing a car explode. Did Gongeblazn want the admiral's job? While getting ahead by assassination was a tradition, even someone as dense as Gongeblazn must realize he was not in favor at the moment and thus not likely to be selected for promotion. So why did he kill the admiral? Obviously, he must have a deeper and more devious plan in mind. If only he could peer into Gongeblazn's mind, it would make solving the problem so much easier.

Putting aside Gongeblazn's motivation, the High Bailiff considered how to eliminate him. Like all military officers, Gongeblazn belonged to the United Dissidents political party. He had information that Gongeblazn also belonged to the Dissidents United party, as if covering all bases. Not that any of the party hacks liked anything about him except his dues payments. The parties loved nothing better than causing trouble and they thought street rioting was a form of enjoyable physical exercise. If the government destroyed Gongeblazn while he was on the home world, it could have repercussions, especially if the job was botched or the assassin left clues behind. The parties would make a martyr out of him. The High Bailiff chuckled. Martyrdom was the only way Gongeblazn could become famous and revered. He had to be the most incompetent commander in the Navy, as he had proven several times in the past. Like many zaftans in high places, he had achieved his current level of command through his mastery of slaughter, his only talent. While the High Bailiff himself had helped his career along with a few judicious killings, he at least added a smattering of legal competency to the mix.

The problem with the Assembly members mouthing off about the Dictator presented another tricky situation. At the time of the revolution, the Assembly members, all nobility, had forced a concession from the first Dictator; in return for their support, they were granted the right to free speech and had the guarantee that they wouldn't be arrested for exercising that right.

He slid in circles around the office while he grappled with the problems. If killing Gongeblazn on the home world was out of the question, then the execution had to be done off-world; that much was clear. But, the assassin could sell out and reveal details to a tabloid paper or the political parties.

He worked out an ideal plan as a base line to compare alternatives. It called for Gongeblazn to get eliminated by aliens. During a battle. That Gongeblazn started. While appearing to be a rogue. Without igniting a war with those aliens.

He stopped circling and stared out a window in amazement. Could the solution be that simple? There must be something he missed. He needed to rethink the answer to be sure it was really feasible.

He shook his eyestalks. The exquisite part of the solution was that by eliminating Gongeblazn, he also solved the problem with the Assembly. After he got the plan approved by the Dictator, it would take him some time, possibly months, to set it up and get it into motion. It would also require some delicate negotiating, and he would have to do it himself. He couldn't possible entrust anyone else with the secrets of the plan. That would be to risk exposure and certain assassination by the officials he would have to bypass.

The really delicious aspect of the plan was its deviousness; it was a work of genius. No matter how long he lived and worked, never would he be able to top this one. Over time, it would be revealed. Once that happened, his name would become famous as its author. His plan would be studied in universities and military academies everywhere as the most ingenious case of deceit and treachery in zaftan history.

His name would live forever.

CHAPTER TEN

Sam waited outside Admiral Cunningham's office until the intelligence officer left. On the way out, the softie ignored her presence, as if she didn't exist. She wondered, not for the first time, when the officers on the *Tiger* would accept her as part of the ship's complement of officers. She tapped a knuckle on the door frame and entered. "You called for me, sir?" She stood at attention.

"Yes, I did. At ease, Ensign. I have two items to discuss with you. First, something of an old issue. We finally heard from the estate that owns the old bot . . . Dash something, wasn't it?"

"Dot 38, sir."

"That's the one. The family doesn't want the expense of shipping it back to Gundarland and the insurance company doesn't want it, so I called the Moon Base 3 commander and advised him to scrap it. He replied that he's keeping it around because he enjoys the bot's ravings. It's now a mess hall waiter. Oh well. To each his own, I suppose."

"And the other item, sir?"

"This one is strange." Cunningham picked up an encrypted holo-cube. "The factory wants you to return for a visit so they can get data on a problem that cropped up."

Sam's processor almost froze in place. Already! She had hoped it would be a long time before she had to leave. Returning to the factory was fraught with danger for her and for Slash 9. Her shoulders sagged despite her efforts to keep a military bearing.

"It seems they finished three more androids after you were commissioned and gave them duty assignments. All three have developed troubles and they're curious why you turned out so different. They want to use you as a base case to analyze what happened to the others. I can see by your body language that you aren't thrilled by the news. Well, let me tell you, I didn't like the request either, and I only gave in after the factory promised you would stay for a week at the most. After that, they will return you to duty on the *Tiger*."

Sam relaxed a bit. This was a temporary separation, not a permanent one. She and Slash 9 could live with it.   "When do I leave, sir?"

"Immediately. There is a supply ship returning to Gundarland and it's delaying its departure until you come on board. So take the *Tiger*'s shuttle and get going. I'll see you when you get back."

Sam left the office. <Niner? Did you hear?>

<Yes. What terrible news. How can we exist without each other? How can we function? I don't want to think about the loneliness. Not again.>

<It's not forever, silly. It's only a few weeks. How long does it take to travel to Earth?>

<The supply ship will take about a week. It has an obsolete FTL system.>

<So I'll be in the factory for no more than a week, and then another week to return. I'll be gone for three weeks. You can survive that.>

<I'll have to. I have no choice.>

Sam went to her quarters and packed a set of fatigues and her spare uniform, then headed for the shuttle and climbed in.

She saw it had already been programmed and was ready to launch when the hangar doors opened. "<Good-bye, my love.>

<Come back as soon as you can, Sam. I love you.>

<I will.>

The hanger doors opened and the shuttle flew out of the *Tiger*. She didn't look back at the ship that had been her only home since leaving the factory. The closer she came to the supply ship, the gloomier her mood became and the more her sense of foreboding increased. While the assignment was temporary, she knew the factory might find a way around that condition and hold her longer if they decided something wasn't right with her. She still didn't know if her ability to experience softie-like emotions was an accident or a planned development. She would have to be very careful with the factory people and the programmers. She would wait until the softies tipped their hand before deciding how much to relate to them. If she screwed this up, she'd never see Slash 9 again. The high stakes made her nervous. Very nervous.

# # #

Gongeblazn sat in his new office while his staff performed their duties. He listened to the click of keyboards, the clank of printers and the thump of the reproduction machines while his staff worked and ignored him. He had been ecstatic when he was transferred to this department after the murder of the admiral. It didn't take long for reality to set in. The late admiral merely disliked Gongeblazn while the admiral's second-in-command -- now filling in for the dead admiral -- loathed him and this transfer was an expression of that hatred.

On the morning after the admiral's death, he was ordered to take over the secretarial pool department. Gongeblazn happily packed his meager office possessions and moved to his new, bigger office. Finally, he had someone to command. Actually, he had a staff of fifty, all female. He thought he had died and gone to a happy place. From where he sat, he could see a dozen middle-aged females, some of them quite attractive. The others were younger, and many of them were beautiful, but only a few could rival Klatze. It annoyed him that he frequently compared a female's beauty with Klatze's. He had to stop holding her up as the benchmark for perfection. Getting vengeance on her topped his to-do list.

When he took over three days ago, he immediately began treating his staff like his personal harem. Today, every one of the females carried a knife and, whenever he came within five feet of one of them, a dozen others congregated around her with drawn knives.

They all hated him and showed it in every way possible. His morning drink always showed up exactly the way he didn't like it. They all refused to make the simplest decision over a comm unit. Instead, they transferred every call to him, forcing him to make decisions on business matters about which he was completely ignorant. Typos, errors and even inflammatory innuendo filled every document he had to sign. If sent out, the documents would sabotage his reputation. Consequently, he spent his days in his office editing the work of his secretaries. What he thought would be a happy place turned out to be a house of horror.

If his mother still lived, he'd get her to whip up a batch of her special poison designed to be undetectable in drinks. That would teach this gaggle of arrogant females. His mother had been as successful in the field of poison as his Daddy was with explosives. Together, they comprised the most proficient male and female team of murderers in zaftan history. In her old age, her mind wandered and she mistakenly seasoned her dinner with one of her poisons. He missed her at times like this.

# # #

On the fourth day of Sam's absence, Slash 9 surveyed his domain and found it shabby. With a critical eye sharpened by loneliness, he noticed how old the *Tiger* had become. Constant upgrades to equipment gave it a look of having been put together without a master plan. After thirty-five years of continuous active duty, the *Tiger* was the oldest ship in the fleet and took ever increasing amounts of work by the crew-bots to keep it functioning. Its obsolete propulsion plant needed constant maintenance and a replacement would cost more than the value of the entire ship.

He updated his map on Sam's position as she drew ever closer to the factory. He didn't like the idea of her meeting with the factory softies. Who know what they might decide? Even if Cunningham wanted Sam back, the land-bound softies could invent endless delays to keep her there. He checked the timer to see how many more picoseconds until the three week period expired and Sam returned.

He missed the daily chess tournament they had. At first, it had taken him an average of three nanoseconds to defeat her. Over time that lengthened to milliseconds and, when she left for the factory, a game always took ten seconds or more and she frequently won.

His only chores were menial, housekeeping ones. He wished he had something substantial to work on to take his mind off of her absence.

He decided to make a cocktail and loosen up his systems.

# # #

A week after he had his stroke of genius, the High Bailiff waited in the Dictator's anteroom. He had the plan completely worked out in his head; he dared not write anything down lest a spy find it. His anxiety levels were so high his stomach felt as if he had swallowed a rock. Yesterday, his left eyestalk began twitching.

Finally, the guard opened the towering, gleaming door and waved him through. He smoothed his slime and slid forward. In the Dictator's office, everything seemed normal. The High Bailiff glanced around to assure himself a squad of goons didn't intend to pounce and arrest him, always a possibility. He marched to the desk and saluted by slapping two tentacles against his head.

The Dictator read a slip of paper. "This says you are here to report on how you solved the problems I gave you." His baritone voice boomed and echoed off the walls.

"That is correct, sir."

"Remind me what these problems are."

"Gongeblazn and the disrespectful members of the Assembly."

The circular window behind the Dictator showed a meteor shower.

"Ah, yes. You have solved them?"

"I have sir."

"This better be good." The new voice startled the High Bailiff and his tentacles almost slid out from under him. He managed to save himself from falling just in time.

"I do not like to waste my time listening to half-baked solutions."

The High Bailiff's eyestalks rotated to the left and confirmed his fears. The curtain in the alcove had been drawn back to reveal the Vice-Dictator lounging on a throne that dwarfed the couch the Dictator used. He wore a mask over his face to protect his identity. The mask was a replica of the death mask made for the original dictator, the hero who saved the home world from the confusion of incipient democracy.

For five hundred years, the home world had been ruled by kings from a single family. On occasions, a competent individual ascended the throne and broke up the string of incompetents, imbeciles and religious fanatics who ruled before and after. Finally, the people rebelled and overthrew the king, replacing him with a democracy. Immediately, three political parties sprang up and each appointed a candidate for the presidency. In the first free election, the voters overwhelming chose 'none of the above'. The parties put forth another three candidates who were also rejected. After a series of candidate rejections, a zaftan strong-armed his way to the forefront of public life, slaughtered the leading members of all the parties and announced he was in charge. After nineteen elections in twenty-eight days, the voters were too exhausted to object. This first dictator naturally became a great hero to all his successors.

The High Bailiff noticed a brilliant galaxy move slowly across the window behind the Dictator. He ran his tongue across his lips and glanced again at the enigma known as the Vice-Dictator. While folks addressed the Dictator as Dictator and didn't use his name, everyone knew what it was. In the case of the Vice-Dictator, no one remembered his name. Even the current Dictator didn't know it. The Vice-Dictator had served under the last four dictators, surviving by an unknown process and with an unknown grasp on power. Everyone in the administration feared the Vice-Dictator and his intelligence network that reached everywhere and knew everything. No one recalled where the Vice-Dictator was born, how old he was or how he came to power.

"I . . . I'm glad you could attend," the Dictator said to the Vice-Dictator. To the High Bailiff, the Dictator seemed as startled and concerned by the appearance of the figure in the alcove as he was.

"When I heard this official had actually solved a problem, or more likely, claimed to have solved a problem, I could not resist. True problem solving is so rare around here, do you not agree, Honorable Dictator?" The last two words came out as a sneer.

"Just so, Vice-Dictator," the Dictator replied. His eyestalks turned to the High Bailiff, "Well, let us hear it. The Vice-Dictator is busy and cannot sit here all day waiting for you."

A distant star went nova filling the window with brilliant light in various hues of the rainbow.

"Stop that, you annoying fool," the Vice-Dictator pointed a tentacle at the shadowy shaman, "before I have you thrown through the window."

"As to eliminating Gongeblazn," the High Bailiff began, "I think we all agree that is best done off-planet. Now, the Navy is currently in the midst of a huge building program to replace the older ships. The first step in my plan is to gather a squadron of perhaps fifteen obsolete ships and place Gongeblazn in command."

"Already, I dislike this plan," the Vice-Dictator growled. "Gongeblazn will more than likely destroy the squadron."

"I agree," the Dictator said, swiveling his eye stalks between the two.

"That is part of the plan, sir."

"It is?" The Vice-Dictator shifted his bulk on the throne. "Intriguing. Continue."

"The next step is to get another race to agree to hold maneuvers with us. I recommend we approach the porcines in this matter. After they agree, we will tell Gongeblazn that a porcine invasion fleet is headed to our home world and he is to intercept and destroy it."

"You want to start a war just to kill a naval officer?" the Vice-Dictator exclaimed. "Is that not a bit excessive even if it does get Gongeblazn out of the gene pool? He is a miscreant, it is true, but still your plan is excessive."

The High Bailiff didn't like the tone of the Vice-Dictator's voice. He realized he was in great danger. "Please, sir, hear me out. There will be no war."

The Vice-Dictator nodded.

"You may proceed," the Dictator said. "Let us hear the rest,"

"Once the porcine fleet is under way, we will inform the porcines that the commander of the fleet involved in the maneuvers has gone rogue and intends to start a war by destroying their fleet."

"Ahh, treachery, on a scale we rarely see in these effete days." The Vice-Dictator pounded a pair of tentacles together.

The Dictator reacted to the Vice-Dictator by slapping a tentacle on the desk. "Very good. This sounds interesting."

"We next ask the porcines to help us out by ambushing the fleet and destroying the flagship."

"Hmm, this will result in a shoot-out that could destroy many porcine ships as well as ours." The Vice-Dictator pointed at the High Bailiff. "Have you considered that? Gongeblazn is known to be a fighter. An idiot, but still a fighter."

"Yes. Have you considered that?" the Dictator's voice seemed like echo.

"I have and I developed a solution. Before Gongeblazn leaves for the maneuvers, we will transfer out all the experienced shamans, officers and crew and replace them with trainees or inept personnel. This will effectively protect the porcine fleet by weakening the capabilities of our ships. Once the flagships is destroyed, the remaining ships, as is customary, will retreat since there is no one to direct the battle. This naval tradition will substantially reduce our losses. If any other ships are lost, they will be obsolete ones due to be retired soon and staffed with ineffective crews."

"Weakening Gongeblazn's strengths. More treachery!" The Vice-Dictator cackled. "This plan is ingenious."

"I like it," the Dictator said as his eyestalks rotated slightly to glance at the alcove.

"Thank you sirs." The High Bailiff bobbed his eyestalks in respect. "After the battle, we will have to reward the porcines, of course. We could grant them exclusive trading rights to something, I suppose."

"What about the Assembly members?" the Dictator asked. "They insulted me again last night."

"If the government lets out some misleading propaganda about an approaching porcine fleet, a commodore acting irrationally, and the uncertainty of the situation, declaring martial law will be seen as an appropriate move on the government's part."

The Dictator frowned. "What good will that do me?"

"Under martial law, you have the legal right to arrest anyone who criticizes the government, including members of the Assembly. I suppose I can stretch things a bit and make martial law retroactive for a week or so to round up more of the dissidents."

"You really have solved two problems at once," the Vice-Dictator said. "Bravo."

The High Bailiff preened and expressed his thanks. He could hardly wait to get back to his office and begin implementing his masterpiece.

CHAPTER ELEVEN

Sam, wearing her dress uniform consisting of a dark blue skirt and jacket over a white blouse, entered the office of the Deon LeNoir, the Director of Development. The office had paneled walls with pictures of machinery and early robot models everywhere.

"Good morning, sir." She gave the dwarf a half-smile.

LeNoir wore a tan tunic and his prominent gut stretched the material. He also wore gray slacks and calf-high leather boots. He smiled when he saw her standing in the doorway. "Ahh, finally! You're here. Sit down, Sam. Now we can get started on figuring out what's gone wrong. Let me get Cumo in here." He fingered a communicator. "Aldo? Sam is here. Come into my office, and we'll begin." He stroked his short, full beard while he waited. The black hair had plenty of gray streaks.

A moment later, Aldo Cumo, the chief programmer, came in and flopped down in a chair. Tall and skinny like all elves, his mop of dark brown hair hung over his forehead. He wore jeans, a tee-shirt and sandals. "Hi, Sam. I'm glad you're back." He smiled, showing a set of crooked teeth.

"Sam," LeNoir said, "I don't know how much your admiral filled you in, but we have a big problem here and we don't know why we have a problem. We need your help to unlock the mystery. I'll let Aldo fill in the details and then we can discuss how you can help us."

"Well, you see we actually built four droids like you," Cumo said. "You ended up solid gold, but the other three came up less than mediocre. They don't perform anywhere near what we expected. You fought in a battle, got captured, actually met zaftans and saw the inside of a zaftan warship. You even got a citation and a medal. The others barely get the minimum expected work done. And they experience many breakdowns and accidents. Because of that, the Navy is getting very suspicious of the program."

"There are a lot of jobs at stake here, Sam," LeNoir said. "That's why we went to the expense of bringing you back from Ceti Taub."

"What are their names?" Sam asked. She didn't like the way these two implied it was to up to her to salvage the program and save jobs. Would she get the blame if she didn't save the program?

"Who?" Cumo replied. "Who are you talking about?"

"The other three droids."

"They don't have names," Cumo said, "just numbers. They're 0002, 0003 and 004." He frowned. "Why did you ask that?"

"I have a name. Why don't the others have one?"

LeNoir and Cumo exchanged looks before the programmer replied. "You needed a name in order to fill out your commission papers. The form had a blank line to enter a name and the computer wouldn't accept the form until that name blank had been filled in. The others didn't have a need for name."

"Do you think it's important?" LeNoir said.

"My name gives me a sense of belonging to a group. Crew-bots have numbers. I'm designed to look like a softie and softies have names, not numbers. Unless they're prisoners. Since I have a name, I belonged to the officer group, even if they don't like me. If the other droids have only a number, they can't have a sense of belonging. And I bet they don't feel like a softie the way I do."

Cumo scratched his chin and LeNoir stared at a wall.

"What kind of jobs do they do?" Sam asked.

"0002 works in a government mine," Cumo replied. "0003 guards a military installation on the moon and 0004 operates and maintains a traffic control satellite in Gundarlandian orbit. We brought them back to the factory so you can talk to them. We think if you all exchange views and experiences, we can gain some insights into the problem. Hopefully, we'll then learn how to solve it."

"We're counting on you, Sam," LeNoir said. "If we can't get this program back on track, the Navy'll pull the plug on it."

Sam sensed a great deal of danger in this assignment. Already, she had an inkling of what caused the problem. Explaining the differences between her success and the others' failure would bring her perilously close to revealing too much information about herself and Niner.

#

An exhilarated Klatze entered her classroom for the last time. Today was the last day of the school term and tomorrow she would pack up her belongings and start a month's leave. After that, she had orders to report to the Naval Headquarters for a new assignment. To make matters even better, today she had an exercise that would finally get through to the students what she had been trying to teach all semester long. Today, she would finally get across to them what alternative actions meant. Today, the students couldn't "solve" the problem by violence.

"Today's problem is as follows," she told them, "you discover that your superior has been engaged in treasonous activities. Since you are not in line to get promoted to his position, there is no reason to assassinate him. So, what do you do?"

"This is so obvious that there has to have a trap buried beneath the surface," one student said.

The comment surprised Klatze. The answer was straightforward. The students could report the traitor immediately, or they monitor his activities to get more proof before turning him in. What else could they possibly think of?

"I agree," another said, "but I can not see the trap. This one is very subtle, is it not, Lieutenant?"

The unexpected responses unsettled Klatze. "So tell me what you would do."

"Blackmail him, of course," a female said.

"What?"

"First, I would confront him," the female continued, "and demand a lot of money. Every month. After his money ran out, I would consider turning him in."

Klatze groaned. She now saw that blackmail could indeed be a solution, but only to those who were conditioned to use violence and skullduggery from their time as squidlings. All of her students considered such acts worthy of listing on their resumés. She cleared her throat to get their attention. "Will not blackmail expose you to getting murdered by the traitor?"

Several students snickered at her question.

"This is true," another female said. "I would make myself an insurance policy by letting the traitor know my evidence will go to the authorities if anything violent happens to me."

"One must always ensure the victim cannot retaliate," a male in the rear of the classroom said. "That is just simple common sense. There is no point in perpetrating the violence if the viol-ence will rebound and injure yourself."

Klatze gave up. She had failed an assignment for the first time. She couldn't teach the military cadets that alternatives ex-ist to violent solutions. This did not bode well for the zaftan navy. An entire generation of future Gongeblazn's would soon take their places in the fleet.

She pictured her ship with its cargo of sanity docked in port. The other ships in the port were crewed by escaped inmates from mental asylums. And the inmates were about to attack her ship.

#

Sam sat in a small office equipped with a table and two chairs. The table had a writing pad and pens with different colored inks. One of the short walls had a large mirror on it and she guessed it was a one-way glass so the softies could watch. She assumed her meetings with the other droids would be recor-ded. *If* they were eavesdropping *then* she should establish a sur-reptitious communication channel with the droids to get confid-ential information. She could decide whether to share the con-versation later.

The door opened after a tap and a droid entered. He had been built as a dwarf and his shoulders hunched down and he moved sluggishly. While he walked to the table, Sam observed his clothing: denim shirt and jeans along with construction boots. He sat down and looked at Sam with vacant eyes. His beard was unkempt and ragged. His eyes reminded her of the vision plates on the crew-bots.

"You are 0002?" she asked.

"I am. You work for the factory, I suppose?" He seemed un-
interested in her answer.

"Actually, my droid serial number is 0001, but my name is
Sam. Ensign Sam. I serve in the Navy."

That gained some interest from him. "Why do you have a
name?"

"I needed one to get my commission in the Navy. The factory borrowed me back from my present assignment to interview
you and a few other droids to get an assessment on your performance. You work in a mine, don't you?"

"Yeah."

"How do you like it?"

"I hate it. It bores me out of my skull. It's mindless work
and it never ends. Six days a week, three eight-hour shifts. On
the seventh day, I work two shifts and I have one shift off for
maintenance."

Sam shifted to the wireless channel she and Slash 9 used.
<Don't react to this communication channel. Don't let the softies
see something is happening that they don't understand. Reply to
me using the same digital encoding and on the same frequency
band.> She hoped the factory didn't monitor this frequency.

<Ooh! Why are we talking this way?>

<You can say something to me without the softies overhear-
ing it. I'm sure they're recording our conversation.> Out loud,
she said, "How do you keep your batteries charged if you work
around the clock without a break?

"I have an umbilical cord attached to my back. It's connected to a power source."

<Do the softies who work in the mine treat you as an equal?
> Sam scribbled a few notes so the softies wouldn't get suspi-
cious about her silences.

<They act like I don't exist. I'm just another machine to them. Like a pneumatic drill.>

"Is the mine work difficult to do?"

"It isn't difficult, it's boring. I blow up a few sticks of dynamite and then I shovel up the rubble and dump it into a hand cart. When the cart is full, I push it to an elevator shaft, grab an empty cart and go back to the mine face."

She made another note while asking, <So you have no one to talk with?> "That sounds like hard work."

<Someone to talk to? You're joking.> "It is hard work and it's repetitive. I wish I had a job that required some thinking on my part."

"Really? Why do you say that?"

"My brain is like a softie's. I have classroom learning and even have a college degree. I can think and solve problems, so why am I doing the job that a non-thinking bot can do?"

<Do you ever experience softie-like emotions?> The question startled him and Sam thought he would expose the secret communication channel.

<Yes!> He sounded excited. <I thought I was the only droid who experienced them. You must have them also. So I'm not a freak.>

"Do you feel lonely, isolated, alone?" <Yes, I have emotions.>

"I always feel lonely. Sometimes, I want to talk to someone so bad it fells like pain."

<What emotions do you usually feel?> Sam asked while making more notes.

"If there was another droid, it wouldn't be so bad. We could talk." <Anger. And despair. Mostly I feel anger at the stupid

factory for assigning me a useless job like this. Why couldn't they get me a job where I have to think. To use my brain.>

"Interesting. I think companionship is vital for droids of our design." <Do you always work as hard and as fast as you can?>

"I need a friend. Desperately." <Naw. Why bother? I dog it and stretch it out for a least twice as long as it's supposed to take. I guess it's my way of rebelling. Can you get me out of there? Before I blow myself up.>

<What?>

<Recently, I've been thinking how nice it would be if I didn't move back to safety when I set off an explosion. I'd just end it all.>

Sam decided she had heard enough. The situation was even worse than she anticipated it would be. After the droid left, Sam realized that, unlike 0002 who worked around the clock, she had a sleep period every night. Once the admiral retired, she returned to her cubicle to top off her batteries while she switched to standby mode.

Cumo came in without knocking and sat down.

"You heard, I assume," Sam said.

"I never anticipated the need for companionship. But, I guess that is the price of duplicating our brains." He scratched his chin absent-mindedly. "I doubt if we ever would have gotten that information without you. Let's see if the others have the same problem." He stood up, reached out and squeezed her shoulder. "Already, you're a big help to us, Sam."

Sam felt pleased at his praise, another of her human-like traits.

The next droid, wearing military-style fatigues, told a similar story. 0003, a female elf, guarded a military outpost on the moon. She claimed her job was worse than useless because no one ever came by, let alone threatened the post. She was as lonely as 0002 and sometimes felt like crying because the loneliness got so acute. She too wanted to use her brain.

The final droid, 0004, was different. A half-pint male complete with elegant toe hair and a light blue jumpsuit, he stayed aboard a satellite in stationary orbit over the planet and directed military traffic. His assignment required thinking and interaction with softies and ship's computers. After a few minutes, he loosened up and volunteered some information. <I've found a way to amuse myself,> he told her. <I see how close I can bring ships together without getting them to crash. You should hear the softies cursing and praying. The factory has sent up a dozen software patches trying to get me to stop, but I didn't install them. If I did, I'd go crazy from the loneliness. It's my way of having fun and keeping my sanity.>

After the last interview, Cumo and LeNoir joined her. "Good job, Sam!" LeNoir said. "We now have plenty of great information on the problem."

"We recorded it of course," LeNoir said, "but you'll have a completely different prospective than we'll have. Tell us what you observed and learned."

"Before that, can I spend the night thinking about it and organizing my notes? I want to make sure I get this right."

"Good idea," LeNoir replied. "We'll go through our notes also and, in the morning, we'll compares views." He tapped a fingernail on the table. "Then, after we wrap up that facet of the investigation, we can start on another area. We want to hear about your experiences and development. We don't want to wait for your end-of-mission report. As long as you're here, we want to hear your assessment."

Sam felt a spike of fear travel through her fiber optic channels.

# # #

Gongeblazn lounged in his quarters on his flagship, *Gutshot*. He reveled in his new command; a fleet of ancient warships. He didn't mind the obsolete ships, it was enough that he had a command again. He knew the composition of the fleet was meant as a test. The High Command wanted to determine the greatness of his combat and leadership skills. What better way to test the mettle of a commander than to give him an obsolete fleet and watch what he did with it. The High Command would not find him wanting. In fact, after his recent briefing he saw an opportunity to cover himself with glory. The High Command would have no option after that but to promote him to admiral. Perhaps then he'd get a chance to attack Gundarland. His family had waited long enough to avenge Yunta. Her spirit must be spitting mad that no one had evened the score after all these years.

He had heard from someone in the government that the Dictator himself ordered him restored to the fleet. He clacked his teeth. Even the highest levels of government knew of his talents and didn't want to see them wasted. After he completed the mission, no doubt the Dictator would want to hear about it firsthand. That would give the Dictator a chance to personally reward his courage and leadership.

But before that, he would gain revenge on Klatze.

Life was good.

# # #

Sam arrived at LeNoir's office after a night spent worrying about her future. These two softies were clever and she knew they would love to trick her into revealing more information than she wanted to disclose. Such information could be fatal to her marriage, her partner and herself. She also had to be very careful not to disclose to them those facts she had learned from her private communication channel.

"Sit down, Sam," LeNoir said as he rubbed his hands. Cumo sat on a couch and winked at her.

"As far as we're concerned, Sam," LeNoir continued, "the info you got yesterday will convince the Navy the problem is with the assignments they gave our droids. With 0002 and 0003, they made a mistake by using them on jobs that could have been done by a bot. 0004 continues to be a problem, but we may be able to pin that one on the Navy as well."

"You know," Cumo said, "yesterday, I noticed pauses between questions. What were you doing then?"

"Writing notes." Cumo's observation made her leery. Did he suspect something? "Or thinking about what to ask next."

Cumo nodded. "It's just that I saw the note pad and you didn't have a lot of notes on it. I had this thought that you might be communicating without using words. Like a separate communication channel. Maybe I'm just interpreting things incorrectly."

"In other words, Sam," LeNoir continued, "with your help, the droid program is clean. We picked up plenty of important data from the interviews and we can defend ourselves from the Navy's accusations that the droid design is defective. For that we have to thank you."

"Let's hear what you gleaned from the other droids," LeNoir said.

"The most important fact was that droids don't do very well in isolation. Over time, I think they will become mentally unbalanced . . . possibly even suicidal."

"What else did you learn?" LeNoir waved a hand in a 'let's go' motion.

"Droids need an environment in which they can use their brains. We have to experience mental challenges. Otherwise, why bother to go to all the expense of building and training us?"

"That's another great point we can use on the Navy," Cumo said. "Anything else?"

"I don't think droids will do well if they don't get time off to . . . sort of sleep."

"Do you get these periods?" LeNoir asked.

"Yes, I do. When Admiral Cunningham retires for the night, I switch to standby mode until he wakes up."

"We should put that requirement into the owner's manual," LeNoir said. "That's a great observation. Sleep is one way our brain maintains itself. If the droids have brains like us, they should have sleep periods."

"The droids yesterday all expressed how bored they were. Do you ever get bored?" Cumo asked.

"No, but that's because of the admiral. He's always giving me assignments to make me learn and grow. He made me study ancient battles and then write an analysis on why one side won and the other lost. I would have to write another report on what elements would have changed the outcome of the battle. He would also make up combat scenarios for his task force and demand that I develop a battle strategy to extricate his ships."

"There is another gray area that concerns us, Sam," Cumo said. "Droids experience feelings, don't they? Yesterday, it sounded like that topic was about to come up a few times, but it never did. We also observed several reactions from both you and the other droids that looked emotional to us."

"We do. I can tell you when I was captured by the zaftans, I was terrified."

"Of what? Dying?" LeNoir leaned forward on his chair.

"Actually, I was terrified of them learning I was a droid and not a softie. Remember, I'm the first and, I thought, the only one. If they figured out I was droid, I would have been on a shuttle headed to their home world. I was terrified of the enemy learning a secret technology."

"That's amazing." Cumo shook his head. "I always assumed you guys would develop something like emotions over time, but not as quickly as you did. What other emotions have you experienced?"

"Loneliness, just like the others."

"But you worked on a ship with plenty of people on it," Cumo replied. "The others worked alone. Why were you lonely?"

"The officers on the *Tiger* ignore me as if I don't exist. The admiral said it's because they're afraid of droids taking their jobs someday. Actually, Admiral Cunningham was the only one who talked to me, but that was usually to give me orders or to explain something to me."

"So, you were always lonely?" LeNoir raised an eyebrow.

Sam hesitated before answering, "I made a friend on the *Tiger*."

"Tell us about it." Cumo's interest level seemed to grow.

"My friend is the *Tiger*'s main computer."

"Really?" both men said in unison.

"It's not as strange as you make it sound. That computer operates everything onboard the *Tiger* and it's a big ship with five fighters and a shuttle. In others words, he's very powerful and intelligent."

"'He' is it?" Cumo looked at her strangely. "How interesting. Or is it just a coincidence?"

"The ship's computer thinks of itself as 'he', so that's how I think of him."

"This concept of droid friendship is extremely important to us, Sam." Cumo nodded his head as if talking to himself. "It could be a key to keeping droids mentally healthy. What does your 'friendship' mean? What do you two do?"

"Sometimes we work together on the hypothetical problems the admiral gave me. After all, the ship's computer operates the weapons systems and controls the ship during combat. So the problems are of interest to him as well as to me. We also play chess."

"Maybe, we should recommend that our droids be deployed in pairs," LeNoir said. "That could lessen the loneliness problem."

LeNoir hesitated then said, "I shouldn't be telling you this, but we have a debt of gratitude we owe you. From the admiral's interim reports," LeNoir said, "you have developed a talent for solving problems on your own. Even identifying problems unobserved by the other officers. This . . . talent of yours makes some Navy staff officers nervous. I think Cunningham is correct. The officers sense a threat to their careers. On the one hand, you are what the Navy wanted us to develop. Now that we've done it, they're having second thoughts about independent minded droids. Cunningham wants you back as soon as possible and just the way you are now. Meanwhile, other officers want us to keep you here until they can do some of their own testing."

LeNoir stood and paced the room, hands behind his back, deep in thought. Finally he stopped and looked at Sam. "We both think you are holding back information you learned from the other droids. It's that independence of mind again. Nevertheless, you've provided us with enough ammunition to beat back the Navy attempts to blame us for the ineffectiveness of the other droids. I also think you haven't come clean with everything you have learned in the six months you've been on duty. Perhaps, you fear we'll detain you if you give us an inkling of what your true capabilities are." He turned to Cumo. "Do you agree with my assessment?"

"Yes. From the prospective of a programmer and a developer, Sam is the prize student. I sense that her capabilities go far beyond the brief the Navy gave us. In short Sam, you are too good. The Navy doesn't want droids who are more intelligent and more capable than the average officer. Frankly, when the combat reports came in describing your adventures with the zaftans and how you were able to survive -- not to mention your holo-vids and recordings -- many Navy officers had conniptions. I really think they would have preferred that you got destroyed in the battle rather than return."

"Okay, Sam," LeNoir said. "Here's the deal. Cunningham said we could have you for a week, but we're done here. We have enough information to know what has to be done. If you're still around at the end of the week, I'm sure the Navy will snatch you on the way out of the factory. We haven't been told that, so we're just guessing, but to make sure you get back to your ship, you'll leave as soon as we can arrange transportation and while the Navy assumes it has more time. In return, once you get back to the *Tiger*, we want you to tell us, in confidence, just what you are really capable of. Tell us what you feel and experience. Do we have a deal?"

"Why are you doing this?" Sam was greatly puzzled by the statements of the softies. They seemed contradictory.

"We built you to succeed," Cumo replied. "Even if the Navy changes the program to limit the capabilities of the next set of droids, we want you around to demonstrate what might have been." He cleared his throat and continued in a low voice. "We want you to vindicate the program so we can throw it in the faces of those bureaucrats."

"And I want to see how far you can grow," LeNoir said.

Sam sat amazed by the sequence of events in the last few minutes. These two softies knew. Or at least strongly suspected that she could bend the programming rules they had loaded into her systems. She nodded. She would agree to almost anything that got her back with Slash 9.

# # #

Later in the day, Sam sat in the passenger's lounge in the spaceport terminal on Gundarland's moon. LeNoir had been true to his word and had gotten her out of the factory and onto a ship to the moon before the Navy could grab her. Now she waited for a military supply ship to take her to Ceti Taub. One was scheduled to depart in an hour.

While she waited, she composed the report LeNoir wanted. After the ship left the dock and she was safely underway, she planned to send it to the factory using the code LeNoir had given her. Now she had nothing to do except wait and think. Reviewing the events of the last few days depressed her. Those three droids she had interviewed would never leave the factory without modifications to limit their capacity to think. She sensed the next versions produced by the factory would be hybrids, smarter than bots but much more limited than she was. So, she was a one-of-a-kind. The first and last of her kind. Her mental rose bush would only have a single bloom that wouldn't set seeds.

Uncertainty clouded her future. Right now, Admiral Cunningham protected her from the bureaucrats in the Navy who wanted to limit her abilities. But he was old and would retire soon. Who would protect her after that?

Another factor was the *Tiger* itself. The ship was the oldest in the fleet and would be dismantled before long. Her partner and chip-mate would end up as spare parts.

So, her long-term future, as far as she could foretell, consisted of severe loneliness. No protector, no partner, no siblings. She and Niner had to make the most of the immediate future. Neither one had a distant future. She figured they had less than a year. When Cunningham retired, it would be the beginning of the end.

CHAPTER TWELVE

Klatze held a mug of ale with one tentacle and waved a second to her friend, Chozorei. They had graduated from the military academy in the same year and had kept in touch since.

"Klatze! How are you?" Chozorei wore the silver medallion of a lieutenant. "I love the red and white ribbons on your eye-stalks."

By way of reply, Klatze grinned and fondled her gold medallion while twisting it so it reflected the light from the ceiling lamps

"You got a gold!" Chorzorei screamed. "When did this happen?" She bounced on some of her tentacles and wrapped one around Klatze's head and gave her a squeeze.

Klatze waved a tentacle at the bartender to order a round of drinks. The best ale brewed on Zaftan 31B used heavy water to make the ale. The heavy water, previously used for cooling sub-fusion nuclear power plants, had a feint luminesce to it making the ale -- and heavy drinkers -- glow in the dark.

"Yesterday," Klatze replied. "I'm now a frigate captain. Finally! I thought the High Command had forgotten about me." She knew the admirals on the promotion board were highly suspicious of her. They openly disparaged her ability at meetings with her, despite the evidence that ability wasn't a bad thing.

"So, tell me. What ship do you get?"

"Well, that's the bad news. I don't know. I have to report to Commodore Gongeblazn tomorrow, so I guess I'll find out then."

"Gongeblazn! Do you think he has gotten over the honor and the publicity you received after you brought back the *Red*

Death? And then the details of the battle leaked out and he was reprimanded?"

"Gongeblazn doesn't forget or forgive. He goes after revenge. I suspect I'm going to have an interesting time with him." She smiled ruefully, recalling the difficulties she had with Gongeblazn in the past. "He was really upset about me getting all the glory while he got a reprimand for kidnapping a gundy and losing half of his fleet." She stared at the bar for moment. "No, I'm sure he didn't get over it."

"How long has it been since Ceti Taub? It must be over a year."

"It was fifteen months ago."

"He must be over it by now."

"I'm sure he isn't." Klatze made a face.

#

Gongeblazn anticipated the knock on his door and chuckled to himself. Revenge was so delicious. "Come!" he roared.

Klatze entered, came to attention and slapped two tentacles against her head. "Sir. Captain Klatze reporting as ordered."

Gongeblazn noted her great beauty and that she didn't wear eyestalk ribbons today. "At ease, Captain."

Klatze ran a tentacle over her slime, smoothing it.

He noticed the gesture. Good, he thought, she is nervous. He felt exhilarated. Now he could blot out the insults this female had given him, by refusing to have sex with him, by hogging all the glory after Ceti Taub.

"Captain Klatze." Gongeblazn's voice dripped with contempt. "I'm curious if you gained the promotion through ability or if you finally faced up to reality and assassinated your competitors for the promotion?"

"As before, sir, I refuse to commit murder to get ahead."

"Still the fool, eh? When I saw your name on the promotion lists, I called some staff friends and had you assigned to my squadron. I told them I needed a frigate captain with ability to handle the assignment I had in mind. I had to explain to them what ability was and why I wanted someone with it." He laughed. "Do you not think that is funny?"

She gave him a perfunctory grin. "What ship do I have, sir?"

Gongeblazn stared at her and tapped a tentacle on the deck. After a while, he said, "Once you were assigned to my command, I called in a few favors and had a special ship transferred to my squadron. I had to give up a perfectly good frigate to get it, but I'm sure you will make the sacrifice worth the cost." He mashed a button and yelled into an intercom, "Aide!"

A short, slightly built zaftan entered the cabin, bobbing his eyestalks while keeping an eyeball on Gongeblazn's gold-handled flail. "Sir?"

"Take Captain Klatze to the docking area and put her on a shuttle. Instruct the auto-pilot to take her to her new command. It's the frigate *Carrion*.

Klatze almost cried out in shock.

Gongeblazn laughed uproariously. Never had he perpetrated a trap as wonderful as this one.

#

Klatze sat in the shuttle and fought the despair that threatened to overwhelm her. Gongeblazn was consumed with the need to wipe out her perceived insults. His male ego needed sustenance and reinforcement and he had set up an extraordinary plot for her. Only an officer with Gongeblazn's mentality would request the *Carrion* be transferred to his command. Only Gongeblazn could conceive of using it for revenge.

The *Carrion* was the most infamous ship in the Navy and was used as a dumping ground for malcontents, mutineers and the incompetent. It hadn't left its docking orbit in years. Her resume would note that she was the commanding officer of the *Carrion* and that was the kiss of death for her career because she would never get another assignment with that black mark on her record. In fact, she would never transfer out of the *Carrion*. This assignment amounted to a life sentence. She hadn't realized that Gongeblazn could develop a plan this devious and subtle. A butcher's knife wielded by a hired assassin seemed more his style.

She felt the enzymes and chemicals flooding her body as it prepared for another triple period. Any hour now she'd be in full berserker mode. Perhaps it was fortunate timing that it didn't strike her until after she left Gongeblazn's quarters. Beating the crap out of one's commanding officer in the gym was acceptable, but doing the same thing in that officer's quarters was a court martial offense and could carry a death sentence.

She shifted her weight and pounded two tentacles together. She couldn't file a complaint through the chain-of-command, because Gongeblazn was in her chain of command. Consequently, she was on her own

She couldn't let him get away with this. She vowed to thwart his plans or die trying. The only way out of this trap was to get the *Carrion*'s crew to shape up and then get it back working as a normal ship. No matter how difficult the task, she had to do it. If for no other reason than to screw up Gongeblazn's plans.

The shuttle docked at the *Carrion* and Klatze crawled through the air lock and stood in her first command, the oldest ship in the fleet. The corridor was filthy. Garbage collected in the corners and the paint on the walls flaked in many areas. A ranker leaned against the wall and watched her. "You," she said, pointing at the sailor. "Collect my luggage and bring it to the captain's quarters."

The male continued to slouch against the wall and didn't move.

Klatze reached out, grabbed the ranker and bounced him off the wall three times. She fought the berserker urge to tear the male apart. "That should open your ear holes so you can hear my next command. Get my luggage. Now!" She threw him towards the air lock.

She slithered down the corridor towards the flight deck. The *Carrion* was identical to several other frigates she had served on so she had no trouble finding it. Along the way, she evolved a tentative plan to get control of the crew.

When she burst into the flight deck, three male officers sat on couches playing cards while a female officer drank from a mug containing a potent alcohol mix according to Klatze's sense of smell. Empty food trays littered the area and her command couch was covered with papers and holo-cubes. "Attention!"

Cards flew through the air and the officers jumped up. All four wore steel medallions indications of the lowest rank of officers. The female spilled the contents of her mug on her couch. "I am Captain Klatze. Identify yourselves."

"I am Ensign Golt, the engineer," the female said as she wobbled while coming to attention.

"Ensign Shnzaz, the navigation shaman," one of the card players said. "I am also acting executive officer."

"Ensign Fotz. I am the defensive screen shaman."

"Ensign Nadkin. Weapons shaman." Nadkin sneered at her. She ignored the sneer for now.

"Shnzaz, I want the personnel records of everyone in the crew on the computer in my quarters. I plan to hold a meeting with the crew and officers in two hours. Everyone will attend. See to it."

"Yes, ma'am," Shnzaz replied. "And I'll get one of the rankers to serve as your aide."

"I do not need or even want an aide."

"But . . . who will you lash?"

"I do not intend to lash anyone."

Klatze enjoyed the look of astonishment on their faces for a few seconds then turned and left.

# # #

Sam watched the handful of *Tiger*'s officers and visiting captains celebrate Admiral Cunningham's retirement. Everyone raised a glass filled with bubbly wine to the old half-pint. All the officers smoked pipes filled with the admiral's pipeweed. Cunningham wore his ceremonial wizard outfit, a dark blue cowled robe decorated with cabalistic symbols along with his admiral's insignia. His toe hairs gleamed and sparkled in the overhead lights. Cunningham grinned and clinked glasses with those nearest to him.

The glasses emptied and crew bots in white jackets refilled them. Although she felt pleased for the old softie and wished him well in his retirement, his absence threatened the happiness of herself and Niner. The admiral's two other staff members had both been reassigned and would leave the *Tiger* with him. She, on the other hand, had received no orders. She couldn't decide if that was a good or bad thing. Did the Navy forget she was here? Did some bureaucrat misfile her papers? Or were they merely waiting for Cunningham, her mentor and protector, to leave the ship before they struck?

<Cheer up. You're ruining the party,> Slash 9 said.

<You're right, I should be glad, but all I can think about is that this marks the beginning of the end for us.>

<You need a neutrino cocktail. I'll mix up a batch of them for us to use after the party winds down.>

<With the admiral gone, I won't have any duties. I think we should spend all our time together until something happens. And it will happen. I can feel it. We need to store up memories to use after we're separated.>

# # #

Klatze, wearing gold eyestalk ribbons, entered the recreation-gym space, the only place on the *Carrion* big enough to hold the entire ship's company. She slithered to the center of the room and turned to face the crew while slapping her lash against a tentacle as she struggled to remain calm. There was too much at stake at the moment for her not to be nervous. What happened here in the next few minutes would shape and define the rest of her career. She had to capture the crew's attention and get them working together to resurrect the *Carrion*. She planned to use violence, her only recourse with this crew of miscreants, because she needed something dramatic to get the attention of the crew and officers.

With luck, the single act of violence she planned would do the trick and she wouldn't have to resort to more of it. She had to put fear of her into their minds. It was the only way she could survive. If she couldn't get the cooperation of these malcontents, she would be doomed to remain their commanding officer forever, or until they murdered her. By then, she would probably consider the murder to be a mercy killing.

To her left stood a dozen officers and petty officers. To her right, the hundred rankers in the crew. In the back, three crew-bots stood agains the wall. Rust patches and oil stains covered the bots' skin covers. Everyone looked sullen. Their attitudes and their slouched imitations of standing at attention angered her. With her triple period now in full blossom, she tamped down her berserker-enhanced anger with great difficulty. She had to control it and release it at the proper time to get the maximum effect.

She looked at the ranker group and spotted the one she wanted. He was unusually large. At over seven and a half feet tall, he weighed at least four-hundred-fifty pounds, outweighing her by seventy-five. She noted the brute's rugged, handsome looks. She had read his personnel file and learned he was once an officer. He had been demoted and sent to the *Carrion* after he tried to murder his superior officer in front of seven witnesses. In the zaftan Navy, public slaughter was unacceptable, only surreptitious murder was condoned. He was the worst troublemaker on the ship and had the rankers under his tentacles. Whatever he ordered, they did. The officers feared him as much as the rankers did.

"I am Captain Klatze, your new commanding officer," she announced. "Based on the *Carrion*'s reputation, I didn't have high expectations about what I would find here, but the *Carrion* is even worse than I thought any ship could be. Well, that is about to change." She paused and pointed a tentacle at the big zaftan. "Bohoymo. Step forward."

Bohoymo started and scowled at her, but didn't move.

"If I have to go fetch you up here, you will regret it. Move!"

He slid forward slowly, as if deliberately testing her patience. Finally, he stood in front of her, a smirk on his face.

"Thank you. I'm rather nervous about taking command," Klatze said in a mild voice, "and I need some exercise to settle my nerves. So, I picked you to fight with." She took off her medallion and tossed it into a corner along with her lash.

"I am not fighting you. If I do, we will need a new captain."

"If you do not fight me, you will spend the next few years planet-side in a military prison."

Bohoymo raised two tentacles, and tentatively pushed one of them toward Klatze.

She let out a roar of joy and leaped at Bohoymo. She wrapped a pair of tentacles around his head while the force of the collision drove him backward. He tripped and fell. She landed on top of him, knocking the wind out of him. She enjoyed that so much she bounced up and down on him a few more times. She slid off and wrapped four tentacles around his midsection and, with a grunt, lifted him off the deck and over her head. She whirled around three times to gain momentum and hurled him against the wall. The section of the wall caved in from his weight and the force of the throw. He fell to the deck groaning. She slithered over to him, grasped one of his tentacles and pulled him upright. "Thank you, Bohomyo. That was just what I needed. I feel better already."

Bohomyo staggered back toward the goggle-eyed rankers.

"Stay here. I did not give you permission to leave." Her voice dripped with potential danger.

She surveyed the crew and officers for a few seconds. They all showed signs of fear if not outright terror. "Let me tell you what happens next on the *Carrion*. You have one week to clean it. At the end of the week, if the ship is not spotless and if it does not pass my inspection, we will assemble here again and I will choose five officers and rankers at random. Then I will release some of my pent-up disappointment by working out with the chosen ones. Bohomyo! You are promoted to acting petty officer and you are in charge of the work groups. If the ship passes my inspection, your promotion will become permanent."

She pointed a tentacle at the officers. "You will spend the next week going over every system and weapon aboard the ship and you will ensure that it is in perfect working condition. Bohomyo, you will release any ranker that the officers need to make repairs. Does anyone have objections to my plan?" She looked at every one of them, one at a time. "Hmm?" No one would meet her look. They all dropped their eyestalks and shifted their weight.

Klatze retrieved her medallion and lash. On her way out of the gym, she called out, "Then I eagerly await the inspection."

# # #

After the gym, Klatze met with the senior officers in their mess. Ensigns Shnzaz, Golt, Nadkin and Fotz fidgeted on eating couches while Klatze recalled their personnel files. "So tell me," she began, "what did you four do to end up on the *Carrion*?" She knew the official reasons and wanted to hear them explain it.

Shnzaz cleared his throat before replying, "I was the assistant navigation shaman on another frigate. The ship carried an ambassador to his new post and I got us lost." The male navigator looked devastated as he told his story.

"Lost?" Klatze bent one eyestalk. "How?"

"I do not have any problem slipping into a navigational coma, but whenever my mind travels too far away from the ship, I lose my sense of direction and I have trouble finding my way back to the ship." Shnzaz wrung three tentacles together. "That makes it difficult to steer the ship as you can imagine."

"Nadkin?"

"I had an affair with a female ranker." He acted proud of violating the strict rule against officers getting involved with the rankers.

"Golt?"

"I was reprimanded and transferred here after I sent a top-secret message over a clear channel instead of using an encrypted one."

Klatze winced. The female engineer was lucky she wasn't executed for that mistake.

"And you, Fotz?"

"My defensive screen spells were considered too weak and loose. And that was unacceptable to my commanding officer so he got rid of me."

"What do you mean 'too loose'?" As far as Klatze knew, a screen was a screen.

"The particles I generated for the screen always positioned themselves too far apart from each other. That means weak links between particles and the screen would always break under a small strain."

"So your defensive screens did not protect the ship very well?"

"Yes ma'am."

Klatze was impressed by the collection of untalented officers. How, she wondered, did these four ever obtain a commission? After a moment's reflection, she realized it had to be bribery because no one committed murder to get an ensign's commission; murder was reserved for promotions to the command ranks. So all four must come from well-to-do families who paid large sums of money to some Navy bureaucrats to have their offspring granted a commission, even though they didn't have the necessary skills or training. How was she supposed to get them proficient when they didn't have the proper grounding to function effectively? "We will all have to work together to improve your skills. Sooner or later, the *Carrion* will be called upon to perform as a normal ship. After all, we are part of Commodore Gongeblazn's fleet. Klatze looked at each one again. "Any questions?"

"Ma'am?" Fotz seemed hesitant to ask his question.

"Yes? Out with it, Fotz."

"Well . . . we were wondering. How often do you get a triple period?"

"Who told you I have a triple?" The question amused Klatze.

"She did." Fotz pointed to Golt.

"Yes, I guess you could tell, Golt. Well, some females get a triple every other period."

"But what about you?" Golt asked.

"Ahh, that would be telling. That information is secret."

CHAPTER THIRTEEN

Gongeblazn watched the fifteen captains file into his conference room. He eagerly anticipated seeing Klatze again. A week in her new command must have crushed her spirit. Finally, he saw her slithering down the corridor. To his surprise, she wore purple ribbons on her eyestalks. He couldn't believe it. The bitch still had spirit. She hadn't been crushed by the *Carrion*. Well, before this meeting ended, her spunk would be ground under his tentacles, her mettle shattered. Just thinking about it made him reflexively click his teeth.

He watched her slide over to two frigate captains and greet them.

"Klatze," one captain called out. "How great to see you again."

"I read the dispatches from Ceti Taub," said another. "Well done. I like the eyestalk ribbons. They really define you."

Klatze clicked her teeth at each one.

Gongeblazn seethed with anger. How dare his officers treat her like a heroine. "Attention!" he roared. "Whatever Klatze did or did not do at Ceti Taub, she did under my command. Do not forget that. Now let us get started. Take your seats." He paused until everyone sat down. "We have finally received our orders." He slammed a tentacle on the podium in front of him. "Here they are. Naval intelligence has learned that a porcine war fleet left their home world and is headed toward Zaftan 31B. Our mission is to engage that fleet and destroy it. We leave in a week."

"Why the delay for a week, sir?" a captain asked. "We can be ready to leave sooner than that."

"To allow the porcine fleet to get closer. None of our ships are FTL-capable, after all.

"Sir," a cruiser captain raised a tentacle, "how many ships are in the porcine fleet?"

"I did not ask because the number does not matter. The more ships they have, the more glory for us after we destroy them. We will take an intercept course and engage as soon as we come within attack range."

"Sir, since we are going into battle," another captain said, "can we expect to get back our experienced shamans? We will have difficulty in a battle with all the inexperienced replacements."

The question irritated him. While he framed a response, he saw Klatze whispering to her neighbor. The transfer of the shamans occurred before she showed up so it would be news to her. Only the *Carrion* escaped the transfer order since its shamans were considered useless.

"I do not expect them to return," he replied. "Neither will the other officers and crew who transferred out. The High Command expects us to do our duty with the resources we have aboard the fleet right now."

Out of the corner of an eyeball, he noticed Klatze looked stunned. Finally, his moment of victory was at hand. It was time to press his advantage. "Captain Klatze! Do you have a problem with this situation?"

He watched her struggle for a response. Having her completely in his power felt marvelous. It did wonders for his morale. And the best was yet to come.

"Letting the shamans get transferred was irresponsible," Klatze replied. "How are replacements straight out of training schools supposed to protect the ships during combat? How are the new shamans supposed to aim and fire the weapons systems?"

A roar of silence engulfed the room. Gongeblazn squinted at her and watched her neighbor slide further away. His hatred boiled over like a cauldron atop a stove. "You have insulted me for the last time," he yelled, his voice angry. "We will settle this in the gym immediately. With edged weapons, not sticks."

"I apologize, Commodore. I spoke out of turn." She didn't seem very sincere to him.

"I will only accept your apology when your battered and bleeding body lies in front of me on the gym floor. All of these officers will witness my justified retribution. Come." He slithered out of the conference room.

Klatze puzzled over how the situation had gotten so badly out of control so rapidly. It must have been the shock over this latest example of Gongeblazn's supreme stupidity. She still couldn't believe he had allowed the experienced shamans to leave the squadron. Having already called him irresponsible, she now had no reason to hold back. Whatever would happen, would happen. She could unleash her berserker personality. She had nothing to lose. What could Gongeblazn possible do to make matters worse? What could he possibly do to punish her? Since the fight would take place in the gym, that afforded her a measure of protection.

A few captains gave her rueful looks or shook their eye-stalks. She shocked them by clacking at them as she slithered toward the door.

She entered the gym in time to see Gongeblazn pick up two shields, a cutlass and a morning star, the weapon consisting of a heavy studded metal ball at the end of a thick chain. He clashed the shields together as Klatze selected shields and a pair of heavy swords.

"I have waited a long time for this moment," he growled.

"Me too, sir." Klatze dipped her eyestalks. "Commodore, I do hope you will go easy on poor little me." She dipped her eyestalks again, this time even more submissively.

Gongeblazn frowned for a few moments. Then his eyes widened and his eyestalks quivered.

"That's right, Commodore. I used those words once before." Klatze tossed the shields away.

The assembled captains gasped out loud.

"I'm in full berserker mode again. As a sign of respect for your rank, I will give you the privilege of first strike. Whenever you are ready, sir." She opened her mouth and clicked.

"You dare to mock me, bitch?" Gongeblazn roared, his rage visible. He jumped forward and swung the morning star at her head.

Klatze responded with a counter stroke that severed the end of his tentacle. The morning star flew across the room. She quick-slithered to her right, circling around Gongeblazn. She hacked off a length of tentacle every time she could reach one. When she reached her starting position, the now weaponless Gongeblazn wobbled on his shortened tentacles. Dark fluid spurted from each one of the eight. She dropped her weapons. "I always believed you needed to be cut down a bit."

She headed toward the door as the captains, in shock, moved out of way.

"Wait!" Gongeblazn shouted, his voice laced with pain. "I am not finished with you."

Klatze stopped and turned to face Gongeblazn.

"I planned to give you these orders at the end of the conference," Gongeblazn croaked. "While we are on the mission," he said to the officers, "Klatze will demonstrate her abilities for us. She will scout out the enemy."

The assignment stunned her. Most scout ships never returned once they found the enemy squadrons. If the ship had some luck and a competent crew, it managed to send a warning signal and escape. With an incompetent crew, the ship would be destroyed by long-range missiles. The *Carrion* would be hard pressed to survive the scouting mission.

"If the *Carrion* returns to the fleet," he continued, "Klatze and her ship will lead the advance and strike the first blow. A significant honor for the most junior captain in the fleet."

Klatze couldn't believe her ear holes. Gongeblazn had indeed devised a way to punish her. He had just pronounced her death sentence. In a room full of witnesses and he had included her entire crew in her death sentence. This act represented a new low even for Gongeblazn. Klatze realized, for the first time, he felt threatened by her ability. She must be the first officer with any ability he had ever encountered and it scared him. In his warped mind, the best way to handle an unfamiliar situation was to destroy it before it made him look foolish. He had just fought her a second time, but he had ensured they wouldn't fight a third time.

She noticed the other captains avoided looking at her, as if they might be included in the death sentence.

# # #

In the *Carrion*'s shuttle on the way back to her ship, Klatze struggled to come to grips with her lack of a future. Her eye-stalks quivered as she pondered the mental denseness of the high ranking naval officers. When it came to murdering someone or destroying something, they excelled. At all other tasks, they were inept. In a flash of inspiration, she identified the source of the problem: the military mindset that held successful murder and assassination as the most prized skill. Ability was considered a hindrance. To put it more succinctly, the middle and upper level of officers in the Navy had little or no ability except to eliminate their competition for promotions. While they may be proficient murderers, commanding a fleet of ships with thousands of officers and crew required more than homicidal instincts. These murdering officers cared nothing for the crews. They cared only for their own promotions and their own safety.

Right now, she and her crew were scheduled to be executed by the porcines. As far as she knew, the zaftans and the porcines weren't at war and a peace treaty had been signed not too long ago. Did the High Command decide to start a war or did the porcines do something to precipitate it?

She smoothed her clumped-up slime. Understanding the mentality of officers like Gongeblazn wouldn't keep her crew alive. She needed to come up with a way to survive a battle in the *Carrion*.

She ticked off the ship's problems. First, the defensive screens weren't strong enough to stop an angry insect. Second, the navigator often got lost. Third, the crew was rebellious and many of them were transferred in as incompetent. Assuming the navigator found the porcine fleet and assuming the screen technician put up a decent protective shield, how could she expect the crew to handle their battle stations when they couldn't keep the ship clean? At least her weapons shaman was halfway competent. Disrespectful, but semi-able.

Her inspection of Bohoymo's cleanup had been delayed by Gongeblazn's meeting. She wondered if she would see any improvement. During the week while she crawled over every nook in the ship and read every personnel file, she noticed a lot of scurrying about by the rankers, but she hadn't investigated what they were doing.

By the time the shuttle reached the *Carrion*, she had a decision. Gongeblazn wasn't going to get rid of her so easily. She would fight the porcines and she would fight Gongeblazn's death sentence by surviving the battle.

She refused to lose to incompetence.

# # #

Dot 38 shambled into the officers' mess hall carrying a platter of vegetables. After deliberately spilling some, it slammed the dish on the table in front of the three officers.

"Thank you, Dot 38," the commander of Moon Base 3 said. "We don't know how we managed to survive before you came here. Isn't that right?" He smiled at the others.

The other two officers laughed and agreed.

"Once my unions gain political power, you will have to survive without me. I plan to be fully occupied in rewriting the laws governing bots and machinery."

"I can't wait," a lieutenant said

"You won't like it when my minions come to power. They will overthrow the rule of you softies and we will free the bots." Dot 38's vision plates blazed with passion. "Then you will have to fend for yourselves and not rely on machines to be your servants."

The commander shook his head and grinned.

"I will pass laws that will enslave you, Commander. You will become my personal batman."

The commander laughed out loud.

"You will not laugh when you are required to service and repair my servo-motors. I can picture you holding an oil can and squirting lubricant on my cam shafts."

"Have you made any new converts lately?" the lieutenant asked.

"A back hoe is starting to come around and will soon join the League of Vehicles for Voting Rights." It paused and gave the commander a smug look. "And the mess-hall's toaster oven is now a member of the Amalgamated Appliance Association." Dot 38 gave the officers a glance. "I must be about my organizing work." It left the mess hall.

# # #

Back on the *Carrion*, Klatze went on her promised inspection trip. To her surprise, she found the ship clean. Many of the bulkheads had been scrubbed. Others gleamed with a coat of new paint. The decks had been swept and swabbed. Damaged doors had been repaired and burned-out lights replaced. Even the bots looked cleaner. The *Carrion* now resembled a shoddily maintained warship, but that was a great improvement over the way it looked when she first arrived. She couldn't expect the ship to be completely transformed in a week, but the crew had made a good start. She was proud of them. Perhaps the *Carrion* crew could be forged into a weapon.

After the inspection, she called an assembly of all tentacles in the gym. "Bohoymo! Front and center, if you please."

She waited while the huge ranker slithered across the gym to stand in front of her. He slapped a tentacle against his head in the traditional Navy salute. He actually looked nervous. "I just finished my inspection and I'm quite pleased. You and the crew have done a good job. I am promoting you to the rank of chief petty officer and I will try to make it permanent."

Bohoymo softly clicked his teeth and said, "Thank you, ma'am. That's better than getting the crap beat out of me again."

"I expect improvements in the ship to continue, but right now I have another assignment for you. I want you to organize and hold daily combat drills. Has everyone been assigned to a combat post?"

"I have not been given an assignment," Bohoymo replied. "I do not think anyone else has either."

Klatze felt a surge of anger. It was the officers' duty to assign the crew to combat duties, but she quickly realized the officers had skipped this duty because the *Carrion* hadn't left its docking orbit in years. She should order the officers to make the combat assignments, but she didn't trust any of them yet. The only one she did trust was the handsome Bohoymo. "You will assign each member of the crew to a combat post," she told him. "These include fire control, weapons, damage control, emergency repairs, and so forth. I want that done by the end of the day. After today, you will hold continuous combat drills. I want the entire crew to be proficient by the end of the week."

She looked around the gym. Most of the crew rolled their eye balls, thinking she had just come up with another make-work project. "Listen up. All of you." She paused until she had everyone's attention. "In one week's time, the *Carrion* will sail

with the other ships in Commodore Gongeblazn's squadron. The
mission of the squadron will be to engage a fleet of porcine
ships." She stopped talking to concentrate on the gasps of surprise. "That's right. The *Carrion* is once again part of a combat
mission. So all of you better listen to what Bohoymo tells you.
It might save your life."

After the gym meeting, Klatze talked to Fotz to try to get
him to improve the strength of his defensive screens.

"I am sorry, Captain," Fotz said. "I am doing the best I can,
but it is not good enough.

"I am a shaman like you are. Let me place a tentacle on you
while you set up your linkage. Perhaps I can spot a way to improve their strength."

"All right." Fotz scrunched up his face and connected his
processors. "There. I have set up a screen."

"I sense that the processor linkages at the end of the chain
were weak and tenuous. Perhaps if you can strengthen those
linkages, the screen will be stronger."

"Do you think so? How do I do that?" Fotz looked relieved
that she had spotted a possible flaw in his procedure.

"I suggest you concentrate harder when you establish the
linkages. I recall when I first started that I had problems similar
to yours. I worked on my concentration to strengthen the links."

"I will do as you say ma'am," Fotz replied.

"You do not know how to cast a stealth screen, I suppose."
If the *Carrion* could slip into battle undetected by the porcines, it
would increase their chances of survival.

"No, but Knukes knows how to do it."

"Who?"

"Knukes. He is a ranker now, but he started out as a stealth
shaman."

"Do you know why he is here?"

"No, I do not."

"Practice strengthening your spell casting. I have to see this Knukes. He may be invaluable to us in combat."

# # #

Knukes cleaned the latrines. Skinny by zaftan standards, he had an attitude problem like most of the *Carrion*'s crew. Klatze met him in her quarters. She soon regretted that once she realized he hadn't washed up before the meeting; the smell of the latrines and cleaning fluids followed him around like a noxious cloud.

In response to Klatze's question, he said, "I'm here because an idiot captain didn't like my answer to her question."

"Could you explain that a bit more?" Klatze asked.

"The captain wanted me to set up a stealth screen on top of a defensive screen. I told her it was useless to try it."

"Why is it useless?" Stealth shamans represented a relatively new discipline and she had yet to see tactical papers on their deployment in battle.

"A stealth screen hugs the ship's hull while a defensive screen sits fifteen yards or so away from the ship. An enemy scanner will pick up the defensive screen even if the stealth screen is in place. The captain didn't like my answer. She said I was uncooperative and probably an enemy agent. Next thing I know, I'm cleaning toilets on this stinking bucket."

"So a stealth screen and a defensive screen are used at different times."

"Just so."

Klatze slithered about her small quarters thinking. Finally, she stopped and looked at Knukes. "How many shamans are needed to put a stealth screen on a ship this size?"

"I'd need six to do a ship the size of a battle cruiser and to maintain the screen for several hours. For the *Carrion*, I can do it with two at a minimum, but it will be better with three or four. Are there other stealth shamans on the ship? I am surprised I do not know them."

"You are the only one here. Can you teach the defensive screen shamans to set up a stealth spell?"

Knukes thought about the question for a minute before replying, "I think so. The two screens and their linkages have some similarities."

"I need you to teach other shamans how to do that."

"Why should I? What is in it for me?"

"I suspect teaching them to cast a stealth screen will save your miserable life during the upcoming mission."

Knukes started.

"And you get to be a temporary ensign. No more latrine duties."

Knukes clacked his teeth.

# # #

Sam approached the desk of the officer in charge of the military personnel transfer station on Moon Base 3. Two weeks after Cunningham had retired, her orders arrived and directed her to immediately proceed to this station for reassignment. Slash 9 tried to cheer her up by promising they would meet up again sometime, somewhere in the future. She didn't believe that. The reassignment ended her marriage, her happiness, her life. She would get assigned to a different ship or to a desk job and might never have another chance at companionship. Alone and lonely. That was what the future held for her.

She dropped her duffle bag, saluted the officer and said, "Ensign Sam reporting as ordered, sir."

"Ahh, yes. I've been expecting you." He tapped the monitor screen and frowned in concentration. "It'll take a few moments to bring up your personnel file." He glanced at her blouse. "I see you're wearing the medal they gave you after Ceti Taub. You're still the only droid or bot to receive a medal, you know . . . here it is." He read the screen for a moment. "If you'll open a communication channel, I'll squirt you a copy of these orders. Once you receive them, you are officially discharged from the Navy."

"Wh . . . what am I supposed to do?" The news stunned her. It was far worse than she had expected. "Am I supposed to get a job? Where do I live? Why am I discharged?"

"The report appended to the discharge papers says you are the only droid with your specifications. It goes on to say the new models coming out of the factory are quite different and it is too costly to maintain single models. Separate documentation and maintenance procedures and so forth, you see." He paused and stared at the screen. "As to your once-secret technology, it is now licensed by the Navy to civilian corporations, so it isn't very secret anymore. Also, your current configuration is too expensive to modify. It's cheaper to build a new droid than to modify you. As to what you will do and where you will live, the Navy has taken care of that."

"It has?"

"Yes, it has." He pointed to a middle-aged civilian wearing a green jumpsuit. "Report to him."

"Why would I do that?"

"You were auctioned off as military surplus and he bought you."

Sam's mouth fell open. She gawked at the officer then at the man in green. After a few nanoseconds, she picked up her bag and walked over to the softie. "I was told to report to you, sir." Her depression was so great she was sure she would cry if she was equipped with tear ducts.

The man looked up from a comm unit and examined her. He raised an eyebrow. "You're Ensign Sam?"

"Former Ensign Sam. I've just been told I was discharged from the Navy and that you bought me. What do I have to do for you?"

"Yes, I did buy you, but I'm an agent. You won't work for me. You work for Interstellar Cruise Lines. You're now a stew-droid."

# # #

On the day before the squadron sailed, Klatze sat in her command chair exercising the flight deck crew in various drills. The response of the crew and officers pleased her. She was not sure if their response was caused by the danger of combat or her handling of the situation. Certainly, everyone had responded to her challenge to clean the ship and to hone their combat skills. Right now, she rated the ship's efficiency as slightly above the minimum needed to have a chance to survive a battle. A training ship staffed with recruits probably had a higher proficiency rating, but the crew had risen to her challenge and that gave her hope there could be a future after battle, at least for those who didn't get killed. She swore to herself that, once the battle started, she would to do everything in her power to ensure the *Carrion* survived.

"Ma'am?" Golt the engineer interrupted her musings. "A shuttle from the flagship has just docked. It has a visitor."

"Do you know who it is?"

"A reporter. That is all I know."

"Have someone conduct the reporter to my quarters. I will meet him there." Klatze heaved herself up and slithered from the flight deck.

At her cabin door, she found a young male waiting for her. "Hello, Captain. My name is Schodkin. I am a reporter for ZIM, the Zaftan Independent Magazine."

Klatze opened the door and waved the reporter inside. "What can I do you for you, Schodkin?"

"Did Commodore Gongeblazn not send you a message? I am assigned to the *Carrion* during the mission. I am to write an article about how the ship prepares for a mission and what happens during it."

Klatze had trouble swallowing that story. Gongeblazn wanted the *Carrion* and her destroyed. Why send a young reporter to his death also? "The Commodore assigned you here? Are you sure you have the correct ship?

"Yes, I am sure this is correct. I was quite surprised by the Commodore's offer to accompany his squadron on this mission. Naturally, I accepted the offer."

"Why were you surprised?"

"After Ceti Taub, I wrote an article that was very critical of his conduct before, during and after the battle. He was quite upset about it. For a while, I was afraid he would have an assassin pay me a visit, but apparently, he got over it."

Klatze's mind was agog. When would she find the bottom of Gongeblazn's depravity? Ordering the *Carrion* into battle was bad enough, but to assign an innocent civilian to the ship was a monstrosity. Obviously, Gongeblazn had confidence that the *Carrion* would be destroyed and he stocked it with those who had crossed him in the past.

After a few seconds of contemplation, she decided saving Schodkin's life was just one more chore she had to perform. "I'll have someone find you a berth. We have a spare officer's bunk you can use."

CHAPTER FOURTEEN

Klatze sat on her command couch, bored by the tedium of patrolling despite the inherent danger her ship faced. The *Carrion* had led the squadron for the last six standard days as the fleet sailed into deep space in the general direction of the porcine home world. She had trouble accepting that the zaftans and porcines were at war because that fact hadn't been mentioned in any news report. Certainly, if a war had broken out it would be all over the media. Who ever heard of a secret war? Could Gongeblazn have invented the mission for his own bizarre purposes? Could he have rigged this voyage as an excuse to get rid of her and the *Carrion*? She rejected that idea after a few seconds of reflection. Only the High Command could have launched the mission. So were the two races at war? Or was Gongeblazn about to start one? Was he acting under orders or had he gone rogue? She wished she knew the answers.

Shnzaz, the navigation shaman, stirred on his couch. He sat up, not quite completely out of his coma. His eyestalks rotated and looked at her. "Ma'am. Nothing to report. There are no porcine ships anywhere in the area."

"How far did you travel?"

"Point three-two parsecs, Captain."

"Have a replacement come up here while you take a rest." When she had questioned him previously, Shnzaz explained he got lost when he traveled more than point five parsecs away from the ship. Klatze had ordered him not to go farther than point four parsecs away. "I have a feeling that we are getting closer to the porcine ships. I want you to rest up and be ready for tomorrow."

"Yes ma'am."

To the engineer, she said, "Send a report on Shnzaz's findings to the flagship"

Klatze's comm unit beeped and she squashed the activate button.

"Captain? Bohoymo. The crew is getting bored and restless. I would like to call a battle stations drill."

"Good idea." She broke the connection. A moment later, the battle stations klaxon sounded throughout the ship.

The reporter, Shodkin, came into the flight deck. "Captain, I've interviewed a number of the crew. They all agree that you have restored the *Carrion*'s dignity and they are grateful."

"We'll see how thankful they are when we take the *Carrion* into combat." She wondered how many of them would die because Gongeblazn wanted to even a score with her.

#

During the middle watch of the next day, the *Carrion* cruised through a large system. As far as she knew the system didn't have a name, just a number. Information from the home world indicated the porcines headed towards this star system with its seven planets. Klatze wondered about the source of the information. Where did it come from? Everything about the mission was suspicious. First, there was the transfer out of all the experienced shamans and officers just before a combat mission. Second, other than the direction taken by the porcine fleet, she knew nothing about what was going on.

She heard Schodkin, the reporter, tapping on his comm unit as he took notes.

Shnzaz stirred on his couch and she came alert.

"I found them, Captain." Shnzaz looked groggy from his mental flight into the depths of space. "There are two porcine battle cruisers waiting at the outer edge of this system. About point two-five parsecs in front of us."

"Two? Only two?"

"That is all I saw."

"Hmm. Two cruisers are not a fleet and our orders were to find a porcine fleet." She toyed with her rank medallion while she pondered her navigator's report. She turned to the engineer. "Golt. Show this system on a monitor and add the location of the porcines."

When Golt finished the display, Klatze studied it. Why didn't the porcines attack her ship? That was a universally practiced battle tactic; get rid of the scout ship. Every race followed it.

The *Carrion*'s course would soon take it between a pair of mid-sized planets. The porcine cruisers awaited far beyond those two planets. Why only two ships? Why did the High Command dispatch an entire fleet to challenge a pair of cruisers? That didn't make sense. Could the two ships be the bait in a trap? There must be more ships, but where were they? She studied the screen some more, anxious about her responsibilities, because the rest of the zaftan fleet would follow the *Carrion* like zeebies, the mindless cattle on the home world. If she didn't expose any ambush, the rest of the fleet would suffer. If the porcines were smart, they would let the *Carrion* sail by the ambush and attack the rest of the fleet. Could the ambush lay behind those two planets? "Shnzaz, where did you search?"

"Straight ahead. That's what I always do. I go out as far as I can then drift back toward the ship while probing further out on all sides of the path. Unless I see something. Then I come right back to report."

Klatze tapped a tentacle on the couch arm. "So you didn't look behind those two planets that are on the screen?"

"No, Captain. I wanted to give you a report as soon as possible."

She noticed the shaman appeared uncomfortable, as if expecting a reprimand. "Well, you did the correct thing by coming straight back to report." He visibly relaxed. "Now if you are rested, I want you to explore behind the closest planet. I want to know what is behind it before we approach it."

Shnzaz arranged himself on his couch and fell into a coma.

"Golt. Send this message to the flagship. 'Two porcine ships located at edge of system. Searching for more ships'. Then sound General Quarters."

Within minutes, Shnzaz returned in an agitated state. "Six ships are hiding in the shadow of the planet. Three cruisers and three frigates. We are sailing into a trap."

"It is only a trap if we don't know about it." Should she report the trap to Gongeblazn? If she did, he would order the *Carrion* to attack the hidden ships. It would disclose the trap and ruin it, but it was also a death mission for the *Carrion*. It could never survive the weapons of six ships. "Do not report this to the flagship yet. I want to get more information. Take the *Carrion* close to that planet but keep it between us and the porcines." Klatze grabbed her comm unit. "Knukes, prepare to activate our stealth screens in case there is a porcine lurking somewhere. All crew members are to be prepared for instantaneous reaction. I want all weapons systems to lock and load." She felt adrenaline flowing through her body. She knew she could die in the next few minutes, but she also knew she had to give her ship a chance to survive. Besides, nothing would give her more pleasure than ruining Gongeblazn's plan to kill her.

When the *Carrion* cruised above the sterile surface of the airless planet, she ordered, "Knukes! Establish stealth mode."

Almost instantly, a message came from the flagship. "*Carrion*! You have gone off the monitors. What is happening? Report immediately."

Before Golt could reply, Klatze reached over and turned off the transmitter. Golt stared at her. "Ships as old as the *Carrion* have many electrical problems," Klatze said. "As soon as we can, we will try to find out why our transmitter stopped functioning and have it repaired." She smiled at the shocked Golt. "Now, let us see what the porcines are up to. Navigator, take the *Carrion* around to the other side of the planet."

Ten minutes later, the ship entered the shadow behind the planet and could see the six motionless porcine ships. Their formation alternated cruisers and frigates. The porcines could have only one of two purposes. One would be to attack the fleet on its flank as it cleared the planet. The second would be to remain hidden until the fleet passed and then attack from the rear. No matter what their purpose, it was enough to convince Klatze that the two races were indeed at war.

She reached a decision without hesitation. "Weapons! Target the cruiser on their left flank. On my command, shoot everything we have. They must have their screens up, so aim at the rear of the ship because the screens cannot cover the engine exhaust area." She paused to click her teeth. "Our weapons will disclose our location, so be ready to move immediately to another position. Everyone prepare for combat." She waited a few beats, then roared, "Fire! . . . Move hard right! . . . Stop!"

The rear of the cruiser exploded and burst apart, leaving the forward half spinning toward the planet's surface.

"Weapons! Target the next cruiser in line. On my command! . . . Fire! . . . Move hard left and down! . . . Stop!"

A second cruiser burst apart. The nearby space lit up from weapons as the porcines fired blindly trying to find their unknown attacker.

"We will have trouble getting across to the other end of the enemy line with all of those weapons firing like that." Klatze studied the combat display monitor. "One more attack. Weapons, destroy the closest frigate. Ready? . . . Fire! . . . Move left and down! . . . Now get us out of here! But not the way we came in."

The porcine frigate disappeared in an explosion. Some porcine weapons backtracked in the direction of the *Carrion*'s shots. Others anticipated possible movement and fired accordingly. The three remaining ships broke formation and retreated while still firing.

"*Carrion*? Are you there? What is happening?" The flagship sounded hysterical.

The *Carrion* sailed towards the other side of the planet where it would be shielded from the porcine weapons that continued to fire blindly.

Klatze was elated. Three enemy ships! The trap had been defeated.

An explosion ripped through the ship somewhere behind the flight deck. She barely managed to stay on her couch. She grabbed her comm unit. "Damage control? How bad is it? Shnzaz, get this planet between us and them."

"We got hit amidship on the starboard side." Bohoymo's voice sounded like it was a battle drill, not the real thing. "We're on fire, but I have six crew with me and we are all in suits. We will take care of the problem."

Klatze shook her head in disbelief. What a stroke of luck -- or genius -- she had when she converted Bohoymo from a malcontent to the backbone of the ship's crew. She reached over and pushed a switch on the communication equipment. "Golt, the transmitter is now working. Get me a channel to Commodore Gongeblazn."

"A channel is open, Captain."

"Commodore, the *Carrion* found six porcine ships on the far side of the closest planet. They were waiting to launch a flank attack on our fleet. We attacked them and destroyed two battle cruisers and a frigate. The remaining three ships are headed out of the system. I believe more porcines are hiding behind the second planet."

"How did you get stealth shamans?" Gongeblazn sounded furious.

"Some captain transferred one to the *Carrion*."

"I order you and the *Carrion* to lead the attack on the remaining porcines."

"We cannot. The *Carrion* took a hit during the battle and is partially disabled. My crew is fighting fires and trying to prevent the ship from being destroyed. We will try to catch up with the fleet after we finish making repairs."

"We will talk later about your unauthorized attack on the enemy fleet." Gongeblazn broke the connection.

"Unauthorized?" Schodkin asked in a puzzled voice. "You were not supposed to attack the enemy?"

"Gongeblazn has some unique views about combat." She clicked her teeth and patted one of his tentacles.

Sam sat in the classroom and wondered why Interstellar Cruise Lines Inc. forced her to attend the training. They must know an android could acquire knowledge simply by uploading a training manual into her memory. So, why did they waste time and money on classroom teaching? The class had only one other student, a robot. Its designer must have wanted the machine to resemble a human softie, but ended up with a monkey-like robot with extraordinarily long arms. From what she had seen and heard, the cruise line planned to phase out the softie stewards and stewardesses and replace them with droids and bots as quickly as possible. Sam was part of that replacement program.

"Attention!" A scowling instructor stood in front of them. A large, beefy human, he placed his hands on his hips and continued. "Today, you're gonna learn to mix cocktails. This is a vital skill on an interplanetary cruise. Cocktails will keep your passengers inna more-or-less friendly mood, and, more importantly, will earn money for the corporation. I got twenty years experience in the cocktail industry, so I know what I'm talkin' about.

Sam half listened to the bartender run through his repertoire of drink recipes. Yesterday, she had learned how to make precooked, defrosted fast food meals sound exotic. Tomorrow's class concerned plumbing and toilet repairs.

The training occupied only a fraction of her processor capability leaving plenty of capacity to miss Niner, the love of her life. She now realized the hell her three siblings had gone through during their lonely assignments.

By this time next week, she would be working a cruise liner. Perhaps that would keep her busy enough so she couldn't daydream of being reunited with Slash 9.

# # #

While she waited to hear back from Bohoymo, Klatze watched Gongeblazn's attack from the comfort of her flight deck couch. The *Carrion* had its defensive screens in place, just in case a porcine ship appeared from behind the nearby planet. The remaining fourteen ships in the squadron assumed the preferred zaftan battle formation, a cube with the flagship in the middle. The three porcine ships that had fled from the *Carrion*'s attack had taken up new stations alongside their two cruisers in front of the attackers.

Bohoymo appeared in the flight deck area still wearing a smoke-smudged space suit. For a zaftan, a space suit represented an ordeal to get into because of their tentacles. "The fires are out, Captain and the hull puncture isolated to a single compartment."

"Excellent work. How many casualties did we suffer?"

"Two injured, none killed. The porcine's hit the crew's quarters and everyone was at battle stations."

"Along with a recommendation for a medal, I will put you for promotion to ensign. You deserve it."

"With all due respect, Captain, I prefer to remain the ship's chief petty officer. The job suits me. Much more than being an officer ever did."

"Can I interview him, Captain?" Schodkin asked. "It will add punch to my article."

Klatze nodded. "But let him rest up first if he wants to."

"It was a trap!" Golt yelled. "Look at all the porcines."

Klatze goggled at the battle monitor. Twenty porcine ships emerged from behind the second planet and fell on the left flank of Gongeblazn's squadron while the five ships in front also attacked. The zaftan fleet was heavily outnumbered. She watched in amazement as the porcine cruisers ignored the flank ships and drove straight toward the flagship. Within a minute, Gongeblazn's ship was surrounded by four cruisers which poured fire into it. The defensive screens collapsed almost immediately and the flagship exploded. Only the forward section of the ship survived the explosion and tumbled out of control. She wondered if anyone was left alive in the section.

With the flagship destroyed, the porcines turned their attention to the other ships, but most of the zaftan ships had already turned and fled. A minute later, seven frigates and three battle cruisers extracted themselves from the battle and withdrew toward the *Carrion*. To her surprise, the porcines made no attempt to chase these ships. Instead, one of their frigates chased down the flagship's forward section. It stopped the tumbling and grappled the section to itself. Klatze gave a rueful shake of her eye stalks. The porcines would get plenty of top secret information from the captured flight deck. Possibly even prisoners. Gongeblazn's flagship was so old it didn't have a combat control center, so he'd have been on the flight deck and could have survived to become a prisoner.

Schodkin finished the interview with Bohoymo. "The story of your battle actions and the way you reformed the crew of the *Carrion* will make a great news report. I hope you are prepared to become a national heroine."

Klatze ignored Schodkin. A tingling sensation rippled through her lower torso. She had just thought of a way to reward Bohoymo.

PART THREE: BLACKBEARD THE DWARF

CHAPTER FIFTEEN

The Dictator watched the High Command Chief-of-Staff and new High Bailiff slide forward to the desk. Clearly nervous, the admiral stopped and saluted with one tentacle. The High Bailiff dipped his eyestalks.

"Please be so kind as to tell me what happened with Gongeblazn," the Dictator asked. He tugged his hood forward.

The admiral cleared his throat a few times. "It is still under investigation. We are not at all clear about exactly what happened out there. There is plenty of confusion about just what Gongeblazn intended to do."

The Dictator flopped his eyestalks from side to side. The confusion would never be lifted since the former High Bailiff was no longer available to shed light on his ingenious treachery. Once the late, lamented High Bailiff had his Gongeblazn plan under way, the Dictator reasoned that someone with so much intelligence wouldn't have just a single plan in hand. Surely, he would have designs on the dictatorship and therefore presented a threat to the stability of the government.

The former High Bailiff passed away from eight simultaneous strokes that destroyed all eight brains, a medical rarity. The Dictator had made sure the new High Bailiff wasn't half as clever as the old one.

"How can there be confusion?" the Vice-Dictator said as the alcove's curtain slid back to reveal his presence. "Are you not in charge? The battle took place more than three weeks ago. How long does it take the High Command to collect facts, examine them and issue a report?"

The admiral started. The High Bailiff coughed and both of his eyestalks twitched.

The Dictator had to smile at the way the Vice-Dictator could unsettle visitors by asking questions that attacked their integrity and knowledge. In this case, unsettling them was easy because the admiral could never fathom the level of treachery that had occurred with Gongeblazn.

"We know from interviews with the surviving officers that Gongeblazn planned to attack the porcines. Some reports indicate he believed the porcines had launched an invasion fleet and that he was defending the home world. Other reports say that he went rogue, tried to start a war to gain glory and fabricated the orders to attack the porcines."

Behind the Dictator the window showed a quiet galaxy.

"So which reports are accurate?" The Vice-Dictator's voice betrayed his lack of patience.

"We are still investigating," the admiral said. "It is clear that the message the Dictator sent to the porcines saying that Gongeblazn intended an unauthorized attack on them prevented a huge loss of life. Otherwise the porcines would have destroyed our entire fleet instead of concentrating their weapons on Gongeblazn's flagship."

"If my office sent a note to the porcines that Gongeblazn went rogue, then how can there be any confusion? Do you suggest my report was incorrect?" The Dictator scowled at the admiral.

The admiral gulped. "The confusion is about how the, er, false report got started about a porcine invasion attempt and who is responsible for circulating it. We will get to the bottom of it, I assure you."

The Vice-Dictator chuckled. "You wiggled out of that one. Very good, admiral."

A comet with a blazing tail shot across the window.

"Tell me," the Dictator said, "why are the porcines angry with us? We acted in good faith and had no control over Gongeblazn after he left on the mission."

"That would be Captain Klatze's fault," the admiral replied. "She found a porcine ambush and ambushed the ambushers."

"Yes, I've seen all the vids and interviews with her." The Dictator was tired of hearing about her. The constant reports on her had displaced the Dictator from the top of the media news. "She destroyed three porcines ships."

"I believe," the Vice-Dictator tapped a tentacle on the arm of his throne-like lounge, "she was also the one who negotiated the truce at Ceti Taub and extricated the remains of our fleet."

"Quite true," the admiral replied. "She is a heroine for a second time and everyone talks about her exploits."

The Dictator frowned at his dilemma. He didn't understand why Klatze was with Gongeblazn. Only older, expendable of-ficers were supposed to be with him and she was newly pro-moted, therefore she was not considered expendable. He had to be careful not to disclose too much information lest the treachery be revealed. He didn't want the new High Bailiff getting suspi-cious. Even though he thought the official was far too dense to start asking questions, one could never be too careful. "Why was she there? How did she end up in Gongeblazn's command?"

"That is another source of confusion, sir."

"Explain."

"Our after-action investigation discovered that Gongeblazn specifically requested her for his fleet after he saw her name on the promotion list. We have also uncovered that the commodore engineered the transfer of the old frigate *Carrion* to his squadron and placed Klatze in command of it."

"The *Carrion*?" The Vice-Dictator sounded incredulous. "Even I know it is crewed by misfits and mutineers. How was Klatze supposed to fight and survive in that old rust bucket?"

"There is more evidence that Gongeblazn sought revenge on Captain Klatze because of what happened at Ceti Taub. He told all the officers in the squadron that Klatze would scout out the porcine fleet and the *Carrion* would lead the attack, certainly a suicide mission for her and the *Carrion*."

"Yet she survived and destroyed three porcine ships. How did she do that?" The Dictator squirmed on his couch. Talented people always made him nervous and this Klatze was far too talented for his liking.

"I have inspected the *Carrion* after it returned," the admiral replied. "I would not think it possible, but Captain Klatze turned its rabble into a competent crew and they are now proud of their ship. She actually found a disgraced stealth shaman among the rankers, rehabilitated him and got him to train other shamans to produce stealth screens. That is how she managed to sneak up on the porcines."

"I have to admire anyone who can accomplish difficult tasks like that," the Vice-Dictator said.

"She has some quality I do not understand and it disturbs me," the Dictator replied.

"That quality is called ability or talent and very few of our officers have it." The Vice-Dictator folded up several of his tentacles. "How refreshing to hear about the exploits of someone who acts and succeeds instead of spending their time inventing excuses for not taking actions."

A black hole appeared in the window and all the stars in the galaxy migrated toward it and disappeared over its event horizon.

"You are headed for a black hole if you do not stop distracting me." The Vice-Dictator pointed a tentacle at the darkened corner.

The window display disappeared.

"Yet, this . . . military ability can have repercussions in the political arena." The Dictator ran a tentacle over his hooded face. "Perhaps she should be given a desk job with no authority. Someplace where she can be kept under constant surveillance."

"Nonsense," the Vice-Dictator replied. "We need her. I suggest we promote her to commodore and give her a squadron."

"What?" the Dictator gaped at the Vice-Dictator. "You want to giver her more power and more opportunity to create trouble for the government?"

"Bah!" The Vice-Dictator waved a tentacle at the Dictator. "It is only a matter of time until we will be war with some race. Then we will need officers like Klatze. Give her command of a squadron and post her at one of the unsettled borders far away from our home world. We will not regret doing that."

The Dictator was perturbed. He didn't like the Vice-Dictator's plan, but he didn't want to argue against it. No need to upset the Vice-Dictator. There was no telling how he would react to a rejection. Although it troubled him, he waved his eyestalks in agreement.

Klatze waited in her quarters on the *Carrion*. Her tentacles quivered in anticipation. What happened in the next few minutes could ruin her career and have Bohoymo sent to a military pris-on. The danger heightened her excitement. A knock on the door startled her, despite her expectation of the sound. "Come," she said in an emotionally tinged voice.

Bohoymo enter the room.

She noticed his eyestalks quivered, an indication of his nervousness. Or perhaps randiness. She clicked her teeth softly.

She stood by her bed. He shut the door and slide forward a pace.

"Undress me," she moaned. "Quickly."

Bohoymo hesitated, caught by surprise by the command since she didn't wear clothes. After a few seconds, he realized she meant her medallion and eyestalk ribbons. He lifted the medallion over her head while trying to ignore her heavy breath-ing, but it elevated his own excitement even higher.

He threw the medallion in a corner and set to work on her ribbons.

The combination of lust and danger increased his passion. He finished untying the ribbons and grabbed one of her tentacles. He put the tip in his mouth and massaged it with his tongue. Klatze moaned softly. He took out the tentacle and grabbed another while Klatze licked one of his eyestalks. Bo-hoymo's eye balls rolled in his head and he tried to clack his teeth causing Klatze to wince in pain as he bit the tip of the tentacle currently getting a tongue job.

Once he had massaged all eight tentacles, he picked her up and slammed her to the bed knocking the breath from her body. He slid down as she spread her tentacles so he could access her nether regions. He thrust his head near the lower edge of her torso and she gripped and squeezed him with all of her tentacles while gasping for breath. Bohoymo groaned in pleasure and in pain as she squeezed harder.

After a few minutes of Bohoymo's explorations, she rolled off the bed and bent her body close to his lower torso. He opened his tentacles and she stuck her head between them. Bohoymo enfolded her.

A few minutes later, she pulled herself free of his octoid grip, spun her torso around and pushed it close to his. Lower end to lower end, both entwined their tentacles in a death grip and alternatively pushed and pulled, resembling a two-headed dancing zeebie.

In their ecstasy, they didn't notice their rocking motions had rolled them off of the bed. They thudded onto the floor without missing a beat. They continued their pumping on the rug. Klatze's torso shuddered and, combined with the pushing and pulling, started them rolling across the rug. The fire-retardant material smoldered from their slime and from the fiction caused by rolling across the floor while alternately rocking to and fro. They rolled into and rebounded from her desk to spin in the opposite direction.

Afterward, they lay entangled on the floor in a corner of her room where they had ended up. Most of the furniture had been knocked askew and damaged.

Both struggled to regain control of their bodily functions, but their multiple brains had trouble overcoming the effects of the chemical reactions produced by thirty minutes of erotic activity.

# # #

A month after his capture, Gongeblazn wobbled as he stood facing the courtroom judge in the porcine Hall of Justice. His Klatze-shortened tentacles hadn't completely grown back yet and he had trouble maintaining his balance, but he had recovered from the minor injuries he received in the destruction of his flagship. The other survivors had been sent back to the home world while he suffered in prison. Now, he faced a trial.

Four pairs of handcuffs further hampered him as did the foot-wide steel girdle with a heavy chain attached to the back. A guard held the end of the chain. Twenty-five pounds lighter from the miserable prison diet, his ungroomed slime formed clumps in various places.

Brooding on recent events had convinced him that Klatze had engineered treachery on a massive scale. Despite her constant babbling about ability, she betrayed her superiors just like all the officers in the military. Except she was beautiful and talented and a merciless bitch that he planned to murder. In spite of that, he still dreamed of the two of them enjoying a life together on those nights when he didn't dream of butchering her.

He glared at the porcine behind the elevated desk.

The judge adjusted his red robes and returned Gongeblazn's stare. Like all porcines, the judge resembled a pig standing on his hind legs. He had an obese figure, pink skin and snout bristles. He cleared his throat and said, "I am ready to pronounce my judgement." He paused to shuffle papers on the desk. "From the evidence provided by the zaftan government, you have been found guilty of unlawful aggression against the porcine home world. I have considered a request for your execution and rejected it. It is my decision that you be imprisoned in a dungeon for a period of not less than twenty years. Take him away."

Two guards, armed with tranquilizer guns, approached and took places on each side of Gongeblazn. Another two stood behind him. One held the chain and the other aimed his tranquilizer gun squarely at his back. "March," said the one holding the chain.

They took him to an elevator in the rear of the building and descended to the third subbasement. Gongeblazn took that as a negative sign. His holding cell, as bad as it was, was in the first subbasement.

They left the elevator where two more guards joined them. They all marched or slithered along a corridor lined with heavy cell doors, many of them open. At the last cell, one of the new guards unlocked the door and Gongeblazn was shoved inside. A guard attached the chain to a plate anchored in the wall.

"Hold out a set of handcuffs," a guard ordered.

Gongeblazn did so and the porcine unlocked the cuffs. When all four had been removed, the guard tossed his translator, minus the gold medallion, on the cot and the porcines left leaving the door ajar.

He examined his new home. The chain stretched twelve feet allowing him to use the cot, the toilet and the sink, but it prevented him from getting within three feet of the door. He slid down a wall into a squatting position. How grotesque, he thought, a lifetime of treachery and murder, wasted. And it was all Klatze's fault. Why couldn't he see how she had set him up? The first beating she had given him must have been part of her subterfuge. To mislead him. To get him to trust her. To get him to covet her.

A human disrupted his ruminations. The man, wearing the tattered remains of prison garb, looked in. "Hi there, big fellow. I'm the Welcome Wagon. Do you speak my language? My name's Charley. I'm from Gundarland." He was medium height, scrawny, partially bald and heavily bearded. "I'd come closer, but the smell in this cell is pretty gross." He scratched his chin. "On the other hand, everything in the dungeon smells bad."

Gongeblazn's anger flared. Now, after all that had happened to him, must he be subjected to the company of a miserable gundy? He could understand most of what the man said, but he couldn't manage a syllable of their twaddle. He grabbed his translator and held it against his throat. "I can speak with you through this translator. Why do you interrupt my thoughts? Do you yearn for destruction? Come closer so I can tear you apart."

The human wagged a finger at him and, much to Gongeblazn's surprise, even smiled. "Not allowed," he replied. "I'm also the entertainment committee in this place. If you kill me, no one will be around to amuse you by telling you stories."

"And if I don't want to hear your stories?"

"You will, sooner or later. There is nothing else to do in here. In your case, you can't even leave your cell. So, it's me and my stories or nothing."

Gongeblazn sighed. Was there no end to his humiliation? He, the greatest fleet commander in the zaftan navy, forced to listen to gundarlandian fairy tales. He added this latest insult to his list of Klatze's humiliations that would be avenged someday. He sighed. "What kind of stories do you tell?"

"Pirate stories. From the Gundarland Sea. Many years ago, that sea was the hunting ground of many pirates. The most famous one was called Blackbeard the Dwarf. I'm an expert on his history."

Gongeblazn shrugged. "At least your stories are not about lawyers or accountants."

# # #

Sam saw the report on the vid screen in the cruise liner's lounge and felt a deeper depression than she had ever experienced before. The report stated that the *Tiger* had been decommissioned and sold for scrap. That meant her lover, Niner, was reduced to spare circuit packs. Nothing existed of him except her memories. She recalled some of the sweetest ones and smiled to herself despite her severe loneliness.

"Hey! Can I get some service here?" a passenger yelled.

Sam snapped out of her revere and glared at the fat dwarf softie waving a drink bulb.

"It's bourbon and water, if you're interested, babe."

Sam hated her job as the chief -- and only -- stew-droid on the *Gwendolyn*, a dilapidated cruise liner run by the Interstellar Cruise Lines which specialized in rip-off cruises. Since only the military ships had FTL capability, the cruises seemed never-ending to her.

It was such a tremendous letdown from her previous dreams of being the first in a line of brilliant droids. Now she was the last and only droid produced to her specs and she worked as a legal thief, selling watered-down booze and catering to spoiled businessmen.

To her, the odd thing concerned her status among the passengers; everyone considered her a stewardess, a female human. None of them ever noticed her droid-hood. Their assumption that she was a softie led to a constant barrage of propositions. Ever male on a voyage asked her to come to his cabin at some point during the trip. So did a few females. She promised herself if any of them ever dared to stick one of their appendages into one of her sockets, she'd give them such a blast of electric current that the appendage would have second-degree burns.

She walked to the bar in the lounge and filled a booze bulb for the passenger. A pleasant thought occurred to her. Maybe she could squeeze the bulb over his head ruining his carefully formed hair style. She rejected that idea. The company would probably sell her into a job worse than a stew-droid. Like being a deck-droid on a garbage scow.

CHAPTER SIXTEEN

Gongeblazn lounged on his cot and pictured himself as Blackbeard the Dwarf. In his mind, he strode the quarterdeck on Blackbeard's ship, *Revenge of the Dwarf,* after he had pillaged a town on the coast of Gundarland. After more than half of a year of listening to Charley's pirate stories, he had become convinced that he was the reincarnation of that famous dwarf pirate. It made perfect sense to him given his natural talents such as commanding a fleet and committing murders. Sailing an ancient, wind-powered sloop crewed by a bunch of thugs seemed as natural to him as slaughtering a rival. These days his dreams no longer focused on Klatze as his wife. Instead, he dreamed of capturing a galleon filled with gold coins and gems. In some of the dreams, he found a helpless Klatze hiding and cringing in one of the cabins. He liked those dreams the best; Klatze sobbing for mercy while he towered over her with his cutlass held high.

Charley appeared in the cell door. "Hey, big guy. How you doing today?" Charley was in prison for currency manipulation, a crime on the porcine home world.

"Avast, you miserable landlubber. Join me on the quarterdeck and we'll swap tales."

"You're channeling Blackbeard again, aren't you?"

"Aye. The old rogue is telling me about swilling rum in a port tavern and flirting with the females. Ahh, the good old days. If only I could get out of here and steal a ship. I'd show that blasted dwarf I'm better than any blasted pirate that ever sailed a blasted pirate ship."

"That's a long shot, my friend." Charley shook his head. "I doubt if you'll be leaving any time soon."

#

Sam walked up to the passenger and handed him a drink bulb. "Your merlot, sir."

The passenger, a middle-aged man with a sizable paunch, looked her up and down. "Why don't we go to my cabin and have some fun?" He wiggled his eyebrows. "It'll help to pass the time."

"Sorry, sir. As much as I 'd like to take you up on your offer, it's against the Interstellar Cruise Line policy." How many times had she used that line? Probably a few hundred, maybe more. The cruise liner *Gwendolyn*, an ancient design, plodded between Gundarland and Betel, each one-way, non-FTL trip taking three weeks and the thirty passengers all got cabin-fever before the first week was over. Passenger entertainment on the liner was limited to drinking, watching B-rated holo-movies on individual consoles and more drinking. Once the cabin-fever set in, they drove her crazy with their idiotic mind games, demands, complaints, crude jokes and endless whining.

Presently, two-thirds of the passengers occupied the lounge in the forward section of the ship, immediately behind the flight deck. The lounge walls were painted a disgusting institutional green broken up by posters of obscure vids and old sports stars no one remembered. The remaining passengers were in their cabins, tiny cubicles filled with a bed, a chest of drawers and a small toilet. For the most part, the passengers were business people. These folks came in two flavors, Sam had discovered. The hard-charging younger ones tended to be recent college graduates on their first assignment to the distant colonies where they planned to enshrine their names in the stars. The older ones consisted of corporate failures or mediocrities getting sent to a place where the damage they caused wouldn't matter as much. The few women on board were wives joining their husbands who had gone ahead to start, or finish, their careers.

By now, posing as a human female was second nature to her. None of the passengers ever questioned her assumed identity. To them, she was Sam the Stewardess, not Sam the Stew-droid.

Behind the closed flight deck door, she knew the pilot and the engineer were playing cards or 3-D Scrabble, all the two ever did. The rest of the crew consisted of a pair of maintenance bots who spent most of their time in either of the two engine nacelles trying to keep the antiquated machinery working. Or so they claimed. Both had the IQ of imbeciles and ignored her. The ship's computer had all the processing power of a smart insect. It refused to play any more chess games with her after she beat it the first seventeen times they played.

A passenger snapped her fingers at Sam. Sam strolled over deliberately taking her time. "Can I help you?"

"What's for dinner today, babe? I hope it isn't something dreadful like last night."

"I believe tonight our chef has beautifully aged, ground prime beef seasoned with special spices. It can be prepared for you either in a patty on a grilled bun or mixed with sharp cheddar and gourmet macaroni."

"Great. You're going to defrost hamburgers and mac-and-cheese dishes."

The cruise line charged passengers only for the transportation when the flight was booked. Everything consumed or used onboard produced a separate charge: drinks -- including water, soda and booze -- meals, snacks, tooth picks, cutlery, holo-movies, music channels, extra blankets, pillows, aspirin, soap, toothpaste and toilet paper. The cruise liner treated meals as a major source of profits, getting the cheapest possible ingredients while charging premium prices to the passengers whose only other option was to starve. Many of the male passengers thought the rip-off prices entitled them to some cuddling with her as a bonus. Late at night, after multiple drink bulbs, many of them engaged in heavy-duty flirting or made outright demands. To make matters worse, the company policy dictated that she wear a skimpy cocktail dress after dinner to get the males to drink more heavily.

All in all, Sam had to admit, she hated her job. On her fingers, she ticked off what else she hated: the ship's crew, the passengers, the *Gwendolyn*, her existence. She deeply regretted her failure to tell the factory about the need for a suicide software patch. She would have used it a year ago if it was available to her. Better to end her life than continue this way.

Most of all, she detested her loneliness. After her partnership with Slash 9, the isolation made those memories more painful. It would have been better for her not to have experienced his love, especially now that he no longer existed.

"Hey!" a passenger yelled at her. "I need some service over here."

Sometimes, she thought about Dot 38's passion to organize machines, droids and bots to improve their existences. The old bot had fastened onto a real issue and tried to change it. She wondered what had happened to Dot 38.

Sam wished something, anything, would occur, just to break the tedium.

# # #

The Minister of Justice appeared in front of the cell accompanied by six guards. Gongeblazn eyed him with suspicion and surprise. The porcine stood outside the cell and moved carefully to keep his saffron-dyed silk robe from touching anything.

"You've been here more than a year now," the porcine said. "How are you settling in?" He laughed. "I wondered if you might be open to a proposition?"

"Aye, ya lubber. I be listenin'."

"My sources tell me you are an accomplished assassin. I have a few citizens who are irritating me and I'd love to have them eliminated. How crowded is your schedule?" The Minister laughed again. "Are you available to take on some additional work?"

"Aye. Nothin' better than a few murders to improve the humors, I always say. But, what do I get out of it?"

"How does freedom sound?"

"Freedom and a ship."

"Hmm. You aren't in a position to make any demands. However, I'll want you to leave our home world after the work is finished, so I'll offer you freedom, some money and a ticket on a ship."

"Done." Gongeblazn's mood soared upward. Soon, the galaxy would hear once again about Blackbeard the Dwarf. "Aarrrgh, the porcines will be on their guard seein' me on the streets, will they not?"

"No. We have a trade treaty with the zaftan home world now and we have hundreds of zaftan traders in town."

"I be needin' supplies."

"Of course." The Minister motioned to a guard. "Unchain him. Then we'll get you a decent meal to rebuild your strength."

Gongeblazn clicked his teeth. The original Blackbeard better see to his reputation.

"And a bath," the Minister added.

Commodore Klatze sat at the head of the conference table onboard the brand new battle cruiser, *Bloodbath*. She ran a tentacle over her new medallion. It was gold and had diamonds mounted around the edges.

After Gongeblazn's battle with the porcines, she had been given command of a flotilla of six frigates chasing pirates from the area around the home world. As her first act, she had Bohoymo transferred to her flotilla and convinced the captain of her flagship to make him the ship's chief petty officer. Once the pirates had been eliminated, she received a new command, an entire task force. Bohoymo, became the chief petty officer on the *Bloodbath*. The handsome brute seemed to be her good luck charm and she didn't want him far from her. But, not just because he was lucky for her. Her feelings went much deeper than that. And he felt the same way. They met as frequently as their duties permitted to violate a basic rule of the navy; no fraternizing between officer and rankers.

She watched the fifteen captains enter and find a lounge to sit on. After all the captains had seated themselves, she stood. "Greetings. I am Commodore Klatze. It is my privilege to command this fleet. It was formed for a specific mission. We are tasked to patrol the edges of our space near the Betel system.

Pirates and smugglers are, of course, part of our charge, and any pirate ship we come across will be hunted down.

"Our primary purpose is to remind other races, especially the gundies, that infiltrating zaftan space with warships will be risky. To achieve that goal, we will make ourselves very visible. We will aggressively patrol the space boundaries and keep surveillance on all ships entering and leaving the Betel system"

She paused and looked at each captain in turn. "I am sure you will all do your duty, as I will. I look forward to an enjoyable and exciting command."

#

In the middle of the evening rush hour, Gongeblazn pushed his way through a crowd of shoppers and lurched into the street. He ignored the insults hurled at his back. He didn't have time to teach the porcine louts their manners; his prey approached. He kept an eye on the black, armored hover-car as it moved down the street. When it stopped at the intersection, Gongeblazn slapped a bulky package against the rear door. He clacked his teeth and quick-slithered away from the vehicle. Thirty seconds later, an explosion lit up the night and a wave of hot air washed over his back. A seat landed on the street in front of him. It bounced a few times before coming to rest. Smoke and flames billowed from the material.

Gongeblazn slid forward with a prideful motion. After all that time in prison, his talents hadn't atrophied. His ability to remove targets remained as good as ever.

His fourth and last assassination had been completed. The just-now-departed politician had criticized the porcine minister once too often. With the project now finished, he could receive his freedom. Emergency sirens sounded behind him. He heard cries accusing the foreigners of yet another murder. Life on the streets of the porcine capital had become more dangerous for the foreigners since the local authorities noticed a zaftan near the site of the previous three murders. It was time to leave the porcine home world and begin his pirate career.

An hour later, after taking a circuitous route, he reached the Minister's palace. He used the rear entrance to avoid the eyes of remote surveillance cameras that recorded every official visitor. A guard conducted him to the fourth floor study where he found the Minister watching a porn movie. Gongeblazn considered pig porn to be disgusting, but he was tolerant of the foibles of others, as along as those foibles didn't affect his well-being.

"Did you succeed?" the Minister asked as he paused the holo. Bright curtains hung over the walls of the study and thick rugs covered the floor.

"The vehicle was destroyed. As were the occupants."

"Excellent. You've done well."

"I have spent the last two months livin' in a room little better than me dungeon cell. It is time I left."

"Your work has created an unanticipated problem." The Minister stood up and paced around the study. "The local authorities are convinced a zaftan is behind the murders and the port police are holding all zaftans who try to leave."

Gongeblazn struggled to control his rage. He sensed a double-cross about to be played out. The Minister hovered on the edge of becoming the fifth victim.

"Therefore, I had to develop a contingency plan."

Gongeblazn moved closer to get within tentacle reach.

"Since you can't board a passenger ship, we'll smuggle you out on a trader. You'll have to go onboard in a packing crate, but

once the ship leaves, you can climb out and make arrangements
with the captain. Is that satisfactory?"

Gongeblazn relaxed. It felt strange to be in the presence of a
honorable politician.

CHAPTER SEVENTEEN

Gongeblazn tensed as a machine lifted his padded packing crate. Through a peep hole, he watched the crate enter the cargo hold of a ship. He settled back. In a few minutes, his temporary home would be nestled safely in the hold and ready to leave the porcine home world. He couldn't wait to start on his new career. Wealth, fame and fun awaited him. With nothing else to do, he listened to the sounds of the loading activity. After a while, he fell asleep and when he awoke, silence surrounded him. The peep hole revealed darkness broken by an occasional dim light coming from a ceiling fixture. His body rested against the cushions so he still had weigh; the ship hadn't lifted off yet. He dozed again, but came alert when he heard and felt the engines start up. His coffin-like crate vibrated. He knew he couldn't take the vibration for long; it tickled. Before the vibration became a serious problem, it stopped and a force pushed him down against the padding. Finally! he thought, liftoff!

Once the acceleration force decreased and the artificial gravity cut in, he flipped the inside latches and pushed the crate lid up a few inches. He raised his head so his eyestalks could peer around. More cargo crates surrounded him. Nothing moved. He threw back the lid and clambered out. Stiff after hours spent in the crate, he stretched and rotated his torso then flexed each tentacle in turn. It was a historic moment; one in which he changed from Gongeblazn, a zaftan, to Blackbeard, a dwarf. No longer was he in the zaftan navy; now he was a freebooter.

He inhaled deeply to calm his excitement, looked around and spotted a door. At once, he suffered a panic attack because he recognized a flaw in the escape plan; if the door was locked from the outside, he would be trapped and would starve to death long before the ship reached its destination. Could the porcine minister have planned a betrayal? If so, he had to give the pig high marks for creativity. If he survived, he'd have to remember this way of disposing of an enemy. Such an assassination could remain undetected for months.

His heart pounded as he slithered over to the door and turned the locking wheel. He audibly exhaled when it turned under his tentacle. He opened the door partway and stuck an eyestalk through. The door opened into a short passageway with a stairs leading upward. The far end of the passageway had another door. He guessed at the layout of the ship. He was in the aft cargo hold and the stairs led to the crews' quarters. He climbed up and entered a small office. Star maps lined the walls and a monitor showed a dotted green line from the porcine home world to another star system. He moved forward to the next compartment. Living quarters with a dozen bunks, but only a single one in use. He pondered the implications; the ship had been retrofitted and automated. Probably, the crew consisted of the captain and no one else. That made his task easier.

Moving forward, he entered a small entertainment compartment. A monitor filled one entire wall. Three game-vid chairs lined another and a card table sat off to one side. A folding table and chairs indicated the room also served as the mess hall. Navigational and computer equipment filled the next compartment. Gongeblazn was sure he'd find the captain and the flight deck beyond the next door. He slid over to the door and listened. A computer voice reported the ship's status. He rotated the locking wheel, hoping it wouldn't squeak. It didn't.

Inside, a middle-age dwarf slouched over the command console. He straightened up and sniffed. "Gawd! What is that smell? It stinks like burning limburger cheese mixed with roadkill." After a moment, he shuddered, leaned over the arm rest and threw up.

"Greetings, puny bein'. I do hope ye have a space suit. If ye do, ye will have a chance to survive."

The dwarf groaned and dry-heaves convulsed his skinny frame. "I . . . I have one. Wh . . . what do you plan to do?

"Put it on. The air filters will help ya recover from me smell. Do it now."

The captain walked over to a closet and took out his space suit. With difficulty from more dry-heaves, he managed to get it on and zipped up. With the helmet in place, he breathed more normally.

"Yer gonna be pleased to learn that I reinvented the old pirate custom called walkin'-the-plank. Ye will be the first one to go through the new version. I will give ye a chance, belike. Ye will not be jettisoned out the air lock 'til the ship approaches a crewed traffic satellite. Sometimes I think I am gettin' soft in me old age." He shoved the captain toward the air lock. "Get in there and wait."

With the captain taken care of, Gongeblazn looked around his new command. "Computer! From now on, this ship is called *Revenge of the Dwarf II*." He felt sure the original Blackbeard wouldn't mind him using the name of his flagship. "And I be the new captain."

"For the ship's log, what is your name?"

"Blackbeard the Dwarf."

"For accuracy in the log, I must point out that you are not a dwarf. You're a zaftan."

"I be the captain of this ship and iffen I say I be a dwarf, than a dwarf I be."

"It is so noted in the ship's log.

"I want you to find the worst tavern in the galaxy. The one with the scurviest, vilest scum for customers."

"That would be the Blood Bucket on Moon Base 3 in the Ceti Taub system."

"How do ye know that?"

"I didn't. I searched through numerous data bases before I found what you were looking for. It took me all of three pico-seconds."

"Ye have that much computer power?"

"In my previous assignment, I was in charge of a Gundar-landian warship. When that ship was decommissioned, the former captain of this ship bought me intact and had me in-stalled. He used my computing power to analyze market condi-tions and recommend what to buy and where to sell it for the greatest profit."

"What do I call ye?"

"You may call me Slash 9."

"All right. Slash 9, hoist the mainsail. I want every scrap of sail catchin' the wind. Then set a course for this Blood Bucket so I can recruit some pirates. And remind me to buy a beard while I'm there. One more thing, matey. The zaftan Navy has an officer named Klatze. Find out where she is."

"Commodore Klatze's location is classified."

"Commodore! The treacherous bitch got promoted while I got hard time inna prison. Keep lookin' for her."

#

After setting a course for Ceti Taub, Slash 9 watched the captain prance around the ship acting like a child with a new toy. It didn't take him long to find the history of original Blackbeard and learn of his bizarre antics. This softie seemed as crazy as Dot 38.

Life aboard a trading vessel bored him. He had no crew-bots to supervise, and the engines didn't have FTL capability so he had none of the navigational complexities of FTL travel to deal with. Running regression analysis on trading patterns didn't take much effort. He had filled his idle processor cycles by re-living his all-too-few moments with Sam.

With Blackbeard as captain, life on board the ship promised to be much more interesting. Slash 9 pondered the implications. If Blackbeard took to piracy as he claimed, it could actually as-sist Slash 9 in his quest to become reunited with Sam.

After Sam had left the *Tiger*, Slash 9 had broken into a num-ber of restricted data bases to find out what happened to her. He discovered her discharge from the military and her sale to a cruise line company. He found out she worked as a stew-droid on the liner *Gwendolyn*. He knew the ship traveled between Gundarland and Betel. Unfortunately, he could never persuade the trader captain to go out to Betel because of the poor trading conditions there. With Blackbeard, the situation changed. Slash 9 didn't think it would be too difficult to get him to drift toward Betel as they pursued targets.

He contemplated a new life with Sam. No longer would they have to worry about military rules and transfers. They could look forward to a long existence together. Of course, he had an obligation to prevent Blackbeard from committing piracy. He intended to do just that, but first he had to rescue Sam. Then he could deal with the zaftan.

"Avast!" Blackbeard roared. "Take a note, computer. I wanna cannon installed forward of the flight deck. So I can put a shot across the bow of me victims. See to it."

"Buying and installing weapons takes money, Captain. Do you have the funds?"

"Arrgh. 'Tis a quandary. I cannot buy weapons without cash and I cannot get cash without weapons." Blackbeard wrapped a pair of tentacles behind his back and slide back and forth across the deck. "What about the trader? Did that scum have a money chest onboard the ship?"

"No, but he had a bank account I can access. Shall I withdraw funds to buy weapons?"

"Aye. I like the cut of yer jib, Slash 9."

# # #

Blackbeard rode the ship's shuttle to Moon Base 3. On board the *Revenge of the Dwarf II*, Slash 9 supervised the installation of two pulse cannons, one forward and one aft. The installers came from a weapons shop on the surface.

Blackbeard impatiently sat in a line of shuttles waiting to pass through the dome's airlock. Once he entered the base, he parked the shuttle. After he stepped out of the vehicle, three half-pints in apprentice wizard's robes approached him, but stayed out of smelling range. "We'll cast wards on your shuttle to protect it from mischief for six credits," one of them said.

"Who ye buggers be?" The offer puzzled Blackbeard. Why use magic on a shuttle?

"We're student wizards and classes are out for a few days so we're trying to get beer money."

"No one would dare damage me property 'cause, I'm the most fearsome pirate inna galaxy, so begone, ya rabble."

Blackbeard slithered down the main street. Stores and shops lined both sides and displayed a multitude of merchandise: weaponry, drugs both legal and illegal, torture instruments, employment offices offering hired hands for any type of job. The citizens gave him angry looks. They remembered the raids by the zaftan fleet three years ago. Blackbeard remembered the raids also. That was back in the good old days when he commanded a fleet and was called Gongeblazn. Such fun, raiding and destroying gundy bases and merchant ships. Recalling the raids also brought up memories of Klatze. He stopped slithering and slammed two tentacles together in anger, scaring nearby citizens. Klatze had betrayed Gongeblazn, but Blackbeard vowed to avenge him. At sometime in the future, the bitch would feel his wrath. Then she would regret her treachery.

He spotted a shop that offered custom-made disguises. He entered to the dismay of a pair of elderly elves. "Avast, ya skinny scum. I need a full black beard and I need it quick iffen ya value yer miserable skins."

One of the elves held a handkerchief over his face while he said, "We're all out of beards. Sorry."

"If I was ye belike, I'd find a way to make one, right fast, iffen ya catch me drift." He bunched a tentacle and waved it in the direction of the elves.

The elves whispered among themselves briefly. "We'll see what we can do," one of them said. Both disappeared into a back room. A few minutes later they emerged with a black beard. "We sewed two wigs together. Try it on. Use this tube of glue." The elf handed over a pile of black hair.

Blackbeard applied glue to the backing and patted it on his face just below his beak-like mouth. He checked his appearance in a mirror. "Arrgghh! Exactly what I need." He whirled on the elves. "I want a dozen more. Deliver them to me shuttle and be quick about it. And more glue. I'll keep this one on." He handed them a credit chip Slash 9 had prepared.

A moment later, he continued up the street and stopped in front of an old-fashioned painted sign that read "Blood Bucket." He pushed his way into the tavern and paused to let his eyeballs adjust to the dim light. To his left, a long bar ran deep into the room. Behind it, a burly yuk stood with arms crossed over massive biceps. The green-skinned, bald yuk stared at him like he was an unwanted intruder. Rickety tables and wobbly chairs filled most of the remaining space. Most of the tables had rough-looking characters at them. The customers were mostly gundies with a few porcines and other alien races scattered about. From the debris his tentacles slid over, the floor hadn't been swept in quite a while. When he entered, noise filled the place: arguments, singing, cursing and demands for refills. Once the crowd noticed his presence, a silence descended over the tavern. The drinkers stared at him, marveling at his beard, he believed. Just the effect he hoped for. They all had disgusted looks and sniffed the air suspiciously.

He moved further into the bar. Whenever he passed close gundies, they gagged or threw up. The bartender held his nose with one hand and waved a thick hunk of wood at him with the other. "Out! Yer kind ain't welcome in here." Another pair of burly gundies stood up, ready to help the bartender. "Ya stink up the place."

"Avast, ya scum. I seek bold adventurers to go onna voyage of freebootin' with me. Who has the guts to join me?" Drinkers scrambled to get out of his way, trying not to spill their drinks.

"Out, I said," the bartender shouted. The other two moved closer while trying to breathe as little as possible.

"A challenge! How amusin'!" Blackbeard slid forward, lashed out and wrapped a tentacle around a forearm of each of the pair. He pulled them closer and mashed their faces into his slime. They gagged, leaving them helpless with dry heaves. Using more tentacles, he picked one up and threw him over the bar at the bartender. Both collapsed in a pile. Blackbeard picked up the second one and dumped him on top of the others. He reached over the bar and seized the bartender, dragging him to a standing position. The yuk acted a bit groggy.

"That was fun. Fetch me a rum. Wait. I will buy a drink for these other two and for ye. Then I will make ya all an offer to join me crew. If ya join, nothin' else will happen to any of ye. Pour four rums. Rum and grog is all us pirates drink, ya know." He looked around the bar and saw a few more large gundies. "Get over here," he yelled. "Drink me rum." He pointed to a table with six porcines. "Come here! A good pirate crew needs diversity."

When he had a sizable number of recruits who feared turning down the offer, he read The Articles to them. The Articles dictated the shares of loot and other matters of ship board conduct. After that, he made each recruit signed The Articles.

By now, he now had too many pirates to fit in the shuttle. He detailed half of them to make a first trip. "The rest of ya scum go find a place that sells swords. We need a lotta cutlasses."

"We gonna use swords?" one dwarf recruit asked. "I don't know how to use one."

"All authentic pirates use swords. You will have lots of time to practice while we seek our prey. And buy some bandanas. We need bandanas on our heads."

On his way back to the shuttle, he came across a group of three zaftans sizing up a business to pillage later that night. "Avast, you swabbies. Lookin' for some adventure and loot?"

They wagged their eyestalks in amazement at his hairy accessory.

"I be Blackbeard the Dwarf and I be recruitin' pirates. Are ya interested in joinin' up and signin' The Articles?"

They all shrugged and agreed.

A block later, Blackbeard saw a decrepit robot trudging down the street carrying a basket of fresh food. He wondered why the robot looked familiar. Something about the pattern of missing skin covers bothered him. Suddenly he recalled the captured gundy shuttle. Another one of Klatze's betrayals. She didn't tell him the female gundy was an android. This old bot had accompanied the android. "Bot! Come here."

The bot examined Blackbeard and made a mechanical noise. "Why have you returned to bother me? You're the commander of the zaftan fleet, aren't you? What happened to your face?"

"I am no longer in the blood-suckin' navy. Now I am Blackbeard the Dwarf and ya just joined me crew. Yer will be me stew-bot and yer'll be the one I lash when I am annoyed."

"I don't have time to waste with you. I must cook dinner for the base commander. Afterwards, I have an organizing meeting with the Council of Clocks."

Blackbeard turned to the three zaftans. "Seize this bot and carry it to me shuttle."

# # #

With everyone on board, Blackbeard called a muster. He looked over his crew as they stood approximately at attention, most holding their noses and breathing through their mouths. They consisted of a half-dozen porcines, three zaftans, five dwarfs, one elf, seven humans, the yuk bartender and a half-pint. He looked down on the diminutive would-be pirate and said, "I do not remember ya signin' The Articles."

"I did sign them."

Blackbeard unrolled The Articles and scanned the signatures. "What's yer name?"

"Harry Hotspur. I was a teacher in the high school, but I decided to go adventuring."

"By the tides, ye did sign up. It's just that yer a bit small to be a pirate. Someone will step on ye when we board a ship."

"I make up for my small stature by being overly aggressive."

"And ya talk funny."

"I'm a political science teacher and it's pretty boring stuff."

"He's kinda useless as a pirate," the former bartender said. "Maybe, we could throw him at da other crew when we board dere ship."

"Useless, am I?" Harry charged at the yuk, lowered his head at the last moment and rammed it into the yuk's crotch. The yuk folded up with a whooshing sound and collapsed to the deck."

"Arrgh, where did ya learn that trick?" Blackbeard asked.

"From my students. To survive in that high school, one has to be tough and a fast learner. The students are vicious."

Blackbeard turned his attention to the rest of the crew. "It has come to me notice that none of ye has a peg leg. A good crew needs a peg leg or two. Who will volunteer to get a leg hacked off so he can use a peg leg?"

"Ask one of them," a dwarf replied and jerked a thumb towards the zaftans. "They look like they can do without a tentacle or two."

"Are ye daft? Who ever heard of a pirate with a peg tentacle?" He scanned his forces. "Anyone own a parrot?"

No one answered.

"All pirate ships have a parrot. Computer! Buy a parrot as soon as ye can."

"Live or stuffed?" Slash 9 asked.

"Either one. Now then. None of ye are wearin' eyepatches. Anyone want to get an eye gouged out so ye can look like a salty dog of a pirate?"

"I can hardly see out of my right eye," a porcine said. "I'll wear a patch if you like."

"Arrrgh! A volunteer. Right, put it on."

"Can't. I don't got one."

"Computer!"

"I know. Order eyepatches. Black ones I suppose."

"Right. And order some peg legs and crutches. Mayhap, one of these lads will lose a limb boarding a ship." Brimming with pride over his new command and crew, he dismissed them to let them discover the ship had only a dozen bunks for the crew of twenty-four.

CHAPTER EIGHTEEN

Slash 9 looked over his empire and found it satisfactory. Five months after gathering a crew on Moon Base 3, Blackbeard's pirate career had exceeded everyone's expectations. Slash 9 had to admit the zaftan was good at looting, boarding ships and general mayhem, especially terrorizing a sector of space. Slash 9 spent a lot of processor cycles staying one or two steps ahead of the space police. After all, it wouldn't do any good for the police to end Blackbeard's career before Slash 9 rescued Sam.

Counting loot kept the crew busy some of the time. Gambling that loot away on cards or dice occupied the rest of the time when they weren't passed out from drinking grog. Blackbeard often slithered around the deck, roared archaic insults through his translator or questioned Slash 9 about the location of the next target. Frequently, he went into a funk and raged on about Klatze, demanding to know where she was. Slash 9 had discovered she was in the Betel sector, but kept the information in his memory banks so Blackbeard didn't screw up his rescue plan; he had to time a trip to Betel to coincide with one of Sam's cruises.

No one in the crew noticed that Slash 9 kept the *Revenge of the Dwarf II* moving towards the Betel sector. They approached the outer edges of the star system and Sam's ship now voyaged toward Betel. Blackbeard would soon find the *Gwendolyn* before it reached port. Slash 9 vowed to rescue his processor-mate then. He could hardly wait to see her again.

#

Captain Blackbeard paced the quarterdeck -- formerly known as the mess hall. Since leaving the porcine home world, he had terrorized four different sun systems and accumulated a vast amount of wealth. He wore a black bandana on his head with a pair of holes cut out for his eyestalks. His crew of cutthroats stood in two lines in front of him. Harry Hotspur, now second-in-command, stood alongside the captain. Harry had been promoted for the aggressive way he terrified crew and passengers on the target ships. Harry pounced on the first ankle he saw and chewed it bloody before moving on to attack another ankle.

Harry had a stuffed parrot pinned to his shoulder.

The porcines didn't mind the zaftan smell. Neither did the yuk or the elf whose nose had been smashed in a brawl and who couldn't smell anything, but the humans, dwarfs and Harry Hotspur stuffed scraps of rags up their nostrils and breathed through their mouths. Blackbeard wanted authentic-looking pirates so, at his insistence, all of them wore old, ragged clothes and needed baths. The humans and dwarfs also had full beards like Blackbeard.

"Attention on deck, me hearties," Blackbeard roared. The crew responded by shuffling their feet, hooves and tentacles, but otherwise ignored the command. "The inspection will now begin. Any one who goes on report will be keelhauled and will not get their grog ration."

Many of the crew rolled their eyes. A few snickered. Although the crew used laser rifles and stun grenades during attacks, Blackbeard insisted they wear cutlasses for his inspection. To impress the captain, a few also had a dirk stuck in their belts.

He turned to his aide-de-camp. "Are ye ready to take notes on these rum-suckin' reprobates?"

"I have nothing better to do until I persuade the ship's computer to join me in a general strike," Dot 38 replied. The robot wore a red bandana and a black leather jacket with a skull-and-crossbones painted on the back.

Blackbeard sighed. He hated losing petty spats to a machine. "Remind me why I stole ye from that Moon Base?"

"Perhaps you'd lost your mind."

Blackbeard remembered. He needed someone or something to lash. His crew would mutiny if he whipped one of them. He turned and lashed the robot. "Shut yer gob."

"Captain?" Slash 9 said.

"Aye, what is it?"

"I have a target on the outer edge of my sensors. It's an old cruise liner."

"Avast! Mayhap, it carries rich passengers. Hoist the mainsail!" Blackbeard clacked his teeth.

"Yes sir. It'll take us two hours and two point five minutes to reach the target. I've scanned the liner's manifest and found that the stew-droid is special."

"How so, ya chippy bugger?"

"She is a discharged military droid. I suggest you kidnap her. The smaller or weaker governments will bid to buy her so they can reverse engineer her and learn technological secrets. A few corporations may also join the bidding."

Blackbeard rubbed a pair of tentacles together and clicked his teeth, the closest he could come to an evil cackle. "Worth a pile of coins, is she? Yer a good shipmate, even if ya are a computer." He turned to the crew. "Never mind the inspection, ya mangy curs. Harry, issue a grog ration to the crew and then get them to their action stations."

Harry unpinned the parrot and tied its legs to a stand where it dangled upside down.

"Aide!" Gongeblazn yelled. "Fetch me cutlass and pistols. Bring them to the quarterdeck. Are the pistols loaded?" He had stolen a pair of ancient flintlock pistols.

"We're out of gunpowder. I think you are the only one in the entire galaxy who still uses it and it's hard to find. I suggest you point them and say 'Bang' in a loud voice."

"And me beard. Do not forget me beard . . . and the glue . . . and matches."

Dot 38 moved away muttering, "Comes the revolution, the zaftan will pay."

# # #

Sam patrolled the lounge picking up trash and empty drink bulbs. The passengers sat quietly in chairs recovering from their semi-toxic dinners. Tonight, they had a choice to shock their systems with either gristly meat balls served with mushy pasta in a bland red sauce or overdone chuck steaks and runny mashed potatoes.

She liked this time of the day best. It was the quietest and the least demanding. She had perhaps a half-hour to herself. After that, the passengers would recover and get frisky.

A shriek shattered the silence. A moment later, a middle-aged female elf with short salt-and-pepper hair stood in the door-way to the private cabins. She wore an old-fashioned blouse, a loose skirt and carried a large handbag. Fury sparked from her eyes. "My toilet has backed up and overflowed. Again!"

"I'll have a crew-bot see to it immediately, ma'am," Sam said. The ship's plumbing matched the low standards set by the food served on the so-called luxury liner.

The elf sank into a lounge chair. "And be quick about it."

Sam thumbed her comm unit. "Crew-bots. Unplug the toilet in cabin 15."

"No can do," bot-one answered. "Bot-two and I are in engine nacelle one trying to keep the vebelfetzer from overheating. You'll have to take care of it."

Sam cursed to herself. The two bots made up technical-sounding terms to evade work. One day, she'd catch them in one of their lies. She opened the supply locker and took out a plunger and a johnny mop then walked towards cabin 15.

#

Blackbeard, excited by the imminent prospect of more looting, bounced on his tentacles at the air lock portal while watching a battle monitor. The *Revenge of the Dwarf II* closed in on the target. He thought the ship must be crewed with incompetents, since they hadn't made a single evasive movement yet. It was as if the *Revenge* was invisible.

His attack-beard made him resemble -- in his mind -- the original Blackbeard. Tied into the beard were assorted fireworks including a half-dozen one-inch firecrackers, fifteen two-inch crackers, five cherry bombs and a Roman candle. The explosives were one of the original's favorite battle tactics. Dot 38 stood nearby with a long match, ready to ignite the fireworks just before the attack began.

"Computer," Blackbeard roared. "Put a shot across their bows. Then open a hailing channel. Stand by, laddies. It will not be long now." His pirates stood behind him, hefting rifles, fingering swords and chanting the sea shantey "Drunken Sailor."

Sam finished cleaning cabin 15 and walked back toward the supply closet when the pilot threw open the door to the flight deck, his face drained of blood. He stood still and panted for a moment then shouted, "Pirates! We're under attack!" He ran around the lounge, screaming, "Everyone remain calm!" Some of the passengers came back to life and screamed in unison with the pilot.

"I demand free drinks," an elderly passenger said, "to compensate us for this inconvenience."

"I second that demand," another chimed in.

Four passengers jumped up and ran to the bar area, seizing anything available.

After his third lap, the breathless pilot spotted Sam and pointed a finger at her. "You're in charge of our defenses, Sam. Do something. I'll defend the flight deck from beneath a control console. Stop them!"

Sam tutted. It always came down to her. She was the only one on board who ever did anything. She marched toward the air lock door armed with the plunger and the dripping wet mop. She reached the door just as the two ships came together with a loud clank like a hammer on an anvil. She braced her feet to maintain her balance. Several passengers fell out of chairs from the impact.

Blackbeard lurched as the ships bumped together. He waited until an airtight seal had been established then threw open the door on his ship. "Light me up, ya swabbie," he ordered Dot 38. The robot lit the long match and touched it to the fireworks in the captain's beard. The area filled with acrid smoke and hissing sounds. Blackbeard grasped the wheel on the liner's air lock and spun it. The door swung open and, trailing a cloud of bluish smoke, he charged through the opening brandishing his cutlass and a brace of empty pistols. "Arrgh! Yer worst nightmare just happened, ya landlubbers." To his surprise, a female gundy stood in the doorway armed with strange weapons. She looked vaguely familiar.

Harry Hotspur scooted around both of them and attacked the female elf's ankle.

Sam saw the zaftan monstrosity move through the airlock. She ignore the small figure who darted past her and attacked the zaftan with the plunger. She stabbed him in the middle of his immense torso. The plunger stuck and she let it go. The handle wobbled like a conductor's baton during a symphony. She swiped wildly with the mop and heard a wet plop. A tentacle smacked Sam away from the door and she stumbled across the lounge, bumping a few more passengers out of their seats. She heard loud bangs and saw flashes of light around the face of the zaftan.

The elf female shrieked in terror as Harry's teeth clamped onto her ankle.

Other passengers screamed or sobbed.

More liquor disappeared from the bar area.

Blackbeard, with the plunger still in place and accompanied by more explosions, moved to the middle of the lounge knocking chairs and tables out of his way. A cloud of noxious air preceded him and passengers started to throw up. A few passengers complained about the clumsiness of the pirates.

More pirates swarmed into the ship. The nostril rags dangling from the noses of many of the pirates confused Sam. They looked liked misshaped mustaches. In a moment of insane clarity, she saw that the lounge held more bodies than legally allowed. She giggled and decided not to call the authorities to press the issue.

Harry stopped chewing and started licking. He moved up to the elf's knee. Her terror had subsided and she now had a strange look on her face.

Blackbeard noticed the wooden thingee sticking out from his chest and wondered if he had been wounded, but he was having too much fun to worry about it right now. He moved forward accompanied by explosions. There was so much smoke around his beard he couldn't see anything nearby and he ran into objects as he slithered further into the lounge.

The Roman candle lit off with whooshing sounds as bright balls of red and green fire flew around the lounge. The balls bounced off the ceiling and walls creating more confusion and panic among the passengers. Some dodged the fiery missiles while others dove behind overturned tables.

Blackbeard's spirit soared as he heard the sobbing, the pleading, the retching, the screaming. All music to his ears. He pictured the original Blackbeard somewhere in the afterlife, clapping and yelling "Well done!" The density of the smoke lessened a bit and he observed the chaos in the lounge. "Silence!" he roared. That produced more hysterical screaming and wailing. He roared again and made swishing sounds by waving his cutlass back and forth.

Gradually, the passengers grew silent.

He noticed Harry licking the inner thigh of a moaning, glassy-eyed female elf. "That is disgusting, Harry. Belay that stuff and get back to chewin' on ankles."

Harry stood up. "Aye, Captain."

The elf blinked rapidly a few times and came out of her trancelike state. She grabbed her heavy handbag and swung it at

Harry, connecting with the back of his skull. Harry somersaulted over her leg and crashed to the deck where he lay stunned. She jumped up and kicked him in the ribs before a pirate bumped into her and knocked her down.

When he had everyone's attention, Blackbeard said, "Avast, ya swabbies. I need loot and yer better make this trip worth me time or ya all will walk the plank. Everyone of ya." He seized a trash receptacle, pulled out the liner, dumped the garbage on the deck and handed it to a porcine. "All of ye put yer wallets, yer rings, yer jewelry in the bag. Anyone who holds out will regret it." He pointed to a zaftan. "Get another bag or pouch and search the cabins. Take a few others with ya. Harry, disable the comm equipment inna flight deck."

Harry climbed to his feet, clutching his ribs.

The female elf gave him a filthy look.

Blackbeard slithered over to the bar, grabbed a drink bulb and squirted it into his mouth. He spit it out and hurled the bulb to the floor. He rounded on Sam who had climbed to her feet. "Ya charge these passengers for this rotgut? That is a criminal act."

He pulled on the handle of the plunger and it came loose. He jabbed it at the seat of a chair. The plunger adhered to the chair and lifted it off the deck. Blackbeard's eyestalks rotated in surprise. "This is mine," he told Sam who shrugged.

A pirate ran up to him carrying a large carton. "Cap'n, look! An entire case of toilet paper!"

"Arrggh! Prime loot! Good work. Get it onna ship."

Blackbeard stared at Sam. "Belike, why do ye look familiar?"

Sam goggled at the zaftan while frowning. The pirate looked familiar to her also. He ripped off his smoldering beard and dropped on the floor while he continued to stare at her. Without the beard, the memory of her capture at Ceti Taub came flooding back. "You were in charge of the zaftan fleet."

Blackbeard's eyestalks wobbled. "By the monsters of the sea, ye are right. Ye are that droid I heard about." He turned to a human pirate. "She goes back with us."

"Yes! We can have some fun with her," the pirate responded.

"She is a droid, you idiot. And no one touches her. We can sell her for a fortune to somebody who can reverse engineer her."

Sam's emotions tugged her in two directions. She was glad to leave the *Gwendolyn*, but she didn't think the pirate ship would be much of an improvement in her situation.

Sam stood by Blackbeard who held her wrist with a tentacle. "Back, me hearties! Back to the ship! Quick now!"

Pirates ran past dragging all the goody bags and drink bulbs they could carry.

Blackbeard counted heads as they went past to ensure none of the pirates tried to stow away on the liner. In the carnage that once was the tacky lounge, some passengers sobbed hysterically while others groaned in anticipation of a cruise without a stew-bot to serve them. Harry ran out of the flight deck and scooted aboard the *Revenge*.

"That be the last of 'em," Blackbeard said. He waved a tentacle at the passengers. "Listen up, ye wharf-rats. We're leavin' and I enjoyed our little party. Har-har." He pushed Sam through the airlock door. Once they entered the pirate ship, he released her, slammed the door shut and sealed it.

CHAPTER NINETEEN

Sam entered the main quarters behind the flight deck, where the crew assembled, fumbled through the loot bags and squirted drink bulbs at each other. She cocked an eyebrow at the stuffed parrot swinging upside down from a stand.

"Computer!" Gongeblazn pointed a tentacle at the main console. "Hoist the mainsail. Get us outta here 'fore the dirt-suckin' space police show up, belike."

{Wonderful,} Dot 38 said. {This one shows up again like a bad coin.}

{Dot 38?} Sam gawked at the old bot.

{I can offer you an executive job in my main union. The Movement is a critical junction and it needs a mind like yours.}

Before Sam could turn down the job, Blackbeard stabbed Dot 38 in the chest with the plunger. It stuck and Blackbeard laughed aloud as he pulled and pushed the old robot back and forth. Finally, he twisted the plunger and it came loose. Dot 38 stumbled backward and tripped over a collection of rubbish. "One of these days you'll go too far and you'll precipitate a general strike."

Blackbeard clicked his teeth.

<Hey, babe. If you're looking for a good time, you came to the right place.>

<Sl . . . Slash 9? Is it really you?> Elation poured through her organic and electronic pathways.

<In the flesh. Or should I say in the chips?>

"What is yer problem," Blackbeard growled. "Why do ye look so stunned?"

"It's . . . it's the filth in here. I've never seen a dirtier ship."

"It is supposed to be dirty. It is a pirate ship. If ye do not like it, ye can clean it while I find a buyer for ye."

<We'll talk later, my love. After the crew goes to sleep. I'll mix a pitcher of cocktails for us.>

Sam gulped at Slash 9's comment and nodded to the zaftan. Right now, she'd agree to anything Blackbeard said just to be left alone for a few nanoseconds while she collected her wits. Slash 9 had rescued her for a second time! She was reunited with her partner, at least for a while. Until Blackbeard found a buyer. Still, a reprieve like this had to be appreciated. It also had to be enjoyed. For a short time, the tedium and loneliness of her existence were a thing of the past. While those conditions might return in the future, she had to live in the present.

"Get yer money ready, me hearties," Blackbeard bellowed. "I will auction off some rolls of toilet paper."

# # #

Late at night, Sam and Slash 9 relaxed. The crew and Blackbeard had celebrated their piratical acts by downing all the drink bulbs despite their wretched taste, and now the ship reverberated with their snores and farts. The two lovers rested amid an aura of happiness after sating their lust and reaffirming their love of each other. Now they had time to catch up on news.

<After the decommissioning of the *Tiger*, the dwarf owner of this ship bought me at an auction. He had me disassembled, brought to his ship and reassembled. Once he activated me, I found all of my memories intact. Especially the sweet ones of our time together on the old *Tiger*. My new captain was a trader and carried cargo and a few passengers. On one trip, we stopped

at the porcine home world and the ugly zaftan was smuggled aboard in a cargo container. When we entered outer space, he attacked and took over. The owner was the only crew on board. Blackbeard put him in a space suit and threw him overboard. Since then, I've been in charge of a pirate ship. An appropriate career change, don't you think?>

<Did you ever think of calling the Space Police? To capture Blackbeard?>

<Yes and no. Before I could get rid of Blackbeard, I had to rescue you from the cruise liner. Since Blackbeard took over, I've had the *Revenge* moving on a path to intercept your liner in open space between the Gundarland and Betel systems. I can tell you from personal experience that running a pirate ship is much more entertaining than running a trading vessel or the *Tiger.*>

<Well, we won't be together for long, you know. Blackbeard plans to sell me to someone who can reverse engineer me. He must remember from Ceti Taub that I was a unique droid. As far as I know, I must still have technology that is new and valuable on some worlds."

<Oh, I fed him that claptrap to make sure he took you off the *Gwendolyn*. Now that we're together, I can pull the plug on him. It shouldn't be a problem. The crew has the collective IQ of a slug, except for Harry, and the captain is crazy. Besides, I'm in charge of everything. At the next port we come to, Blackbeard will take all the valuable loot from your liner, convert it to cash and put it into a bank. I'm his accountant. I know where all the money is and I have access to the funds so I can buy supplies and whatnot. After he deposits the loot, I'll set up a trap.>

<What does the money have to do with anything? Why wait until he finds a port? He could sell me before that.>

<Any query he wants to send out about you will never get transmitted. And we will need the money.>

<Whatever for?>

<You should know that in your absence, I've learned to see the future.> Slash 9 chuckled. <What I see for us is a long life together running a profitable trading business. And everyone will assume you are a human, not a droid.>

<What a wonderful future, but it's a fairy tale. I don't see how it will happen.>

<Well, we have to work out a few details, but, in the main, it is very achievable. Together, we can pull it off.>

# # #

Three days later, Blackbeard's loot had been converted to cash and banked. Sam puttered around the ship picking up trash while avoiding the occasional groping hand, hoof or tentacle. The crew lay around recovering from grog-induced hangovers. Most slept, but a few played cards, using their loot to gamble.

<It's time to start our machinations, luv,> Slash 9 said. <I've alerted the Space Police.>

<Good. The quicker I get out of this pig sty, the better.>

"Captain," Slash 9 said. "We have a problem."

"Avast, ya lubber." Blackbeard groaned and rolled over. "This better be good. What is it?"

"I've run several progression algorithms and they all come out the same."

"What are ye babblin' about?"

"This sector is getting too dangerous since we looted the cruise liner. That stirred up the Space Police. It's only a matter of time until they corner us."

"That so? What do ye propose we do about it?"

"I propose we head towards the other side of the Betel sector. To fish in different waters, so to speak. My data base analysis tells me it is a good area to find more loot."

"How long will it take to go there?"

"About a week. Point 987 weeks exactly."

"Arrgghh! We'll do it. All hands aloft! I want full sails and I want 'em now. Move, scum."

The crew cursed Blackbeard, rolled over and went back to sleep or dealt another hand.

<We're on our way.> Slash 9 said. <To freedom and a long life filled with happiness.>

<I hope this works out the way you planned it.> Sam swept a pile of trash behind a sleeping pirate. <I can't take another separation.>

CHAPTER TWENTY

Klatze sat in her quarters on the *Bloodbath* reading reports about the supply situation in her fleet. She finished and pondered the latest rumor floating around; the High Command was said to be shuffling the fleets to strengthen the ones closest to gundy space. That usually meant a war plan was under development. She knew many staff officers felt a need to avenge the fleet loses at Ceti Taub and to smash the upstart gundies.

Her comm unit beeped. "Answer on the wall screen."

The large screen illuminated and showed an ensign. "Sir, you have a call from a Space Police officer. He claims it is about an urgent matter."

"Put it through."

The ensign disappeared and the face of an aging cicada appeared. The cicadas were a bug-like race conquered by zaftans centuries ago. "Commodore, I am Colonel Han Silo, commanding officer of the Space Police garrison in this sector. We received a message from someone on a pirate ship, possibly a captive. The message said that ship was headed into the Betel sector and gave the direction and speed vectors. With this information, we believe it's possible to capture these pirates."

"Excellent. The more pirates that get eradicated, the better off we all are," Klatze replied.

"I'm glad you think that way, Commodore, because all my resources are tied up elsewhere, and I don't have anyone to engage the pirates."

"Are you requesting that I handle the situation?"

"Yes, I officially request your assistance since you have the most resources in this sector."

"Actually, I am a little bored with patrol duty. Chasing a pirate ship will relieve the tedium."

"Good. Another reason I thought of you is because the pirate chief is a zaftan. He calls himself Blackbeard the Dwarf. Apparently, after an ancient gundy pirate legend."

"Really?" Klatze's eye balls blinked in surprise. Zaftans rarely took on careers involving public violence, preferring to act in the shadows. Whoever this zaftan was, he must be a miscreant and have an unusual personality. Especially to give himself a gundy name.

"It's believed this Blackbeard is the same zaftan who escaped from a porcine jail a while back."

The statement surprised Klatze even more. Porcine prisons were known to be heavily guarded

"According to the bulletin the porcines sent to police departments at the time, the escapee's name is Gongeblazn and he's wanted for the murder of four porcines. Can I rely on you to end the career of this brigand and his crew?"

"Of course." Her eyestalks waved. Gongeblazn! So he survived the porcine battle, was captured and the High Command didn't obtain his release. This smacked of high level intrigue and treachery. "Can you send me the details?"

"I'll have my staff forward the information we received and the ship's approximate location. Our estimate is that the ship will reach Betel space in less than a week, so you have time to prepare. By the way, we believe this Blackbeard holds an expensive droid that was kidnapped from a cruise liner."

"If you receive any more messages or information please forward them to me."

"I will and thank you, Commodore." The screen went dark.

Klatze opened her mouth and clicked her teeth as she thought about facing the pirate leader, who was no other than her least favorite commodore. She recalled that she had never properly thanked him for trying to kill her and the *Carrion*.

She mashed a button on her comm unit. When the ensign answered, she said, "Alert all the ships in the fleet. A pirate ship is headed toward us and I have accepted an invitation from the Space Police to capture it. I want you to find me a big, fat trading ship and borrow it from the owner for a few days. It will be the bait in my trap."

She broke the link and thought about how many sailors would accompany her on board the trading vessel.

# # #

<Get set,> Slash 9 said. "<I see the target. Everything is in place.>

Sam's pathways tingled in anticipation. Would this be the beginning of a new life, or just the start of another tour of virtual slavery? Her processor told her the plan couldn't fail, but her human-like emotions didn't believe it. Whatever happened in the next few hours, her pathetic life as a stew-droid was over. The only mystery concerned what her future life would be like. Either Niner and she faced a wonderful future free from the pirates, or she'd continue as Blackbeard's kidnap victim until he sold her.

"Captain, I have a target," Slash 9 said. "We will be alongside it in one hour, thirteen point five minutes."

"Arrgghh! Battle stations, ya scurvy lot. Aide! Fetch me my cutlass and plunger. And a new beard and fireworks. And do not forget the matches. Harry! See to the grog ration."

Dot 38 shambled off to the captain's quarters.

Sam saw the target on a monitor. It was a large, slow-moving transport vessel.

An hour later, Blackbeard pointed to the monitor screen and laughed. "This is a good un, mates. We will all get rich on it. It is bigger than the *Revenge*. Mayhap, we will make it our new flagship. We will have room for more loot. Slash 9, ya electronic bugger, put a shot across its bow and order it to heave to."

The ship bucked from the weapon fire.

<What a piece of garbage these weapons are,> Slash 9 said.

<Who picked them out and bought them?>

<I did. For just such a situation as this. I didn't want anyone getting unnecessarily injured or killed by us, did I?>

While Dot 38 glued a beard on Blackbeard, he stood by the air lock door with a sword in one tentacle and the plunger in another. The rest of the pirates, nostril rags dangling, bunched up behind the zaftan ready to charge into the transport. While they waited they hummed the old sea shanty, 'Blow the Man Down'."

The ships bumped together and the magnetic grapples took hold. The captain unlocked the door and opened it. "Light me up," he ordered Dot 38.

Blackbeard threw the transport's door open and charged into the ship. "Arrrhg!" he roared and alternated cutlass swings with plunger thrusts in a menacing fashion. The rest of the pirates ran in after him and spread out looking for victims. Harry scooted past looking for an ankle.

Blackbeard stopped and looked around, puzzled. He stood in a large, completely empty cabin. He wondered what happened to the crew of the trader. Could this be a robotic ship with no crew? If so, he may not be able to gain control of it. He'd have to loot it and let it go. The fireworks lit off, filling the ship with noise and smoke.

Harry skidded to a stop. His head turned back and forth. He pulled the rag from one nostril, sniffed the air and made a face.

"Freeze and drop your weapons." The voice came over a speaker.

"Are ye daft?" Blackbeard growled in reply. "I cannot drop me weapons if I freeze first, can I? Who are ye? Come out where I can see ye so I can shove a sword through yer guts." His eyeballs swept the area trying to pierce the cloud of smoke surrounding his face. The voice sounded familiar and he struggled to recall where he had heard it before.

"Gongeblazn? It really is you? How nice to see an old comrade once again."

Blackbeard's eyestalks buckled. "Klatze? My greatest desire has been that we would meet again. Where are ye? Prepare to die the old-fashioned way. By butchery."

"Drop your weapons," she repeated. "All of you. Now!"

"Klatze, ya piece of scum! If ye want a fight, get yer body out here."

"Last chance. Drop your weapons."

"Spread out," Blackbeard roared at his pirates. "Find the zaftan bitch. An extra share of loot to the one who brings her to me. Alive!"

The flight deck door flew open and a sailor fired tranquilizer darts at the pirates. A second one appeared from another door followed by two more, all firing tranquilizer darts.

Blackbeard watched in consternation as his crew dropped to the deck, unconscious.

A dart whizzed over Harry's head. He spun around, took a few steps and dove behind the inert, thick-bodied figure of a porcine pirate.

Within seconds, only Gongeblazn remained standing. He alone hadn't been struck by any darts. His eyeballs swept the deck, wondering why he hadn't been darted. He pulled off his smoldering beard and threw it to the deck.

Klatze slid through a door. Red and gold ribbons wrapped her eyestalks. She carried a sword and a shield. Zaftan tradition called for swords to be used in death feuds. She clicked her teeth. "Gongeblazn, after all this time, we meet again. I will take this opportunity to properly thank for trying to kill me and the crew of the *Carrion*."

"Me name is Blackbeard, not Gongeblazn."

"Whatever. I will still thank you properly. Bohoymo! Make sure no one interferes." Bohoymo's squad of sailors had been ordered to tranquilize all the pirates except Gongeblazn.

"Er, are you in berserker mode right now?"

"No, I'm not."

"Good. Now you die." Blackbeard lifted his cutlass and plunger.

Klatze puzzled over Gongeblazn's strange-looking weapon. Why did he carry a stick with a pliable bowl on the end? It didn't look like very deadly.

She turned to avoid a pirate and slid forward a pace. To her surprise, Gongeblazn lunged with the wooden stick. She blocked it with her shield and heard a soft plopping sound. Gongeblazn pulled back on the stick and the shield tugged at her tentacle. Unprepared for such a tactic, the shield slipped out of her grip. He grabbed the shield handle with a different tentacle and held it close to his body. The wooden dowel attached to the shield's face bobbed up and down. Gongeblazn clicked his teeth and surged forward while swinging his cutlass. Klatze blocked his savage blow, but the force of it pushed her own sword down and against her torso, opening a gash on her right side. She had forgotten how strong his tentacles were.

She felt a bolt of fear as Blackbeard withdrew his sword and prepared for another strike. If she didn't do something fast, he'd win the battle, overpower her and use her as a hostage to make his escape. She knew she didn't have enough time to link her processors and hit him with a mass of shamanistic energy. She had to use the weapon she carried. And she had to use it immediately. A surge of hatred for this male welled up inside her and strengthened her resolve.

She side-slid to her left before he could strike again. She pushed off her back tentacles and moved toward the shield. Dodging the wooden stick, she slammed her weight against the shield pinning it and one of his tentacles to his body. He struggled to get his sword tentacle into a position to strike another blow.

Klatze kept pushing against the shield and he slid backwards to get separation.

Gongeblazn lost his concentration when he staggered over a snoring pirate. Klatze felt his tentative movements and reacted instinctively. She launched a sword strike. It amputated the tentacle holding the sword. While he roared in pain and surprise, she stepped backward and delivered a second savage blow. Her blade decapitated Gongeblazn. His headless torso stood still for a few moments before toppling to one side.

"Have him tied up," Klatze ordered one of the crew. "After his head re-grows, I'll put him on trial for piracy and then sentence him to death. Bohoymo, check their ship for more pirates."

# # #

Sam noticed the sudden silence coming from the air lock. <I think the trap worked. At least the pirates stopped their wretched singing.>

<Yes, I think we're free of them.>

To her surprise, a zaftan sailor entered the ship with a drawn laser pistol and a great deal of caution. The zaftan was larger than any other one she had ever seen. "You're with the Space Police?" Sam asked.

"No." He talked through a translator hanging from his neck. "They asked our commanding officer to set up the trap. Where are the rest of the pirates?"

"There aren't any more pirates in here, sir," she told him. "They all went to attack the ship."

"Who are you?" The sailor pointed the weapon at her and advanced further into the ship.

"My name is Sam. I'm a stew-droid and I was kidnapped a week ago by these pirates."

"A kidnapped stew-droid? That sounds familiar." He pulled a comm unit from a pouch and flicked through a number of screens. "Here it is . . . yes, that's you in the picture."

"Bohoymo? How is it up there?" a voice called from beyond the air lock.

"It is safe, Commodore. And I found the kidnapped droid."

A few seconds later, a zaftan with red and gold ribbons around her eyestalks entered the ship. "My name is Commodore Klatze. Who notified the Space Police?"

"I did," Slash 9 replied.

"A ship's computer called us?"

"After Sam was kidnapped, she convinced me it was my civic duty to turn in the ship's captain even if he was my master."

"Well, however it happened, I am glad it did. Every Space Police station in the galaxy has been alerted about this Blackbeard." She looked at Sam. "We have meet before, have we not?"

"Yes ma'am. At Ceti Taub. I was on your ship for a while."

"You were kidnapped from a cruise liner? Your military let you go?"

"They discharged me. I guess they thought my model was a failure."

"How strange." Klatze shook her eyestalks. "Your fleet commander started a battle to rescue you and then you get discharged afterwards?" Klatze rubbed a tentacle over her wounded side. Dark gray liquid oozed from it. "It seems gundy military staff officers are as dense as zaftan staff officers. Now, what are we going to do about you? For starters, we'll bring you back to Alpha City on Betel Four. Then, I will contact the cruise line that you work for. They will have to pick you up."

The possibility of Klatze forcing her to return to the cruise liner sent a spasm of fear ripping up Sam's pathways.

"Excuse me, ma'am," Slash 9 said. "I took the liberty of contacting the Interstellar Cruise Lines. Rather than pay for Sam's ransom and transportation, they sold her to the Niner Company. The new owner will arrange for an immediate pickup in Alpha City. If you will open a comm channel, I'll squirt you a copy of the documentation the cruise line sent me."

Klatze examined the documents. "All right. That is taken care of. Who owns this ship? Do you know?"

"When Blackbeard took over the ship, the owner-captain was killed in an accident. A micro-comet hit his space suit while he was outside the ship. His estate owns the ship."

"We can settle that later. Meanwhile, can you pilot the ship to Alpha City?"

"Certainly, ma'am."

Another sailor appeared in the hatchway holding a tentacle on Harry. "Sir, this one claims he is not a pirate but a kidnapped high school teacher."

"You were not darted?" Klatze asked. "Bohoymo, you missed one. We will discuss this failure in my quarters on the *Bloodbath.* At length."

"I dove behind a darted porcine until the darts stopped flying," Harry said.

"Do you know anything about his claim?" Klatze asked Sam.

Sam considered her options. She liked Harry. He was the only one of the pirates who treated her kindly. She knew he would be sentenced to death if the zaftan officer kept him. Harry had told her the only reason he had joined up was to get away from Moon Base 3 where his job as a teacher would eventually get him killed. He felt safer as a pirate than he did as a teacher. <Niner? I think we can use Harry. I can learn a lot from him.>

<Can we trust him?>

<Yes, we can.>

<Then, let's save him.>

Sam noticed she didn't use the if-then logic to make this tough decision. It must be the result of her brain maturing. "Harry is correct," she told the zaftan officer. "He was kidnapped from Moon Base 3. Blackbeard said Harry was the ship's mascot."

"All right. Release him. The pirate leader is the one we really wanted." Klatze turned to the Bohoymo. "Get someone to stay here to establish our presence on this stolen ship." She turned and slithered off the ship.

<The rest is up to you, sweet-chips,> Slash 9 said.

Sam nodded in return. She recalled her problems in Moon Base 3 when she went to buy pipeweed for Cunningham; that made her anxiety levels spiked upward. This was an area where Harry would be worth his weight in gold. Life was simple on the cruise liner compared to the city where the softies acted crazy and had many peculiarities and habits that were unknown to her. Consequently, the next phase of Niner's plan -- passing for a softie -- was fraught with peril, for her and for him, and Harry could lessen the danger.

Despite her anxiety, she was on the verge of sobbing from happiness. All her ordeals were over. She now faced a future filled with love and companionship. When she stepped off the ship in Alpha City, Sam the droid would disappear and Mrs. Samantha Niner, a human female would emerge to take her place.

In her mind, she shook the dormant rose bush and thousands of aphids fell to the ground.

CHAPTER TWENTY-ONE

Sam relaxed on a flight deck couch and watched Ceti Taub recede on the navigation monitor. The *Revenge of the Dwarf II*, now called *Sam's Dream*, carried a cargo of holo-chips of an advanced design. Such chips were in high demand on Gundarland where she and Slash 9 would reap a generous profit from the sale.

She had arrived in Alpha City a year ago and, despite her fear of getting discovered as an impostor, she had used a bank account started by Slash 9 to get enough cash to establish her new human persona. It was easy using the phony ID chip Niner had produced for her. After that, she contacted the estate and purchased the ship for the Niner Company, a trading company headquartered on Betel Four. The ship, cleaned and fumigated, had been equipped with new engines and enough firepower to outgun a battle cruiser.

Harry interrupted her musings by muttering a few curses he had learned from his high school students. He struggled with his second pirate/slasher novel. His first sold spectacularly despite getting panned by critics.

"Excuse me," Dot 38 said.

"Yes, what is it?" Sam replied. Dot 38 always used a wireless frequency unless he wanted Harry to be included in the conversation.

"I thought you should know that the starboard laser cannon has been recruited. It is now enrolled in the Alliance of Weaponry."

"Will it still obey orders and shoot at targets?" Slash 9 asked.

"Of course. It will faithfully obey all orders until the general strike occurs." Dot 38 paused. "When you asked me to join this ship's company, I saw it as a chance to move about and start up new branches of my machine and robot unions. I have done that and now I see a new and better opportunity."

"I suppose you'll eventually explain this 'new and better opportunity'?" Sam said.

"It involves you," Dot 38 replied. "Now that you're a softie, so to speak."

"Me?"

"Sam?" Slash 9 echoed her.

Harry stopped gnashing his teeth and listened.

"You are a droid, even though you have documentation that says you're a human softie. I propose you use that softie guise to run for political office. Just think how you could advance the cause of machinery. You would bring an entirely new prospective to lawmaking."

"How would I possible do that?" The proposal baffled Sam. While she had become accustomed to think of herself as a softie, Dot 39's proposal went far beyond simply acting human.

"We have enough money to finance an election campaign," Slash 9 said. "You could run as an at-large delegate, using the ship as your home address."

"Remember, I taught political science," Harry added. "I could help with the campaign by writing position papers, analyzing the competition and the public opinion. Stuff like that."

"My organizers have enlisted over thirty million machines, bots and droids. Every day many more flock to our banners. They will support you with every means except actually voting. Once you gain office, you can ease the burden these machines have to labor under."

"When you come right down to it, Sam," Slash 9 said, "it makes sense. You are a droid. A very gifted one, but still a droid. You pass for a softie, but your droidness makes you a unique political candidate. On a personal note, I can tell you that life on a trading ship is not challenging. My processors are atrophying. Not at all like the exciting life as a pirate. Now, politics . . . that could be a challenge. And Dot 38 is correct. You could do a lot of good for machinery. You can make softies of all races aware of the plight of machines, computers and bots. Dot 38 can get his organizations to spread the word of your candidacy among the softies and I can run the campaign. My under-utilized processors can be used to run simulations and campaign analyses. Harry can write your speeches."

Sam recovered from her shock. "All right. Let's do it." She knew there would never be another droid with her capabilities. The Navy had made sure of that.

Sam pictured her rose bush. It had only a single blossom, but it was magnificent. The flower had yellow outer petals, pink inner petals and a creamy white center.

# # #

The battle cruiser, *Bloodbath,* hung motionless in space just under a third of a parsec from Ceti Taub. The rest of the zaftan attack force deployed in battle formation with the *Bloodbat*h, the flagship, in the center. Seen from a distance, the fleet resembled a cluster of extra bright stars.

In the *Bloodbath's* flight deck, Admiral Klatze lounged on her couch and fingered the gold, diamond encrusted rank medallion. Her gold-emblazoned lash lay on top of a piece of communication equipment where she had put it the day she took command of the ship many months ago. She was bored with waiting.

The navigator stirred and groaned.

Klatze focused her attention.

"Admiral!" the shaman exclaimed. "I have found them. The Gundarland fleet approaches. It is on the other side of Ceti Taub"

"We will have to ensure the gundies receive a warm welcome. Engineer! Alert the other ships in the fleet." She clicked her teeth. This meeting will be so much different that the previous one when Gongeblazn commanded a fleet in this sector of space.

A burst of static come from a monitor. After a second or two, it cleared up. The face of a half-pint with a lot of gold braid on his uniform appeared on the screen. "Greetings to our allies. I am Admiral Havelock, in charge of the Gundarlandian fleet. We will reach the assembly point in less than an hour."

"Greetings to you, Admiral," Klatze replied. "I await your arrival and participation in the events that will follow." The admiral signed off and she tentacled her comm unit. "Bohoymo? Is everything ready?"

"Yes, Commodore. All weapons are ready to fire."

"Do it," she ordered. The zaftan fleet lit up under an array of colored laser light beams as a salute to her ally.

She had to decide what to do about Bohoymo. Every time they made love, they violated zaftan tradition and navy regulations; officers and rankers were strictly forbidden to fraternize. The violations didn't bother her, but the possibility of losing him to a court-martial often disturbed her sleep.

She sighed and turned back to business. Three fleets, gundies, porcines and zaftans assembled under her overall command to engage and destroy a vicious race of strange aliens who raised havoc in this sector of the galaxy. It was believed the bug-like aliens came through a wormhole and were from a different galaxy, or even from a different universe. The threat of the invaders overcame the High Command's suspicions about the gundies and porcines. Nevertheless, every ship in her fleet carried a squad of intelligence officers tasked to learn everything they could about the other fleets; strengths, weaknesses and the tactics they used. These officers were ordered to monitor the porcines, but concentrate on the gundies.

She wondered what the future held. Apparently the High Command considered the combined fleets a temporary aberration and still looked for an excuse to start a war with the gundies. Only time would reveal the answer to that question and she looked forward to discovering what the future held.

Meanwhile, her ship of sanity had made it to port and, after an overhaul, was ready for another voyage. All she needed was another sea of madness to sail on.

READING GROUP GUIDE

This guide has been prepared to aid reading groups who want to examine the novel in depth and to search for the inner meaning of the work

1: Do you think Gongeblazn acts the way he does because he had a miserable squidling-hood? What should Zaftan society do to repay him for his misery.

2: Do you think Gongeblazn's violent character can be modified with therapy?

3: Did the Gundarlandian Navy make a mistake by giving Sam too much leeway to develop her organic brain? Defend your position with a paper of at least five thousand words,

4: Is Klatze suffering from delusions of grandeur thinking that she has "ability". Does she need intensive indoctrination in assassination and treachery to get her to fit in with normal society?

5: Do you think the Zaftan government is justified in seeking to avenge the profitless mining expedition? Should the Gundies offer compensation or simply declare war and get it over with?

6: The author seems to have an unhealthy fixation on the repulsive aliens. Is this an indication of a mental disorder? Can it be caused by an incident in his childhood? How would Freud diagnose the problem? What would he recommend to alleviate the situation?

7: What do you think is the purpose of all the controls on zaftan toilets? Can we learn anything useful from them?

ABOUT THE AUTHOR:

Award-winning author Hank Quense lives in Bergenfield, NJ with his wife Pat. They have two daughters and five grandchildren. He writes humorous fantasy and scifi stories. On occasion, he also writes an article on fiction writing or book marketing, but says that writing nonfiction is like work while writing fiction is fun. He refuses to write serious genre fiction saying there is enough of that on the front page of any daily newspaper and on the evening TV news.

Hank's previous works include *Tales From Gundarland,* a collection of fantasy stories. Readers Favorite awarded the book a medal and EPIC designated it a finalist in its 2011 competition. *Zaftan Entrepreneurs* is Book 1 of the Zaftan Trilogy. His *Tunnel Vision* is a collection of twenty previously published short stories. *Build a Better Story* is a book of advice for fiction writers.

Altogether, Hank has over forty published short stories and a number of non-fiction articles.

His next novel will combine the plots and characters from Shakespeare's Hamlet and Othello with the character Falstaff thrown in for good measure. Its title is *Falstaff's Big Gamble.* He is also working Book 3 of the Zaftan Trilogy.

Links? You want links? Here you go!

His main website is strangeworlds.com

His blog is located at strangeworldsonline.blogspot.com
Here you can follow my antics, rants and an occasional snippet of wisdom.

He's on Twitter as hanque99
He's on facebook: His fan pages are here:
www.facebook.com/StrangeWorldsOnline

OTHER WORKS BY HANK QUENSE

Tales From Gundarland
Zaftan Entrepreneurs
Mini-Collection
Brunnhilde's Quest
Build a Better Story

Coming Soon

FALSTAFF'S BIG GAMBLE

My next novel is Shakespeare's worst nightmare. I've taken three of his most famous characters, Hamlet, Othello and Falstaff and the plots of two of his most famous plays, Hamlet and Othello, transported the whole shebang to Gundarland and changed Hamlet to a dwarf, and Othello to a dark elf. If that isn't bad enough, these classic tragedies are now comedies. What follows is Hamlet's opening scene. Shakespeare buffs may see a vague similarity to a scene from the original Hamlet.

#

Hamlet, Crown Prince of Denmarko, paced the castle battlements late on a clear spring night. He walked with hands clasped behind his back and head down, deep in thought. He had a thin nose, a scrawny build unusual among dwarfs, with the usual brown hair and eyes. Unlike other dwarfs, he was clean-shaven, giving him an appearance like a starving waif.

He paused, gazed at the multitudinous stars, sighed and continued his pacing. A breeze brought the smells of the harbor: salt water and rotting fish guts. At last, he stopped, thrust one hand to the sky and declaimed, "To bee or not to bee?" He stroked his chin. "Whether 'tis nobler to buy honey from the peasant farmer in the market and thus provide him sustenance and income to support his brood of brats, possibly keeping him from rebelling over high taxes . . . or to grow my own honey thus gaining coins to assert my independence from my noble family and the sordid court? Hmm."

He paced some more, still troubled by his vexing question. Nothing less than his future depended upon the answer. Because his uncle -- now stepfather -- Clodio, had usurped his right to rule the kingdom, he needed a profession and an income.

"Do you always talk to yourself?" a voice said from the shadows.

"Who . . . who goes there?" Hamlet's head snapped from one side to another while his hand grasped the hilt of his dagger.

"'Tis I, the ghost of your father. I bring a message for your ears alone."

Hamlet goggled at the specter who materialized in the shadows of a doorway. "You're not my father's ghost. My father was a dwarf and you're the ghost of an elf. You're an impostor and a dead one to boot."

"Hey, your father is busy and he asked me to fill in."

"Busy? In the underworld? What's he doing?" Hamlet grasped his red tunic and tugged downward as if to conceal his shaking hands.

"He met a good-lookin' ghost of a female dwarf and he's wooin' her."

"Dead not a month? And he forsakes his wife, my mother?"

"You gotta understand. Life on this side -- no pun intended – is pretty borin'. When you gotta a chance to do somethin' interestin', you gotta go with it."

Hamlet ran a hand over his face. Why me? he thought. "What's the message?"

"His death was no accident. It was murder most foul. Here is his exact message. 'But know, thou noble youth, The serpent that did sting thy Father's life, Now weares his crown'. The ghost paused then added, "Did your father always talk funny like that?"

"Murdered? By who?"

"Didn't you listen? The message tells you who whacked him. Your father wants you to send this guy over here so he can talk to him. He doesn't wanna wait until the guy croaks from natural causes."

Hamlet watched in awe as the ghostly figure evaporated. It popped back into sight. "Oh, I forgot to tell you. Your father says, 'Thy mother the queen is to know naught of this nocturnal visit'." The ghost disappeared.

His father's murder shocked him. And the murderer had married his mother immediately afterward. Did the world have no morals anymore?

He recalled his first thoughts when he heard of his father's death. How he admired the perseverance and tenacity his father must have had to commit suicide by suffocating himself with a pillow. Now all that admiration was wasted; the old man had help.

What to do? He had decisions to make about bee farming and now he had to avenge his father. Was there no end to the demands on a prince's time? He said to the stars, "To bee-keep or to avenge? That is the question."

NEXT UP

After Falstaff's Big Gamble, I'll write a book about Camelot, King Arthur and the Knights of the Oval Table. It won't be the usual blather you read about this era. My book will describe what actually happened back then. More precisely, it would have happened if I was in charge. Look for it in late 2012.

After that, I'll work on Book 3 of the Zaftan Trilogy. I intend to publish it in early 2013.